WITHDRAWN

As he raced over the uneven prairie he fumbled with the saddle string. FRONTISPIECE. *See Page 83.*

LONESOME LAND

BY

B. M. BOWER

WITH ILLUSTRATIONS BY

STANLEY L. WOOD

Introduction to the Bison Books Edition
by Pam Houston

University of Nebraska Press
Lincoln and London

⊖ The paper in this book meets the minimum require-
ments of American National Standard for Information
Sciences—Permanence of Paper for Printed Library
Materials, ANSI Z39.48-1984.

WES
Bower

First Bison Books printing: 1997
Most recent printing indicated by the last digit below:
10 9   8   7   6   5   4   3   2   1

Library of Congress Cataloging-in-Publication Data
Bower, B. M., 1874–1940.
Lonesome land / by B. M. Bower; introduction to the Bison
Books edition by Pam Houston.
p. cm.
ISBN 0-8032-6134-9 (pbk.: alk. paper)
I. Title.
PS3503.08193L66   1997
8138.52—dc21
96-49022 CIP

Reprinted from the original 1912 edition by Little, Brown
and Company, Boston.

INTRODUCTION

PAM HOUSTON

On her deathbed in Hollywood in 1940, Bertha Muzzy Bower told her daughter Dele, "Don't be pious," advice that by all accounts she lived by. Those who remember her say she liked men, *maybe too much*, and that most of the stories they remember about her are *unprintable*. She started writing stories in 1900 so that she could earn enough money to get divorced. The day after her death the *San Francisco Examiner* called her "One of the greatest western writers of them all."

Sensible, gutsy, fiercely independent, and decades ahead of her time, B. M. Bower loved the stories of western men and women. She wrote about the land she loved with humor, grace, and honesty. She took on subjects—divorce and spouse abuse among them—that few writers of the time, male or female, would touch with a ten-foot pole. She was private, much talked about, and, like most frontier artists, probably very little understood.

If her parents had moved to Paris in 1889 instead of Big Sandy, Montana, she would have likely found many kindred spirits. In Montana she found three husbands, two of whom she divorced, a few good friends, C. M.

Russell among them, and the land, which she loved and feared and in which she found both her self and her stories.

"Did you ever get to the point, Mr. Cowboy, where you—you dug right down to the bottom of things, and found that you must do something or go mad—and there wasn't a thing you could do? Did you ever?"

These are the words the heroine of *Lonesome Land*, Valeria Peyson, utters in exasperation to Kent Burnett, the man she befriends when the isolation that her alcoholic and carousing husband leaves her to nearly drives her insane. Kent Burnett loves Val Peyson, though whether or not she loves him back is a question never answered by the novel. ("I don't know why I should deny myself a friend," she says, "just because that friend happens to be a man, and I happen to be married. I never did have much patience with the rule that a man must be perfectly indifferent, or else make love.")

Kent comes to Val's rescue when the ranch catches fire, and he listens to her stories and comes to visit her when she thinks the solitude of the Big Sky country will drive her mad. But in the end it isn't Kent, or any other man, who saves her. Val Peyson does what B. M. Bower herself did, what so many of us who live in places where the square miles number more than the population do to stave off the loneliness and longing for contact that we're afraid sometimes will swallow us whole: she begins writing.

B. M. Bower had little tolerance for the popular romanticized view of the West, although her vision of it was not particularly bleak. Her descriptions of place have a matter-of-factness to them, a quiet assertion that anyone who didn't live there couldn't have the slightest idea about the land and all that it meant to those who did.

To the passengers on the through trains which watered at the red tank near the creek, the place looked crudely picturesque—interesting, so long as one was not compelled to live there and could retain a perfectly impersonal viewpoint. . . . Many of them imagined that they understood the West and sympathized with it, and appreciated its bigness and its freedom from conventions.

Bower understood the power of the western landscape to shape the lives of the people who chose to live there. She understood its wildness, its vastness, its utter indifference to the microscopic communities that were trying to tame it, and both her characters and her sentences seem fueled by the way they encounter the land around them, with a mixture of equal parts rapture and terror and awe.

She stood still in the doorway with her fingers doubled into tight little fists, and stared out over the great, treeless, unpeopled land which had swallowed her alive.

Bower also understood that there was not a great difference between the people who survived the land's beauty and brutality and the ones who did not. A brush fire, a glass of whisky, some unpublished words on a white page; these were the differences between sanity and madness in that big country. People who went down went down slowly, irretrievably, and the ones who didn't were not free from days when they thought they might.

So the months passed. The winds blew and brought storm and heat and sunshine and cloud. Nothing, in

*that big land, appreciably changed, except the people;
and they so imperceptibly that they failed to realize it
until afterward.*

Some years ago I left my apartment and job in the
San Francisco Bay Area to move to a ranch at nine
thousand feet on the Continental Divide in a county
that has nearly a thousand square miles and less than
five hundred people. I drive 90 miles to the nearest
grocery store, 250 miles to the nearest airport. I have a
phone, a fax machine, a computer, running water, in-
door plumbing, propane heat, four-wheel drive, gortex
weather gear, and sixteen inches of fiberglass insula-
tion. My life is nothing like B. M. Bowers'—except in
the ways it is everything like it.

When she writes about the isolation, the loneliness,
the strangeness of being a smart and articulate woman
in a place where people would just as soon you weren't
that way; about the way her fear and love for the sur-
rounding lonely land get so balled up together there
ought to be a single word for it; about the way it is the
land, finally, that makes her what she is—then I know
that there is little more than the better part of a cen-
tury between us and that she has left *Lonesome Land*
like a message in a bottle for me and for all of those
like me to find.

*She was not the prim, perfectly well bred woman he
had met at the train,* Kent Burnett says of Val. *Lonesome Land was doing its work. She was beginning to
think as an individual—as a woman; not merely as a
member of conventional society.*

When a woman comes west for the first time and
falls in love with the landscape, it isn't the same as her
first view of Paris or the New York City skyline or even

Niagara Falls. Even today the West is still big and free and marvelous in a way our East Coast upbringing and our liberal arts colleges can't ever prepare us for.

Our first response, often, is to be overwhelmed by it. Our second response, sometimes, is to find a man who will translate that beauty for us. But one day we hear it whispering to us when the man is not around. We begin to marvel daily at the beauty and the wildness of it. We learn to fight for it and against it. We put out the fires, we pray for rain. We wait and we wait for the wind to stop blowing. We pray that this winter is not as cold as the last. We dance alone in the first sweet grasses of spring. We walk on the land, we raise children in it, we curse it, we love it, we make it our own. One day we realize it has been a very long time since we needed a translator. Our lives have become so bound up in the land that we can no longer find the separation; that the land speaks to us and through us in a way that it hasn't before spoken; that our woman's ears hear it differently than it has ever been heard before.

Our next response, if we're lucky, is to write.

Contents

CONTENTS

List of Illustrations

Lonesome Land

CHAPTER I

THE ARRIVAL OF VAL

IN northern Montana there lies a great, lonely stretch
of prairie land, gashed deep where flows the Missouri.
Indeed, there are many such — big, impassive, impressive
in their very loneliness, in summer given over to the winds
and the meadow larks and to the shadows fleeing always
over the hilltops. Wild range cattle feed there and grow
sleek and fat for the fall shipping of beef. At night the
coyotes yap quaveringly and prowl abroad after the long-
eared jack rabbits, which bounce away at their hunger-
driven approach. In winter it is not good to be there;
even the beasts shrink then from the bleak, level reaches,
and shun the still bleaker heights.

But men will live anywhere if by so doing there is
money to be gained, and so a town snuggled up against
the northern rim of the bench land, where the bleakness
was softened a bit by the sheltering hills, and a willow-
fringed creek with wild rosebushes and chokecherries

made a vivid green background for the meager huddle of little, unpainted buildings.

To the passengers on the through trains which watered at the red tank near the creek, the place looked crudely picturesque — interesting, so long as one was not compelled to live there and could retain a perfectly impersonal viewpoint. After five or ten minutes spent in watching curiously the one little street, with the long hitching poles planted firmly and frequently down both sides — usually within a very few steps of a saloon door — and the horses nodding and stamping at the flies, and the loitering figures that appeared now and then in desultory fashion, many of them imagined that they understood the West and sympathized with it, and appreciated its bigness and its freedom from conventions.

One slim young woman had just told the thin-faced school teacher on a vacation, with whom she had formed one of those evanescent traveling acquaintances, that she already knew the West, from instinct and from Manley's letters. She loved it, she said, because Manley loved it, and because it was to be her home, and because it was so big and so free. Out here one could think and grow and really live, she declared, with enthusiasm. Manley had lived here for three years, and his letters, she told the thin-faced teacher, were an education in themselves.

The teacher had already learned that the slim young woman, with the yellow-brown hair and yellow-brown eyes to match, was going to marry Manley — she had forgotten his other name, though the young woman had mentioned it — and would live on a ranch, a cattle ranch. She smiled with somewhat wistful sympathy, and hoped the young woman would be happy; and the young woman waved her hand, with the glove only half pulled on, toward the shadow-dappled prairie and the willow-fringed creek, and the hills beyond.

"Happy!" she echoed joyously. "Could one be anything else, in such a country? And then — you don't know Manley, you see. It's horribly bad form, and undignified and all that, to prate of one's private affairs, but I just can't help bubbling over. I'm not looking for heaven, and I expect to have plenty of bumpy places in the trail — trail is anything that you travel over, out here; Manley has coached me faithfully — but I'm going to be happy. My mind is quite made up. Well, good-by — I'm so glad you happened to be on this train, and I wish I might meet you again. Isn't it a funny little depot? Oh, yes — thank you! I almost forgot that umbrella, and I might need it. Yes, I'll write to you — I should hate to drop out of your mind completely. Address me Mrs. Manley Fleetwood, Hope, Montana. Good-by — I wish —"

She trailed off down the aisle with eyes shining, in the wake of the grinning porter. She hurried down the steps, glanced hastily along the platform, up at the car window where the faded little school teacher was smiling wearily down at her, waved her hand, threw a dainty little kiss, nodded a gay farewell, smiled vaguely at the conductor, who had been respectfully pleasant to her — and then she was looking at the rear platform of the receding train mechanically, not yet quite realizing why it was that her heart went heavy so suddenly. She turned then and looked about her in a surprised, inquiring fashion. Manley, it would seem, was not at hand to welcome her. She had expected his face to be the first she looked upon in that town, but she tried not to be greatly perturbed at his absence; so many things may detain one.

At that moment a young fellow, whose clothes emphatically proclaimed him a cowboy, came diffidently up to her, tilted his hat backward an inch or so, and left it that way, thereby unconsciously giving himself an air of candor which should have been reassuring.

"Fleetwood was detained. You were expecting to — you 're the lady he was expecting, are n't you?"

She had been looking questioningly at her violin box and two trunks standing on their ends farther down the platform, and she smiled vaguely without glancing at him.

"Yes. I hope he is n't sick, or —"

"I 'll take you over to the hotel, and go tell him you 're here," he volunteered, somewhat curtly, and picked up her bag.

"Oh, thank you." This time her eyes grazed his face inattentively. She followed him down the rough steps of planking and up an extremely dusty road — one could scarcely call it a street — to an uninviting building with crooked windows and a high, false front of unpainted boards.

The young fellow opened a sagging door, let her pass into a narrow hallway, and from there into a stuffy, hopelessly conventional fifth-rate parlor, handed her the bag, and departed with another tilt of the hat which placed it at a different angle. The sentence meant for farewell she did not catch, for she was staring at a wooden-faced portrait upon an easel, the portrait of a man with a drooping mustache, and porky cheeks, and dead-looking eyes.

"And I expected bearskin rugs, and antlers on the walls, and big fireplaces!" she remarked aloud, and sighed. Then she turned and pulled aside a coarse curtain of dusty, machine-made lace, and looked after her guide. He was just disappearing into a saloon across the street, and she dropped the curtain precipitately, as if she were ashamed of spying. "Oh, well — I 've heard all cowboys are more or less intemperate," she excused, again aloud.

She sat down upon an atrocious red plush chair, and wrinkled her nose spitefully at the porky-cheeked portrait. "I suppose you 're the proprietor," she accused, "or else the proprietor's son. I wish you would n't squint like that. If I have to stop here longer than ten minutes, I shall certainly turn you face to the wall." Whereupon, with another grimace, she turned her back upon it and looked out of the window. Then she stood up impatiently, looked at her watch, and sat down again upon the red plush chair.

"He did n't tell me whether Manley is sick," she said suddenly, with some resentment. "He was awfully abrupt in his manner. Oh, you —" She rose, picked up an old newspaper from the marble-topped table with uncertain legs, and spread it ungently over the portrait upon the easel. Then she went to the window and looked out again. "I feel perfectly sure that cowboy went and got drunk immediately," she complained, drumming pettishly upon the glass. "And I don't suppose he told Manley at all."

The cowboy was innocent of the charge, however, and he was doing his energetic best to tell Manley. He had gone straight through the saloon and into the small room behind, where a man lay sprawled upon a bed in one corner. He was asleep, and his clothes were wrinkled as if he had lain there long. His head rested upon his folded arms, and he was snoring loudly. The young fellow went up and took him roughly by the shoulder.

"Here! I thought I told you to straighten up," he cried disgustedly. "Come alive! The train's come and gone, and your girl's waiting for you over to the hotel. D' you hear?"

"Uh-huh!" The man opened one eye, grunted, and closed it again.

The other yanked him half off the bed, and swore. This brought both eyes open, glassy with whisky and sleep. He sat wobbling upon the edge of the bed, staring stupidly.

"Can't you get anything through you?" his tormentor exclaimed. "You want your girl to find out you're drunk? You got the license in your pocket. You're supposed to get spliced this evening — and look at you!" He turned and went out to the bartender.

"Why did n't you pour that coffee into him, like I told you?" he demanded. "We've got to get him steady on his pins *somehow!*"

The bartender was sprawled half over the bar, apathetically reading the sporting news of a torn Sunday edition of an Eastern paper. He looked up from under his eyebrows and grunted.

"How you going to pour coffee down a man that lays flat on his belly and won't open his mouth?" he inquired, in an injured tone. "Sleep 's all he needs, anyway. He 'll be all right by morning."

The other snorted dissent. "He 'll be all right by dark — or he 'll feel a whole lot worse," he promised grimly. "Dig up some ice. And a good jolt of bromo, if you 've got it — and a towel or two."

The bartender wearily pushed the paper to one side, reached languidly under the bar, and laid hold of a round blue bottle. Yawning uninterestedly, he poured a double portion of the white crystals into a glass, half filled another under the faucet of the water cooler, and held them out.

"Dump that into him, then," he advised. "It 'll help some, if you get it down. What 's the sweat to get him married off to-day? Won't the girl wait?"

"I never asked her. You pound up some ice and bring it in, will you?" The volunteer nurse kicked open the door into the little room and went in, hastily pouring the bromo seltzer from one glass to the other to keep it from foaming out of all bounds. His patient was still sitting upon the edge of the bed where he had left him, slumped forward with his head in his hands. He looked up stupidly, his eyes bloodshot and swollen of lid.

" 'S the train come in yet?" he asked thickly. " 'S you, is it, Kent?"

" The train 's come, and your girl is waiting for you at the hotel. Here, throw this into you — and for God's sake, brace up! You make me tired. Drink her down quick — the foam 's good for you. Here, you take the stuff in the bottom, too. Got it? Take off your coat, so I can get at you. You don't look much like getting married, and that 's no josh."

Fleetwood shook his head with drunken gravity, and groaned. "I ought to be killed. Drunk to-day!" He sagged forward again, and seemed disposed to shed tears. "She 'll never forgive me; she —"

Kent jerked him to his feet peremptorily. "Aw, look here! I 'm trying to sober you up. You 've got to do your part — see? Here 's some ice in a towel — you get it on your head. Open up your shirt, so I can bathe your chest. Don't do any good to blubber around about it. Your girl can't hear you, and Jim and I ain't sympathetic. Set down in this chair, where we can get at you." He enforced his command with some vigor, and Fleetwood groaned again. But he shed no more tears, and he grew momentarily more lucid, as the treatment took effect.

The tears were being shed in the stuffy little hotel parlor. The young woman looked often at her watch, went into the hallway, and opened the outer door several times, meditating a search of the town, and drew back always with a timid fluttering of heart because it was all so crude and strange, and the saloons so numerous and terrifying in their very bald simplicity.

She was worried about Manley, and she wished that cowboy would come out of the saloon and bring her lover to her. She had never dreamed of being treated in this way. No one came near her — and she had secretly expected to cause something of a flutter in this little town they called Hope.

Surely, young girls from the East, come out to get married to their sweethearts, were n't so numerous that they should be ignored. If there were other people in the hotel, they did not manifest their presence, save by disquieting noises muffled by intervening partitions.

She grew thirsty, but she hesitated to explore the depths of this dreary abode, in fear of worse horrors than the parlor furniture, and all the places of refreshment which she could see from the window or the door looked terribly masculine and immoral, and as if they did not know there existed such things as ice cream, or soda, or sherbet.

It was after an hour of this that the tears came, which is saying a good deal for her courage. It seemed to her then that Manley must be dead. What else could keep him so long away from her, after three years of impassioned longing written twice a week with punctilious regularity?

He knew that she was coming. She had telegraphed from St. Paul, and had received a joyful reply, lavishly expressed in seventeen words instead of the ten-word limit. And they were to have been married immediately upon her arrival.

That cowboy had known she was coming; he must also have known why Manley did not meet her, and she wished futilely that she had questioned him, instead of walking beside him without a word. He should have explained. He would have explained if he had not been so very anxious to get inside that saloon and get drunk.

She had always heard that cowboys were chivalrous, and brave, and fascinating in their picturesque dare-deviltry, but from the lone specimen which she had met she could not see that they possessed any of those qualities. If all cowboys were like that, she hoped that she would not be compelled to meet any of them. And *why* did n't Manley come?

It was then that an inner door — a door which she had wanted to open, but had lacked courage — squeaked upon its hinges, and an ill-kept bundle of hair was thrust in, topping a weather-beaten face and a scrawny little body. Two faded, inquisitive eyes looked her over, and the woman sidled in, somewhat abashed, but too curious to remain outside.

"Oh yes!" She seemed to be answering some inner question. "I did n't know you was here." She went over and removed the newspaper from the portrait.

"That breed girl of mine ain't got the least idea of how to straighten up a room," she observed complainingly. "I guess she thinks this picture was made to hang things on. I'll have to round her up again and tell her a few things. This is my first husband. He was in politics and got beat, and so he killed himself. He could n't stand to have folks give him the laugh." She spoke with pride. "He was a real handsome man, don't you think? You mighta took off the paper; it did n't belong there, and he does brighten up the room. A good picture is real company, seems to me. When my old man gets on the rampage till I can't stand it no longer, I come in here and set, and look at Walt. 'T ain't every man that's got nerve to kill himself — with a shotgun. It was turrible! He took and tied a string to the trigger —"

"Oh, please!"

The landlady stopped short and stared at her. "What? Oh, I won't go into details — it was awful messy, and that's a fact. I did n't git over it for a couple of months. He coulda killed himself with a six-shooter; it's always been a mystery why he dug up that old shotgun, but he did. I always thought he wanted to show his nerve." She sighed, and drew her fingers across her eyes. "I don't s'pose I ever will git over it," she added complacently. "It was a turrible shock."

"Do you know," the girl began desperately, "if Mr.

Manley Fleetwood is in town? I expected him to meet me at the train."

"Oh! I kinda *thought* you was Man Fleetwood's girl. My name 's Hawley. You going to be married to-night, ain't you?"

"I — I have n't seen Mr. Fleetwood yet," hesitated the girl, and her eyes filled again with tears. "I 'm afraid something may have happened to him. He —"

Mrs. Hawley glimpsed the tears, and instantly became motherly in her manner. She even went up and patted the girl on the shoulder.

"There, now, don't you worry none. Man 's all right; I seen him at dinner time. He was —" She stopped short, looked keenly at the delicate face, and at the yellow-brown eyes which gazed back at her, innocent of evil, trusting, wistful. "He spoke about your coming, and said he 'd want the use of the parlor this evening, for the wedding. I had an idea you was coming on the six-twenty train. Maybe he thought so, too. I never heard you come in — I was busy frying doughnuts in the kitchen — and I just happened to come in here after something. You 'd oughta rapped on that door. Then I 'd 'a' known you was here. I 'll go and have my old man hunt him up. He must be around town somewheres. Like as not he 'll meet the six-twenty, expecting you to be on it."

She smiled reassuringly as she turned to the inner door.

"You take off your hat and jacket, and pretty soon I'll show you up to a room. I'll have to round up my old man first — and that's liable to take time." She turned her eyes quizzically to the porky-cheeked portrait. "You jest let Walt keep you company till I get back. He was real good company when he was livin'."

She smiled again and went out briskly, came back, and stood with her hand upon the cracked doorknob.

"I clean forgot your name," she hinted. "Man told me, at dinner time, but I'm no good on earth at remembering names till after I've seen the person it belongs to."

"Valeria Peyson — Val, they call me usually, at home." The homesickness of the girl shone in her misty eyes, haunted her voice. Mrs. Hawley read it, and spoke more briskly than she would otherwise have done.

"Well, we're plumb strangers, but we ain't going to stay that way, because every time you come to town you'll have to stop here; there ain't any other place to stop. And I'm going to start right in calling you Val. We don't use no ceremony with folk's names, out here. Val's a real nice name, short and easy to say. Mine's Arline. You can call me by it if you want to. I don't let everybody — so many wants to cut it down to Leen, and I won't stand for that; I'm *lean* enough, without havin' it throwed up to me. We might jest as well start in the way we 're likely to keep it up, and you won't feel so much like a stranger.

"I 'm awful glad you 're going to settle here — there ain't so awful many women in the country; we have to rake and scrape to git enough for three sets when we have a dance — and more likely we can't make out more 'n two. D' you dance? Somebody said they seen a fiddle box down to the depot, with a couple of big trunks; d' you play the fiddle?"

"A little," Valeria smiled faintly.

"Well, that 'll come in awful handy at dances. We 'd have 'em real often in the winter if it was n't such a job to git music. Well, I got too much to do to be standin' here talkin'. I have to keep right after that breed girl all the time, or she won't do nothing. I 'll git my old man after your fellow right away. Jest make yourself to home, and anything you want ask for it in the kitchen." She smiled in friendly fashion and closed the door with a little slam to make sure that it latched.

Valeria stood for a moment with her hands hanging straight at her sides, staring absently at the door. Then she glanced at Walt, staring wooden-faced from his gilt frame upon his gilt easel, and shivered. She pushed the red plush chair as far away from him as possible, sat down with her back to the picture, and immediately felt his dull, black eyes boring into her back.

"What a fool I must be!" she said aloud, glancing reluctantly over her shoulder at the portrait. She got up resolutely, placed the chair where it had stood before, and stared deliberately at Walt, as if she would prove how little she cared. But in a moment more she was crying dismally.

CHAPTER II

WELL-MEANT ADVICE

KENT BURNETT, bearing over his arm a coat newly pressed in the Delmonico restaurant, dodged in at the back door of the saloon, threw the coat down upon the tousled bed, and pushed back his hat with a gesture of relief at an onerous duty well performed.

"I had one hell of a time," he announced plaintively, "and that Chink will likely try to poison me if I eat over there, after this — but I got her ironed, all right. Get into it, Man, and chase yourself over there to the hotel. Got a clean collar? That one's all-over coffee."

Fleetwood stifled a groan, reached into a trousers pocket, and brought up a dollar. "Get me one at the store, will you, Kent? Fifteen and a half — and a tie, if they've got any that's decent. And hurry! Such a triple-three-star fool as I am ought to be taken out and shot."

He went on cursing himself audibly and bitterly, even after Kent had hurried out. He was sober now — was Manley Fleetwood — sober and self-condemnatory and penitent. His head ached splittingly; his eyes were heavy-lidded and bloodshot, and his hands trembled so that he could scarcely button his coat. But he was sober. He did not even carry the odor of whisky upon his breath or his person; for Kent had been very thoughtful and very thorough. He had compelled his patient to crunch and swallow many nauseous tablets of "whisky killer," and he had sprinkled his clothes liberally with Jockey Club; Fleetwood, therefore, while he emanated odors in plenty, carried about him none of the aroma properly belonging to intoxication.

In ten minutes Kent was back, with a celluloid collar and two ties of questionable taste. Manley just glanced at them, waved them away with gloomy finality, and swore.

"They 're just about the limit, and that 's no dream," sympathized Kent, "but they 're clean, and they don't look like they 'd been slept in for a month. You 've got to put 'em on — by George, I sized up the layout in both those imitation stores, and I drew the highest in the deck. And for the Lord's sake, get a move on. Here, I 'll button it for you."

Behind Fleetwood's back, when collar and tie were in place, Kent grinned and lowered an eyelid at Jim, who put his head in from the saloon to see how far the sobering had progressed.

"You look fine!" he encouraged heartily. "That green-and-blue tie 's just what you need to set you off.

And the collar sure is shiny and nice — your girl will be plumb dazzled. She won't see anything wrong — believe *me*. Now, run along and get married. Here, you better sneak out the back way; if she happened to be looking out, she 'd likely wonder what you were doing, coming out of a saloon. Duck out past the coal shed and cut into the street by Brinberg's. Tell her you 're sick — got a sick headache. Your looks 'll swear it 's the truth. Hike!" He opened the door and pushed Fleetwood out, watched him out of sight around the corner of Brinberg's store, and turned back into the close-smelling little room.

"Do you know," he remarked to Jim, "I never thought of it before, but I 've been playing a low-down trick on that poor girl. I kinda wish now I 'd put her next, and given her a chance to draw outa the game if she wanted to. It 's stacking the deck on her, if you ask *me!*" He pushed his hat back upon his head, gave his shoulders a twist of dissatisfaction, and told Jim to dig up some Eastern beer; drank it meditatively, and set down the glass with some force.

"Yes, sir," he said disgustedly, "darn my fool soul, I stacked the deck on that girl — and she looked to be real nice. Kinda innocent and trusting, like she has n't found out yet how rotten mean men critters can be." He took the bottle and poured himself another glass. "She 's sure due to wise up a lot," he added grimly.

"You bet your sweet life!" Jim agreed, and then he reconsidered. "Still, I dunno; Man ain't so worse. He ain't what you can call a real booze fighter. This here 's what I 'd call an accidental jag; got it in the exuberance of the joyful moment when he knew his girl was coming. He 'll likely straighten up and be all right. He —" Jim broke off there and looked to see who had opened the door.

"Hello, Polly," he greeted carelessly.

The man came forward, grinning skinnily. Polycarp Jenks was the outrageous name of him. He was under the average height, and he was lean to the point of emaciation. His mouth was absolutely curveless — a straight gash across his face; a gash which simply stopped short without any tapering or any turn at the corners, when it had reached as far as was decent. His nose was also straight and high, and owned no perceptible slope; indeed, it seemed merely a pendant attached to his forehead, and its upper termination was indefinite, except that somewhere between his eyebrows one felt impelled to consider it forehead rather than nose. His eyes also were rather long and narrow, like buttonholes cut to match the mouth. When he grinned his face appeared to break up into splinters.

He was intensely proud of his name, and his pleasure was almost pathetic when one pronounced it without curtailment in his presence. His skinniness was also a matter of pride. And when you realize that he was an indefatigable gossip, and seemed always to be riding at large, gathering or imparting trivial news, you should know fairly well Polycarp Jenks.

"I see Man Fleetwood 's might' near sober enough to git married," Polycarp began, coming up to the two and leaning a sharp elbow upon the bar beside Kent. "By granny, gitting married 'd sober anybody! Dinner time he was so drunk he could n't find his mouth. I met him up here a little ways just now, and he was so sober he remembered to pay me that ten I lent him t' other day — *he-he!* Open up a bottle of pop, James.

"His girl 's been might' near crying her eyes out, 'cause he did n't show up. Mis' Hawley says she looked like she was due at a funeral 'stid of a weddin'. 'Clined to be stuck up, accordin' to Mis' Hawley — shied at hearin' about Walt — *he-he!* I 'll bet there ain't been a transient to that hotel in the last five year, man or woman, that ain't had to hear about Walt and the shotgun — Pop 's all right on a hot day, you bet!

" She 's got two trunks and a fiddle over to the depot — don't see how 'n the world Man 's going to git 'em out to the ranch; they 're might' near as big as claim shacks, both of 'em. Time she gits 'em into Man's shack she 'll have to go outside every time she wants to turn around — *he-he!*

By granny — two trunks, to one woman! Have some pop, Kenneth, on me.

"The boys are talkin' about a shivaree t'-night. On the quiet, y' know. Some of 'em 's workin' on a horse fiddle now, over in the lumber yard. Wanted me to play a coal-oil can, but I dunno. I 'm gittin' a leetle old for sech doings. Keeps you up nights too much. Man had any sense, he 'd marry and pull outa town. 'Bout fifteen or twenty in the bunch, and a string of cans and irons to reach clean across the street. By granny, I 'm going to plug m' ears good with cotton when it comes off — *he-he!* 'Nother bottle of pop, James."

"Who 's running the show, Polycarp?" Kent asked, accepting the glass of soda because he disliked to offend. "Funny I did n't hear about it."

Polycarp twisted his slit of a mouth knowingly, and closed one slit of an eye to assist the facial elucidation.

"Ain't funny — not when I tell you Fred De Garmo 's handing out the *in*vites, and he sure aims to have plenty of excitement — *he-he!* Betcher Manley won't be able to set on the wagon seat an' hold the lines t'-morrow — not if he comes out when he 's called and does the thing proper — *he-he!* An' if he don't show up, they aim to jest about pull the old shebang down over his ears. Hope 'll think it 's the day of judgment, sure — *he-he!* Reckon I might 's well git in on the fun — they won't be no sleepin' within ten mile of the place, nohow, and a feller always sees the joke better when he's lendin' a hand. Too bad you an' Fred's on the outs, Kenneth."

"Oh, I don't know — it suits me fine," Kent declared easily, setting down his glass with a sigh of relief; he hated " pop."

"What's it all about, anyway?" quizzed Polycarp, hungering for the details which had thus far been denied him. "De Garmo sees red whenever anybody mentions your name, Kenneth—but I never did hear no particulars."

"No?" Kent was turning toward the door. " Well, you see, Fred claims he can holler louder than I can, and I say he can't." He opened the door and calmly departed, leaving Polycarp looking exceedingly foolish and a bit angry.

Straight to the hotel, without any pretense at disguising his destination, marched Kent. He went into the office — which was really a saloon — invited Hawley to drink with him, and then wondered audibly if he could beg some pie from Mrs. Hawley.

"Supper 'll be ready in a few minutes," Hawley informed him, glancing up at the round, dust-covered clock screwed to the wall.

"I don't want supper — I want pie," Kent retorted, and opened a door which led into the hallway. He went down the narrow passage to another door, opened it

without ceremony, and was assailed by the odor of many
things — the odor which spoke plainly of supper, or
some other assortment of food. No one was in sight, so
he entered the dining room boldly, stepped to another
door, tapped very lightly upon it, and went in. By this
somewhat roundabout method he invaded the parlor.

Manley Fleetwood was lying upon an extremely uncomfortable couch, of the kind which is called a sofa. He
had a lace-edged handkerchief folded upon his brow, and
upon his face was an expression of conscious unworthiness
which struck Kent as being extremely humorous. He
grinned understandingly and Manley flushed — also understandingly. Valeria hastily released Manley's hand and
looked very prim and a bit haughty, as she regarded the
intruder from the red plush chair, pulled close to the
couch.

"Mr. Fleetwood's head is very bad yet," she informed
Kent coldly. "I really do not think he ought to see —
anybody."

Kent tapped his hat gently against his leg and faced
her unflinchingly, quite unconscious of the fact that she
regarded him as a dissolute, drunken cowboy with whom
Manley ought not to associate.

"That's too bad." His eyes failed to drop guiltily
before hers, but continued to regard her calmly. "I'm
only going to stay a minute. I came to tell you that

there's a scheme to raise — to 'shivaree' you two, to-night. I thought you might want to pull out, along about dark."

Manley looked up at him inquiringly with the eye which was not covered by the lace-edged handkerchief. Valeria seemed startled, just at first. Then she gave Kent a little shock of surprise.

"I have read about such things. A *charivari*, even out here in this uncivilized section of the country, can hardly be dangerous. I really do not think we care to run away, thank you." Her lip curled unmistakably. "Mr. Fleetwood is suffering from a sick headache. He needs rest — not a cowardly night ride."

Naturally Kent admired the spirit she showed, in spite of that eloquent lip, the scorn of which seemed aimed directly at him. But he still faced her steadily.

"Sure. But if I had a headache — like that — I'd certainly burn the earth getting outa town to-night. *Shivarees*" — he stuck stubbornly to his own way of saying it — "are bad for the head. They are n't what you could call silent — not out here in this uncivilized section of the country. They're plumb —" He hesitated for just a fraction of a second, and his resentment of her tone melted into a twinkle of the eyes. "They've got fifty coal-oil cans strung with irons on a rope, and there'll be about ninety-five six-shooters popping, and eight or ten horse-fiddles, and they'll all be yelling to beat four of a kind. They're going," he said quite gravely, "to play the full orchestra. And I don't believe," he added ironically, "it's going to help Mr. Fleetwood's head any."

Valeria looked at him doubtingly with steady, amber-colored eyes before she turned solicitously to readjust the lace-edged handkerchief. Kent seized the opportunity to stare fixedly at Fleetwood and jerk his head meaningly backward, but when, warned by Manley's changing expression, she glanced suspiciously over her shoulder, Kent was standing quietly by the door with his hat in his hand, gazing absently at Walt in his gilt-edged frame upon the gilt easel, and waiting, evidently, for their decision.

"I shall tell them that Mr. Fleetwood is sick — that he has a horrible headache, and mustn't be disturbed."

Kent forgot himself so far as to cough slightly behind his hand. Valeria's eyes sparkled.

"Even out here," she went on cuttingly, "there must be some men who are gentlemen!"

Kent refrained from looking at her, but the blood crept darkly into his tanned cheeks. Evidently she "had it in for him," but he could not see why. He wondered swiftly if she blamed him for Manley's condition.

Fleetwood suddenly sat up, spilling the handkerchief

to the floor. When Valeria essayed to push him back he put her hand gently away. He rose and came over to Kent.

"Is this straight goods?" he demanded. "Why don't you stop it?"

"Fred De Garmo 's running this show. My influence would n't go as far —"

Fleetwood turned to the girl, and his manner was masterful. "I 'm going out with Kent — oh, Val, this is Mr. Burnett. Kent, Miss Peyson. I forgot you two are n't acquainted."

From Valeria's manner, they were in no danger of becoming friends. Her acknowledgment was barely perceptible. Kent bowed stiffly.

"I 'm going to see about this, Val," continued Fleetwood. "Oh, my head 's better — a lot better, really. Maybe we 'd better leave town —"

"If your head is better, I don't see why we need run away from a lot of silly noise," Valeria interposed, with merciless logic. "They 'll think we 're awful cowards."

"Well, I 'll try and find out — I won't be gone a minute, dear." After that word, spoken before another, he appeared to be in great haste, and pushed Kent rather unceremoniously through the door. In the dining room, Kent diplomatically included the landlady in the conference, by a gesture of much mystery bringing her in from the kitchen, where she had been curiously peeping out at them.

"Got to let her in," he whispered to Manley, "to keep her face closed."

They murmured together for five minutes. Kent seemed to meet with some opposition from Fleetwood — an aftermath of Valeria's objections to flight — and became brutally direct.

"Go ahead — do as you please," he said roughly. "But you know that bunch. You'll have to show up, and you'll have to set 'em up, and — aw, thunder! By morning you'll be plumb laid out. You'll be headed into one of your four-day jags, and you know it. I was thinking of the girl — but if you don't care, I guess it's none of my funeral. Go to it — but darned if I'd want to start my honeymoon out like that!"

Fleetwood weakened, but still he hesitated. "If I didn't show up —" he began hopefully. But Kent withered him with a look.

"That bunch will be two-thirds full before they start out. If you don't show up, they'll go up and haul you outa bed — hell, Man! You'd likely start in to kill somebody off. Fred De Garmo don't love you much better than he loves me. You know what him and his friends would do then, I should think." He stopped, and seemed to consider briefly a plan, but shook his head over it. "I could round up a bunch and stand 'em off, maybe — but we 'd be shooting each other up, first rattle of the box. It 's a whole lot easier for you to get outa town."

"I 'll tell somebody you got the bridal chamber," hissed Arline, in a very loud whisper. "That 's number two, in front. I can keep a light going and pass back 'n' forth once in a while, to look like you 're there. That 'll fool 'em good. They 'll wait till the light 's been out quite a while before they start in. You go ahead and git married at seven, jest as you was going to — and if Kent'll have the team ready somewheres, I can easy sneak you out the back way."

"I could n't get the team out of town without giving the whole deal away," Kent objected. "You 'll have to go horseback."

"Val can't ride," Fleetwood stated, as if that settled the matter.

"Damn it, she 's got to ride!" snapped Kent, losing patience. "Unless you want to stay and go on a toot that 'll last a week, most likely."

"Val belongs to the W. C. T. U.," shrugged Fleetwood. "She 'd never —"

"Well, it 's that or have a fight on your hands you maybe can't handle. I don't see any sense in haggling about going, now you know what to expect. But, of course," he added, with some acrimony, "it 's your own business. I don't know what the dickens I'm getting all worked up over it for. Suit yourself." He turned toward the door.

"She could ride my Mollie — and I got a sidesaddle hanging up in the coal shed. She could use that, or a stock saddle, either one," planned Mrs. Hawley anxiously. "You better pull out, Man."

"Hold on, Kent! Don't rush off — we'll go," Fleetwood surrendered. "Val won't like it, but I'll explain as well as I can, without — Say! you stay and see us married, won't you? It's at seven, and —"

Kent's fingers curled around the doorknob. "No, thanks. Weddings and funerals are two bunches of trouble I always ride 'way around. Time enough when you've got to be *it*. Along about nine o'clock you try and get out to the stockyards without letting the whole town see you go, and I'll have the horses there; just beyond the wings, by that pile of ties. You know the place. I'll wait there till ten, and not a minute longer. That'll give you an hour, and you won't need any more time than that if you get down to business. You find out from her what saddle she wants, and you can tell me while I'm eating supper, Mrs. Hawley. I'll 'tend to the rest." He did not wait to hear whether they agreed to the plan, but went moodily down the narrow passage, and entered frowningly the "office." Several men were gathered there, waiting the supper summons. Hawley glanced up from wiping a glass, and grinned.

"Well, did you git the pie?"

"Naw. She said I 'd got to wait for mealtime. She plumb chased me out."

Fred De Garmo, sprawled in an armchair and smoking a cigar, lazily fanned the smoke cloud from before his face and looked at Kent attentively.

CHAPTER III

TO saddle two horses when the night has grown black and to lead them, unobserved, so short a distance as two hundred yards or so seems a simple thing; and for two healthy young people with full use of their wits and their legs to steal quietly away to where those horses are waiting would seem quite as simple. At the same time, to prevent the successful accomplishment of these things is not difficult, if one but fully understands the designs of the fugitives.

Hawley Hotel did a flourishing business that night. The two long tables in the dining room, usually not more than half filled by those who hungered and were not over-nice concerning the food they ate, were twice filled to overflowing. Mrs. Hawley and the "breed" girl held hasty consultations in the kitchen over the supply, and never was there such a rattling of dishes hurriedly cleansed for the next comer.

Kent managed to find a chair at the first table, and eyed the landlady unobtrusively. But Fred De Garmo sat down opposite, and his eyes were bright and watchful, so that there seemed no possible way of delivering a message undetected — until, indeed, Mrs. Hawley in desperation resorted to strategy, and urged Kent unnecessarily to take another slice of bacon.

"Have some more — it's *side!*" she hissed in his ear, and watched anxiously his face.

"All right," said Kent, and speared a slice with his fork, although his plate was already well supplied with bacon. Then, glancing up, he detected Fred in a thoughtful stare which seemed evenly divided between the landlady and himself. Kent was conscious of a passing, mental discomfort, which he put aside as foolish, because De Garmo could not possibly know what Mrs. Hawley meant. To ease his mind still further he glared insolently at Fred, and then at Polycarp Jenks *te-hee*ing a few chairs away. After that he finished as quickly as possible without exciting remark, and went his way.

He had not, however, been two minutes in the office before De Garmo entered. From that time on through the whole-evening Fred was never far distant; wherever he went, Kent could not shake him off though De Garmo never seemed to pay any attention to him, and his presence was always apparently accidental.

"I reckon I'll have to lick that son of a gun yet," sighed Kent, when a glance at the round clock in the hotel office told him that in just twenty minutes it would strike nine;

and not a move made toward getting those horses saddled and out to the stockyards.

There was much talk of the wedding, which had taken place quietly in the parlor at the appointed hour, but not a man mentioned a *charivari*. There were many who wished openly that Fleetwood would come out and be sociable about it, but not a hint that they intended to take measures to bring him among them. He had caused a box of cigars to be placed upon the bar of every saloon in town, where men might help themselves at his expense. Evidently he had considered that with the cigars his social obligations were canceled. They smoked the cigars, and, with the same breath, gossiped of him and his affairs.

At just fourteen minutes to nine Kent went out, and, without any attempt at concealment, hurried to the Hawley stables. Half a minute behind him trailed De Garmo, also without subterfuge.

Half an hour later the bridal couple stole away from the rear of the hotel, and, keeping to the shadows, went stumbling over the uneven ground to the stockyards.

"Here's the tie pile," Fleetwood announced, in an undertone, when they reached the place. "You stay here, Val, and I'll look farther along the fence; maybe the horses are down there."

Valeria did not reply, but stood very straight and dignified in the shadow of the huge pile of rotting railroad ties. He was gone but a moment, and came anxiously back to her.

"They 're not here," he said, in a low voice. "Don't worry, dear. He 'll come — I know Kent Burnett."

"Are you sure?" queried Val sweetly. "From what I have seen of the gentleman, your high estimate of him seems quite unauthorized. Aside from escorting me to the hotel, he has been anything but reliable. Instead of telling you that I was here, or telling me that you were sick, he went straight into a saloon and forgot all about us both. You know that. If he were your friend, why should he immediately begin carousing, instead of —"

"He did n't," Fleetwood defended weakly.

"No? Then perhaps you can explain his behavior. Why did n't he tell me you were sick? Why did n't he tell you I came on that train? Can you tell me that, Manley?"

Manley, for a very good reason, could not; so he put his arms around her and tried to coax her into good humor.

"Sweetheart, let 's not quarrel so soon — why, we 're only two hours married! I want you to be happy, and if you 'll only be brave and —"

"Brave!" Mrs. Fleetwood laughed rather contemptuously, for a bride. "Please to understand, Manley, that I 'm not frightened in the least. It 's you and that horrid cowboy — I don't see why we need run away, like crim-

inals. Those men don't intend to *murder* us, do they?"
Her mood softened a little, and she squeezed his arm
between her hands. "You dear old silly, I 'm not blaming
you. With your head in such a state, you can't think
things out properly, and you let that cowboy influence you
against your better judgment. You 're afraid I might be
annoyed — but, really, Manley, this silly idea of running
away annoys me much more than all the noise those fellows could possibly make. Indeed, I don't think I would
mind — it would give me a glimpse of the real West;
and, perhaps, if they grew too boisterous, and I spoke
to them and asked them not to be quite so rough — and,
really, they only mean it as a sort of welcome, in their
crude way. We could invite some of the nicest in to have
cake and coffee — or maybe we might get some ice cream
somewhere — and it might turn out a very pleasant little
affair. I don't mind meeting them, Manley. The worst
of them can't be as bad as that — but, of course, if he 's
your friend, I suppose I ought n't to speak too freely my
opinion of him!"

Fleetwood held her closely, patted her cheek absently,
and tried to think of some effective argument.

"They 'll be drunk, sweetheart," he told her, after
a silence.

"I don't think so," she returned firmly. "I have been
watching the street all the evening. I saw any number

of men passing back and forth, and I did n't see one who staggered. And they were all very quiet, considering their rough ways, which one must expect. Why, Manley, you always wrote about these Western men being such fine fellows, and so generous and big-hearted, under their rough exterior. Your letters were full of it — and how chivalrous they all are toward nice women."

She laid her head coaxingly against his shoulder. "Let 's go back, Manley. I — I *want* to see a *charivari*, dear. It will be fun. I want to write all about it to the girls. They 'll be perfectly wild with envy." She struggled with her conventional upbringing. "And even if some of them are slightly under the influence — of liquor, we need n't *meet* them. You need n't introduce those at all, and I 'm sure they will understand."

"Don't be silly, Val!" Fleetwood did not mean to be rude, but a faint glimmer of her romantic viewpoint — a viewpoint gained chiefly from current fiction and the stage — came to him and contrasted rather brutally with the reality. He did not know how to make her understand, without incriminating himself. His letters had been rather idealistic, he admitted to himself. They had been written unthinkingly, because he wanted her to like this big land; naturally he had not been too baldly truthful in picturing the place and the people. He had passed lightly over their faults and thrown the limelight on their virtues; and so he had aided unwittingly the stage and the fiction she had read, in giving her a false impression.

Offended at his words and his tone, she drew away from him and glanced wistfully back toward the town, as if she meditated a haughty return to the hotel. She ended by seating herself upon a projecting tie.

"Oh, very well, my lord," she retorted, "I shall try and not be silly, but merely idiotic, as you would have me. You and your friend!" She was very angry, but she was perfectly well-bred, she hoped. "If I might venture a word," she began again ironically, "it seems to me that your friend has been playing a practical joke upon you. He evidently has no intention of bringing any fleet steeds to us. No doubt he is at this moment laughing with his dissolute companions, because we are sitting out here in the dark like two silly chickens!"

"I think he's coming now," Manley said rather stiffly. "Of course, I don't ask you to like him; but he's putting himself to a good deal of trouble for us, and —"

"Wasted effort, so far as I am concerned," Valeria put in, with a chirpy accent which was exasperating, even to a bridegroom very much in love with his bride.

In the darkness that muffled the land, save where the yellow flare of lamps in the little town made a misty brightness, came the click of shod hoofs. Another moment and a man, mounted upon a white horse, loomed indistinct before them, seeming to take substance from the night. Behind him trailed another horse, and for the first time in her life Valeria heard the soft, whispering creak of saddle leather, the faint clank of spur chains, and the whir of a horse mouthing the "cricket" in his bit. Even in her anger, she was conscious of an answering tingle of blood, because this was life in the raw — life such as she had dreamed of in the tight swaddlings of a smug civilization, and had longed for intensely.

Kent swung down close beside them, his form indistinct but purposeful. "I 'm late, I guess," he remarked, turning to Fleetwood. "Fred got next, somehow, and — I was detained."

"Where is he?" asked Manley, going up and laying a questioning hand upon the horse, by that means fully recognizing it as Kent's own.

"In the oats box," said Kent laconically. He turned to the girl. "I could n't get the sidesaddle," he explained apologetically. "I looked where Mrs. Hawley said it was, but I could n't find it — and I did n't have much time. You 'll have to ride a stock saddle."

Valeria drew back a step. "You mean — a man's saddle?" Her voice was carefully polite.

"Why, yes." And he added: "The horse is dead gentle — and a sidesaddle 's no good, anyhow. You 'll like this better." He spoke, as was evident, purely from a man's viewpoint.

That viewpoint Mrs. Fleetwood refused to share. "Oh, I could n't ride a man's saddle," she protested, still politely, and one could imagine how her lips were pursed. "Indeed, I 'm not sure that I care to leave town at all." To her the declaration did not seem unreasonable or abrupt; but she felt that Kent was very much shocked. She saw him turn his head and look back toward the town, as if he half expected a pursuit.

"I don't reckon the oats box will hold Fred very long," he observed meditatively. He added reminiscently to Manley: "I had a deuce of a time getting the cover down and fastened."

"I 'm very sorry," said Valeria, with sweet dignity, "that you gave yourself so much trouble —"

"I 'm kinda sorry myself," Kent agreed mildly, and Valeria blushed hotly, and was glad he could not see.

"Come, Val — you can ride this saddle, all right. All the girls out here — "

"I did not come West to imitate all the girls. Indeed, I could never think of such a thing. I could n't possibly — really, Manley! And, you know, it does seem so childish of us to run away — "

Kent moved restlessly, and felt to see if the cinch was tight.

Fleetwood took her coaxingly by the arm. "Come, sweetheart, don't be stubborn. You know — "

"Well, really! If it's a question of obstinacy — You see, I look at the matter in this way: You believe that you are doing what is best for my sake; I don't agree with you — and it does seem as if I should be permitted to judge what I desire." Then her dignity and her sweet calm went down before a flash of real, unpolished temper. "You two can take those nasty horses and ride clear to Dakota, if you want to. I'm going back to the hotel. And I'm going to tell somebody to let that poor fellow out of that box. I think you're acting perfectly horrid, both of you, when I don't want to go!" She actually started back toward the scattered points of light.

She did not, however, get so far away that she failed to hear Kent's "Well, I'll be damned!" uttered in a tone of intense disgust.

"I don't care," she assured herself, because of the thrill of compunction caused by that one forcible sentence. She had never before in her life heard a man really swear. It affected her very much as would the accidental touch of an electric battery. She walked on slowly, stumbling a little and trying to hear what it was they were saying.

Then Kent passed her, loping back to the town, the led horse shaking his saddle so that it rattled the stirrups like castanets as he galloped. "I don't care," she told herself again very emphatically, because she was quite sure that she did care — or that she would care if only she permitted herself to be so foolish. Manley overtook her then, and drew her hand under his arm to lead her. But he seemed quite sullen, and would not say a word all the way back.

CHAPTER IV

THE "SHIVAREE"

KENT jerked open the stable door, led in his horses, turned them into their stalls, and removed the saddles with quick, nervous movements which told plainly how angry he was.

"I'll get myself all excited trying to do her a favor again — I don't think!" he growled in the ear of Michael, his gray gelding. "Think of me getting let down on my face like that! By a woman!"

He felt along the wall in the intense darkness until his fingers touched a lantern, took it down from the nail where it hung, and lighted it. He carried it farther down the rude passage between the stalls, hung it high upon another nail, and turned to the great oats box, from within which came a vigorous thumping and the sound of muttered cursing.

Kent was not in the mood to see the humor of anything in particular. Had he known anything about Pandora's box he might have drawn a comparison very neatly while he stood scowling down at the oats box, for certainly he

was likely to release trouble in plenty when he unfastened
that lid. He felt of the gun swinging at his hip, just to
assure himself that it was there and ready for business in
case Fred wanted to shoot, and rapped with his knuckles
upon the box, producing instant silence within.

"Don't make so much noise in there," he advised
grimly, "not unless you want the whole town to know
where you are, and have 'em give you the laugh. And,
listen here: I ain't apologizing for what I done, but, all
the same, I 'm sorry I did it. It was n't any use. I 'd
rather be shut up in an oats box all night than get let
down like I was — and I 'm telling you this so as to
start us off even. If you want to fight about it when
you come out, all right; you 're the doctor. But I 'm
just as sorry as you are it happened. I lay down my
hand right here. I hope you shivaree Man and his wife —
and shivaree 'em good. I hope you bust the town wide
open."

"Why this sudden change of heart?" came muffled
from within.

"Ah — that 's my own business. Well, I don't like you
a little bit, and you know it; but I 'll tell you, just to give
you a fair show. I wanted to keep Man sober, and I tried
to get him and his wife out of town before that shivaree
of yours was pulled off. But the lady would n't have it
that way. I got let right down on my face, and I 'm done.

Now you know just where I stand. Maybe I'm a fool for telling you, but I seem to be in the business to-night. Come on out."

He unfastened the big iron hasp, which was showing signs of the strain put upon it, and stepped back watchfully. The thick, oaken lid was pushed up, and Fred De Garmo, rather dusty and disheveled and purple from the close atmosphere of the box and from anger as well, came up like a jack-in-the-box and glared at Kent. When he had stepped out upon the stable floor, however, he smiled rather unpleasantly.

"If you've told the truth," he said maliciously, "I guess the lady has pretty near evened things up. If you haven't — if I don't find them both at the hotel — well — Anyway," he added, with an ominous inflection, "there'll be other days to settle this in!"

"Why, sure. Help yourself, Fred," Kent retorted cheerfully, and stood where he was until Fred had gone out. Then he turned and closed the box. "Between that yellow-eyed dame and the chump that went and left this box wide open for me to tip Fred into," he soliloquized, while he took down the lantern, and so sent the shadows dancing weirdly about him, "I've got a bunch of trouble mixed up, for fair. I wish the son of a gun would fight it out now, and be done with it; but no, that ain't Fred. He'd a heap rather wait and let it draw interest!"

Over in the hotel the "yellow-eyed dame" was doing her unsophisticated best to meet the situation gracefully, and to realize certain vague and rather romantic dreams of her life out West. She meant to be very gracious, for one thing, and to win the chivalrous friendship of every man who came to participate in the rude congratulations that had been planned. Just how she meant to do this she did not know — except that the graciousness would certainly prove a very important factor.

"I 'm going to remain downstairs," she told Manley, when they reached the hotel. It was the first sentence she had spoken since he overtook her. "I 'm so glad, dear," she added diplomatically, "that you decided to stay. I want to see that funny landlady now, please, and get her to serve coffee and cake to our guests in the parlor. I wish I might have had one of my trunks brought over here; I should like to wear a pretty gown." She glanced down at her tailored suit with true feminine dissatisfaction. "But everything was so — so confused, with your being late, and sick — is your head better, dear?"

Manley, in very few words, assured her that it was. Manley was struggling with his inner self, trying to answer one very important question, and to answer it truthfully: Could he meet "the boys," do his part among them, and still remain sober? That seemed to be the only course open to him now, and he knew himself just well enough

to doubt his own strength. But if Kent would help him —
He felt an immediate necessity to find Kent.

"You'll find Mrs. Hawley somewhere around," he
said hurriedly. "I've got to see Kent —"

"Oh, Manley! Don't have anything to do with that
horrid cowboy! He's not — nice. He — he swore, when
he must have known I could hear him; and he was swear-
ing about *me*, Manley. Didn't you hear him?" She
stood in the doorway and clung to his arm.

"No," lied Manley. "You must have been mistaken,
sweetheart."

"Oh, I wasn't; I heard him quite plainly." She must
have thought it a terrible thing, for she almost whispered
the last words, and she released him with much reluctance.
It seemed to her that Manley was in danger of falling
among low associates, and that she must protect him in
spite of himself. It failed to occur to her that Manley
had been exposed to that danger for three years, without
any protection whatever.

She was thankful, when he came to her later in the
parlor, to learn from him that he had not held any speech
with Kent. That was some comfort — and she felt that
she needed a little comforting, just then. Her consulta-
tion with Arline had been rather unsatisfactory. Arline
had told her bluntly that "the bunch" didn't want any
coffee and cake. Whisky and cigars, said Arline, without

so much as a blush, was what appealed to them fellows. If Manley handed it out liberal enough, they would n't bother his bride. Very likely, Arline had assured her, she would n't see one of them. That, on the whole, had been rather discouraging. How was she to show herself a gracious lady, forsooth, if no one came near her? But she kept these things jealously tucked away in the remotest corner of her own mind, and managed to look the relief she did not feel.

And, after all, the *charivari*, as is apt to be the case when the plans are laid so carefully, proved a very tame affair. Valeria, sitting rather dismally in the parlor with Mrs. Hawley for company, at midnight heard a banging of tin cans somewhere outside, a fitful popping of six-shooters, and an abortive attempt at a procession coming up the street. But the lines seemed to waver and then break utterly at the first saloon, where drink was to be had for the asking and Manley Fleetwood was pledged to pay, and the rattle of cans was all but drowned in the shouts of laughter and talk which came from the "office," across the hall. For where is the pleasure or the profit in *charivaring* a bridal couple which stays up and waits quite openly for the clamor?

"Is it always so noisy here at night?" asked Valeria faintly when Mrs. Hawley had insisted upon her lying down upon the uncomfortable sofa.

"Well, no — unless a round-up pulls in, or there's a dance, or it's Christmas, or something. It's liable to keep up till two or three o'clock, so the sooner you git used to it, the better off you'll be. I'm going to leave you here, and go to bed — unless you want to go upstairs yourself. Only it'll be noisier than ever up in your room, for it's right over the office, and the way sound travels up is something fierce. Don't you be afraid — I'll lock this door, and if your husband wants to come in he can come through the dining room." She looked at Valeria and hesitated before she spoke the next sentence. "And don't you worry a bit over him, neither. My old man was in the kitchen a minute ago, when I was out there, and he says Man ain't drinking a drop to-night. He's keeping as straight as — "

Valeria sat up suddenly, quite scandalized. "Oh — why, of course Manley wouldn't drink with them! Why — who ever heard of such a thing? The idea!" She stared reproachfully at her hostess.

"Oh, sure! I didn't say such a thing was liable to happen. I just thought you might be — worrying — they're making so much racket in there," stammered Arline.

"Indeed, no. I'm not at all worried, thank you. And please don't let me keep you up any longer, Mrs. Hawley. I am quite comfortable — mentally and physically, I assure you. Good night."

Not even Mrs. Hawley could remain after that. She went out and closed the door carefully behind her, without even finding voice enough to return Valeria's sweetly modulated good night.

"She's got a whole lot to learn," she relieved her feelings somewhat by muttering as she mounted the stairs.

What it cost Manley Fleetwood to abstain absolutely and without even the compromise of "soft" drinks that night, who can say? Three years of free living in Montana had lowered his standard of morality without giving him that rugged strength of mind which makes a man master of himself first of all. He had that day lain, drunken and sleeping, when he should have been at his mental and physical best to meet the girl who would marry him. It was that very defection, perhaps, which kept him sober in the midst of his taunting fellows. Now that Valeria was actually here, and was his wife, he was possessed by the desire to make some sacrifice by which he might prove his penitence. At any cost he would spare her pain and humiliation, he told himself.

He did it, and he did it under difficulty. He was denied the moral support of Kent Burnett, for Kent was sulking over his slight, and would have nothing to say to him. He was jeered unmercifully by Fred De Garmo and his crowd. He was "baptized" by some drunken reveler, so that the stench of spilled whisky filled his nostrils and

He was jeered unmercifully by Fred De Garmo and his crew

Page 50.

tortured him the night through. He was urged, he was
bullied, he was ridiculed. His head throbbed, his eyeballs
burned. But through it all he stayed among them because he feared that if he left them and went to Val, some
drunken fool might follow him and shock her with his
inebriety. He stayed, and he stayed sober. Val was his
wife. She trusted him, and she was ignorant of his sins.
If he went to her staggering and babbling incoherent
foolishness, he knew it would break her heart.

When the sky was at last showing faint dawn tints and
the clamor had worn itself out perforce — because even
the leaders were, after all, but men, and there was a limit
to their endurance — Manley entered the parlor, haggard
enough, it is true, and bearing with him the stale odor of
cigars long since smoked, and of the baptism of bad whisky,
but also with the air of conscious rectitude which sits so
comically upon a man unused to the feeling of virtue.

As is so often the case when one fights alone the good
fight and manages to win, he was chagrined to find himself immediately put upon the defensive. Val, as she
speedily demonstrated, declined to look upon him as a
hero, or as being particularly virtuous. She considered
herself rather neglected and abused. She believed that
he had stayed away because he was angry with her on
account of her refusal to leave town, and she thought
that was rather brutal of him. Also, her head ached from

tears and lack of sleep, and she hated the town, the hotel
— almost she hated Manley himself.

Manley felt the rebuff of her chilling silence when he
came in, and when she twitched herself loose from his
embrace he came near regretting his extreme virtue. He
spent ten minutes trying to explain, without telling all
of the truth, and he felt his good opinion of himself slipping from him before her inexorable disfavor.

"Well, I don't blame you for not liking the town, Val,"
he said at last, rather desperately. "But you must n't
judge the whole country by it. You 'll like the ranch,
dear. You 'll feel as if you were in another world — "

"I hope so," Val interrupted quellingly.

"We 'll drive out there just as soon as we have breakfast." He laid his hand diffidently upon her tumbled hair.
"I *had* to stay out there with those fellows. I did n't
want to — "

"I don't want any breakfast," said Val, getting up and
going over to the window — it would seem to avoid his
caress. "The odor of that dining room is enough to make
one fast forever." She lifted the grimy lace curtain with
her finger tips and looked disconsolately out upon the
street. "It 's just a dirty, squalid little hamlet. I don't
suppose the streets have been cleaned or the garbage removed from the back yards since the place was first —
founded." She laughed shortly at the idea of "found-

ing" a wretched village like that, but she had no other word at hand.

"*Arline*," she remarked, in a tone of drawling recklessness. "Arline swears. Did you know it? I suppose, of course, you do. She said something that struck me as being shockingly true. She said I 'm 'sure having a hell of a honeymoon.'" Then she bit her lips hard, because her eyelids were stinging with the tears she refused to shed in his presence.

"Oh, Val!" From the sofa Manley stared contritely at her back. She must feel terrible, he thought, to bring herself to repeat that sentence — Val, so icily pure in her thoughts and her speech.

Val was blinking her tawny eyes — like the eyes of a lion in color — at the street. Not for the world would she let him see that she wanted to cry! A figure, blurred to indistinctness, appeared in a doorway nearly opposite, stood for a moment looking up at the reddened sky, and came across the street. As the tears were beaten back she saw and recognized him, with a curl of the lip.

"Here comes your cowboy friend — from a saloon, of course." Her voice was lazily contemptuous. "Only his presence in the street was needed to complete the picture of desolation. He has been in a fight, judging from his face. It is all bruised and skinned, and one eye is swollen — ugh! My guide, my adviser — is it possible, Manley, that you could n't find a *nice* man to meet me at the train?" She turned from the disagreeable sight of Kent and faced her husband. "Are all the men like that? And are all the women like — Arline?"

Manley looked at her dumbly from the sofa. Would Val ever come to understand the place, and the people, he was wondering.

She laughed suddenly. "I 'm beginning to feel very sorry for Walt," she said irrelevantly, pointing to the easel and the expressionless crayon portrait staring out from the gilt frame. "He has to stay in this room always. And I believe another two hours would drive me hopelessly insane." The word caught her attention. "Hope!" she laughed ironically. "What imbecile ever thought of hope in the same breath with this place? What they really ought to do is paint that 'Abandon-hope' admonition across the whole front of the depot!"

Manley, because he had lifted his head too suddenly and so sent white-hot irons of pain clashing through his brain, turned sullen. "If you hate it as bad as all that," he said, "why, there 'll be a train for the East in about two hours."

Val stiffened perceptibly, though the petulance in her face changed to something wistful. "Do you mean — do you want me to go?" she asked very calmly.

Manley pressed his fingers hard against his temples.

"You know I don't. I want you to stay and like the country, and be happy. But — the way you have been talking makes it seem — a-ah!" He dropped his tortured head upon his hands and did not trouble to finish what he had intended to say. Nervous strain, lack of sleep, and a headache to begin with, were taking heavy toll of him. He could not argue with her; he could not do anything except wish he were dead, or that his head would stop aching.

Val took one of her unexpected changes of mood. She went up and laid her cold fingers lightly upon his temples, where she could see the blood beating savagely in the swollen veins. "What a little beast I am!" she murmured contritely. "Shall I get you some coffee, dear? Or some headache tablets, or — You know a cold cloth helped you last evening. Lie down for a little while. There's no hurry about starting, is there? I — I don't hate the place so awfully, Manley. I'm just cross because I couldn't sleep for the noise. Here's a cushion, dear. I think it's stuffed with scrap iron, for there doesn't seem to be anything soft about it except the invitation to 'slumber sweetly,' in red and green silk; but anything is better than the head of that sofa in its natural state."

She arranged the cushion to her own liking, if not to his, and when it was done she bent down impulsively and kissed him on the cheek, blushing vividly the while.

"I won't be nasty and cross any more," she promised. "Now, I'm going to interview Arline. I hear dishes rattling somewhere; perhaps I can get a cup of real coffee for you." At the door she shook her finger at him playfully. "Don't you dare stir off that sofa while I'm gone," she admonished. "And, remember, we're not going to leave town until your head stops aching — not if we stay here a week!"

She insisted upon bringing him coffee and toast upon a tray — a battered old tray, purloined for that purpose from the saloon, if she had only known it — and she informed him, with a pretty, domestic pride, that she had made the toast herself.

"Arline was going to lay slices of bread on top of the stove," she explained. "She said she always makes toast that way, and no one could tell the difference! I never heard of such a thing — did you, Manley? But I've been attending a cooking school ever since you left Fern Hill. I didn't tell you — I wanted it for a surprise. I could have done better with the toast before a wood fire — I think poor Arline was nearly distracted at the way I poked coals down from the grate; but she didn't say anything. Isn't it funny, to have cream in cans! I don't suppose it ever saw a cow — do you? The coffee's pretty bad, isn't it? But wait until we get home! I can make lovely coffee — if you'll get me a percolator. You will, won't you? And I learned how to make the most delicious fruit salad, just before I left. A cousin of Mrs. Forman's taught me how. Could you drink another cup, dear?"

Manley could not, and she deplored the poor quality, although she generously absolved Arline from blame, because there seemed so much to do in that kitchen. She refused to take any breakfast herself, telling him gayly that the odor in the kitchen was both food and drink.

Because he understood a little of her loathing for the place, Manley lied heroically about his headache, so that within an hour they were leaving town, with the two great trunks roped securely to the buckboard behind the seat, and with Val's suitcase placed flat in the front, where she could rest her feet upon it. Val was so happy at the prospect of getting away from the town that she actually threw a kiss in the direction of Arline, standing with her frowsy head, her dough-spotted apron, and her tired face in the parlor door.

Her mood changed immediately, however, for she had no more than turned from waving her hand at Arline, when they met Kent, riding slowly up the street with his hat tilted over the eye most swollen. Without a doubt he had seen her waving and smiling, and so he must have observed the instant cooling of her manner. He nodded to Manley and lifted his hat while he looked at her full;

and Val, in the arrogant pride of virtuous young woman-
hood, let her golden-brown eyes dwell impersonally upon
his face; let her white, round chin dip half an inch downward, and then looked past him as if he were a post by
the roadside. Afterwards she smiled maliciously when
she saw, with a swift, sidelong glance, how he scowled and
spurred unnecessarily his gray gelding.

CHAPTER V

FOR almost three years the letters from Manley had been headed "Cold Spring Ranch." For quite as long Val had possessed a mental picture of the place — a picture of a gurgly little brook with rocks and watercress and distracting little pools the size of a bathtub, and with a great, frowning boulder — a cliff, almost — at the head. The brook bubbled out and formed a basin in the shadow of the rock. Around it grew trees, unnamed in the picture, it is true, but trees, nevertheless. Below the spring stood a picturesque little cottage. A shack, Manley had written, was but a synonym for a small cottage, and Val had many small cottages in mind, from which she sketched one into her picture. The sun shone on it, and the western breezes flapped white curtains in the windows, and there was a porch where she would swing her hammock and gaze out over the great, beautiful country, fascinating in its very immensity.

Somewhere beyond the cottage — "shack," she usually corrected herself — were the corrals; they were as yet rather impressionistic; high, round, mysterious inclosures forming an effective, if somewhat hazy, background to the picture. She left them to work out their attractive details upon closer acquaintance, for at most they were merely the background. The front yard, however, she dwelt upon, and made aglow with sturdy, bright-hued flowers. Manley had that spring planted sweet peas, and poppies, and pansies, and other things, he wrote her, and they had come up very nicely. Afterward, in a postscript, he answered her oft-repeated questions about the flower garden:

The flowers are n't doing as well as they might. They need your tender care. I don't have much time to pet them along. The onions are doing pretty well, but they need weeding badly.

In spite of that, the flowers bloomed luxuriantly in her mental picture, though she conscientiously remembered that they were n't doing as well as they might. They were weedy and unkempt, she supposed, but a little time and care would remedy that; and was she not coming to be the mistress of all this, and to make everything beautiful? Besides, the spring, and the brook which ran from it, and the trees which shaded it, were the chief attractions.

Perhaps she betrayed a lack of domesticity because she had not been able to "see" the interior of the cottage

— "shack" — very clearly. Sunny rooms, white curtains, bright cushions and books, pictures and rugs mingled together rather confusingly in her mind when she dwelt upon the inside of her future home. It would be bright, and cozy, and "homy," she knew. She would love it because it would be hers and Manley's, and she could do with it what she would. She bothered about that no more than she did about the dresses she would be wearing next year.

Cold Spring Ranch! Think of the allurement of that name, just as it stands, without any disconcerting qualification whatever! Any girl with yellow-brown hair and yellow-brown eyes to match, and a dreamy temperament that beautifies everything her imagination touches, would be sure to build a veritable Eve's garden around those three small words.

With that picture still before her mental vision, clear as if she had all her life been familiar with it in reality, she rode beside Manley for three weary hours, across a wide, wide prairie which looked perfectly level when you viewed it as a whole, but which proved all hills.and hollows when you drove over it. During those three hours they passed not one human habitation after the first five miles were behind them. There had been a ranch, back there against a reddish-yellow bluff. Val had gazed upon it, and then turned her head away, distressed because human beings could consent to live in such unattractive surroundings. It was bad in its way as Hope, she thought, but did not say, because Manley was talking about his cattle, and she did not want to interrupt him.

After that there had been no houses of any sort. There was a barbed-wire fence stretching away and away until the posts were mere pencil lines against the blue, where the fence dipped over the last hill before the sky bent down and kissed the earth.

The length of that fence was appalling in a vague, wordless way. Val unconsciously drew closer to her husband when she looked at it, and shivered in spite of the midsummer heat.

"You're getting tired." Manley put his arm around her and held her there.

"We're over half-way now. A little longer and we'll be home." Then he bethought him that she might want some preparation for that home-coming. "You mustn't expect much, little wife. It's a bachelor's house, so far. You'll have to do some fixing before it will suit you. You don't look forward to anything like Fern Hill, do you?"

Val laughed, and bent solicitously over the suitcase, which her feet had marred. "Of course I don't. Nothing out here is like Fern Hill. I know our ranch is different from anything I ever knew — but I know just how it will be, and how everything will look."

"Oh! Do you?" Manley looked at her a bit anxiously.

"For three years," Val reminded him, "you have been describing things to me. You told me what it was like when you first took the place. You described everything, from Cold Spring Coulee to the house you built, and the spring under the rock wall, and even the meadow lark's nest you found in the weeds. Of *course* I know."

"It 's going to seem pretty rough, at first," he observed rather apologetically.

"Yes — but I shall not mind that. I want it to be rough. I 'm tired to death of the smug smoothness of my life so far. Oh, if you only knew how I have hated Fern Hill, these last three years, especially since I graduated. Just the same petty little lives lived in the same petty little way, day in and day out. Every Sunday the class in Sunday school, and the bells ringing and the same little walk of four blocks there and back. Every Tuesday and Friday the club meeting — the Merry Maids, and the Mascot, both just alike, where you did the same things. And the same round of calls with mamma, on the same people, twice a month the year round. And the little social festivities — ah, Manley, if you only knew how I long for something rough and real in my life!" It was very nearly what she said to the tired-faced teacher on the train.

"Well, if that's what you want, you've come to the right place," he told her dryly.

Later, when they drew close to a red coulee rim which he said was the far side of Cold Spring Coulee, she forgot how tired she was, and felt every nerve quiver with eagerness.

Later still, when in the glare of a July sun they drove around a low knoll, dipped into a wide, parched coulee, and then came upon a barren little habitation inclosed in a meager fence of the barbed wire she thought so detestable, she shut her eyes mentally to something she could not quite bring herself to face.

He lifted her out and tumbled the great trunks upon the ground before he drove on to the corrals. "Here's the key," he said, "if you want to go in. I won't be more than a minute or two." He did not look into her face when he spoke.

Val stood just inside the gate and tried to adjust all this to her mental picture. There was the front yard, for instance. A few straggling vines against the porch, and a sickly cluster or two of blossoms — those were the sweet peas, surely. The sun-baked bed of pale-green plants without so much as a bud of promise, she recognized, after a second glance, as the poppies. For the rest, there were weeds against the fence, sun-ripened grass trodden flat, yellow, gravelly patches where nothing grew — and a glaring, burning sun beating down upon it all.

The cottage — never afterward did she think of it by that name, but always as a shack — was built of boards placed perpendicularly, with battens nailed over the cracks to keep out the wind and the snow. At one side was a "lean-to" kitchen, and on the other side was the porch that was just a narrow platform with a roof over it. It was not wide enough for a rocking-chair, to say nothing of swinging a hammock. In the first hasty inspection this seemed to be about all. She was still hesitating before the door when Manley came back from putting up the horses.

"I 'm afraid your flowers are a lost cause," he remarked cheerfully. "They were looking pretty good two or three weeks ago. This hot weather has dried them up. Next year we 'll have water down here to the house. All these things take time."

"Oh, of course they do." Val managed to smile into his eyes. "Let 's see how many dishes you left dirty; bachelors always leave their dishes unwashed on the table, don't they?"

"Sometimes — but I generally wash mine." He led the way into the house, which smelled hot and close, with the odor of food long since cooked and eaten, before he threw all the windows open. The front room was clean

— after a man's idea of cleanliness. The floor was covered with an exceedingly dusty carpet, and a rug or two. Her latest photograph was nailed to the wall; and when Val saw it she broke into hysterical laughter.

"You 've nailed your colors to the mast," she cried, and after that it was all a joke. The home-made couch, with the calico cushions and the cowhide spread, was a matter for mirth. She sat down upon it to try it, and was informed that chicken wire makes a fine spring. The rickety table, with tobacco, magazines, and books placed upon it in orderly piles, was something to smile over. The chairs, and especially the one cane rocker which went sidewise over the floor if you rocked in it long enough, were pronounced original.

In the kitchen the same masculine idea of cleanliness and order obtained. The stove was quite red, but it had been swept clean. The table was pushed against the only window there, and the back part was filled with glass preserve jars, cans, and a loaf of bread wrapped carefully in paper; but the oilcloth cover was clean — did it not show quite plainly the marks of the last washing? Two frying pans were turned bottom up on an obscure table in an obscure corner of the room, and a zinc water pail stood beside them.

There were other details which impressed themselves upon her shrinking brain, and though she still insisted upon smiling at everything, she stood in the middle of the room holding up her skirts quite unconsciously, as if she were standing at a muddy street crossing, wondering how in the world she was ever going to reach the other side.

"Isn't it all — deliciously — primitive?" she asked, in a weak little voice, when the smile would stay no longer. "I — love it, dear." That was a lie; more, she was not in the habit of fibbing for the sake of politeness or anything else, so that the words stood for a good deal.

Manley looked into the zinc water pail, took it up, and started for an outer door, rattling the tin dipper as he went. "Want to go up to the spring?" he queried, over his shoulder. "Water's the first thing — I'm horribly thirsty."

Val turned to follow him. "Oh, yes — the spring!" She stopped, however, as soon as she had spoken. "No, dear. There'll be plenty of other times. I'll stay here."

He gave her a glance bright with love and blind happiness in her presence there, and went off whistling and rattling the pail at his side.

Val did not even watch him go. She stood still in the kitchen and looked at the table, and at the stove, and at the upturned frying pans. She watched two great horse-flies buzzing against a window-pane, and when she could endure that no longer, she went into the front room and stared vacantly around at the bare walls. When she saw her picture again, nailed fast beside the kitchen door, her face lost a little of its frozen blankness — enough so that her lips quivered until she bit them into steadiness.

She went then to the door and stood looking dully out into the parched yard, and at the wizened little pea vines clutching feebly at their white-twine trellis. Beyond stretched the bare hills with the wavering brown line running down the nearest one — the line that she knew was the trail from town. She was guilty of just one rebellious sentence before she struggled back to optimism.

"I said I wanted it to be rough, but I did n't mean — why, this is just squalid!" She looked down the coulee and glimpsed the river flowing calmly past the mouth of it, a majestic blue belt fringed sparsely with green. It must be a mile away, but it relieved wonderfully the monotony of brown hills, and the vivid coloring brightened her eyes. She heard Manley enter the kitchen, set down the pail of water, and come on to where she stood.

"I 'd forgotten you said we could see the river from here," she told him, smiling over her shoulder. "It 's beautiful, is n't it? I don't suppose, though, there 's a boat within millions of miles."

"Oh, there 's a boat down there. It leaks, though. I just use it for ducks, close to shore. Admiring our view? Great, don't you think?"

Val clasped her hands before her and let her gaze travel again over the sweep of rugged hills. "It 's — wonderful. I thought I knew, but I see I did n't. I feel very small, Manley; does one ever grow up to it?"

He seemed dimly to catch the note of utter desolation. "You 'll get used to all that," he assured her. "I thought I 'd reached the jumping-off place, at first. But now — you could n't dog me outa the country."

He was slipping into the vernacular, and Val noticed it, and wondered dully if she would ever do likewise. She had not yet admitted to herself that Manley was different. She had told herself many times that it would take weeks to wipe out the strangeness born of three years' separation. He was the same, of course; everything else was new and — different. That was all. He seemed intensely practical, and he seemed to feel that his love-making had all been done by letter, and that nothing now remained save the business of living. So, when he told her to rest, and that he would get dinner and show her how a bachelor kept house, she let him go with no reply save that vague, impersonal smile which Kent had encountered at the depot.

While he rattled things about in the kitchen, she stood

still in the doorway with her fingers doubled into tight
little fists, and stared out over the great, treeless, unpeopled land which had swallowed her alive. She tried
to think — and then, in another moment, she was trying
not to think.

Glancing quickly over her shoulder, to make sure
Manley was too busy to follow her, she went off the porch
and stood uncertain in the parched inclosure which was
the front yard.

"I may as well see it all, and be done," she whispered,
and went stealthily around the corner of the house, holding up her skirts as she had done in the kitchen. There
was a dim path beaten in the wiry grass — a path which
started at the kitchen door and wound away up the coulee.
She followed it. Undoubtedly it would lead her to the
spring; beyond that she refused to let her thoughts
travel.

In five minutes — for she went slowly — she stopped
beside a stock-trampled pool of water and yellow mud. A
few steps farther on, a barrel had been sunk in the ground
at the base of a huge gray rock; a barrel which filled
slowly and spilled the overflow into the mud. There
was also a trough, and there was a barrier made of poles
and barbed wire to keep the cattle from the barrel. One
crawled between two wires, it would seem, to dip up water
for the house. There were no trees — not real trees.

There were some chokecherry bushes higher than her head, and there were other bushes that did not look particularly enlivening.

With a smile of bitter amusement, she tucked her skirts tightly around her, crept through the fence, and filled a chipped granite cup which stood upon a rock ledge, and drank slowly. Then she laughed aloud.

"The water really *is* cold," she said. "Anywhere else it would be delicious. And that's a spring, I suppose." Mercilessly she was stripping her mind of her illusions, and was clothing it in the harsher weave of reality. "All these hills are Manley's — our ranch." She took another sip and set down the cup. "And so Cold Spring Ranch means — all this."

Down the coulee she heard Manley call. She stood still, pushing back a fallen lock of fine, yellow hair. She turned toward the sound, and the sun in her eyes turned them yellow as the hair above them. She was beautiful, in an odd, white-and-gold way. If her eyes had been blue, or gray — or even brown — she would have been merely pretty; but as they were, that amber tint where one looked for something else struck one unexpectedly and made her whole face unforgettably lovely. However, the color of her eyes and her hair did not interest her then, or make life any easier. She was quite ordinarily miserable and homesick, as she went reluctantly back along the grassy trail. The odor of fried bacon came up to her, and she hated bacon. She hated everything.

"I 've been to the spring," she called out, resolutely cheerful, as soon as she came in sight of Manley, waiting in the kitchen door; she ran toward him lightly. "However does the water keep so deliciously cool through this hot weather? I don't wonder you call this Cold Spring Ranch."

Manley straightened proudly. "I 'm glad you like it; I was afraid you might not, just at first. But you're the right stuff — I might have known it. Not every woman could come out here and appreciate this country right at the start."

Val stopped at the steps, panting a little from her run, and smiled unflinchingly up into his face.

CHAPTER VI

MANLEY'S FIRE GUARD

HOT sunlight, winds as hot, a shimmering heat which distorted objects at a distance and made the sky line a dazzling, wavering ribbon of faded blue; and then the dull haze of smoke which hung over the land, and, without tempering the heat, turned the sun into a huge coppery balloon, which drifted imperceptibly from the east to the west, and at evening time settled softly down upon a parched hilltop and disappeared, leaving behind it an ominous red glow as of hidden fires.

When the wind blew, the touch of it seared the face, as the smoke tang assailed the nostrils. All the world was a weird, unnatural tint, hard to name, never to be forgotten. The far horizons drew steadily closer as the days passed slowly and thickened the veil of smoke. The distant mountains drew daily back into dimmer distance; became an obscure, formless blot against the sky, and vanished completely. The horizon crouched then upon the bluffs across the river, moved up to the line of trees along its banks, blotted them out one day, and impudently established itself half-way up the coulee.

Time ceased to be measured accurately; events moved slowly in an unreal world of sultry heat and smoke and a red sun wading heavily through the copper-brown sky from the east to the west, and a moon as red which followed meekly after.

Men rode uneasily here and there, and when they met they talked of prairie fires and of fire guards and the direction of the wind, and of the faint prospect of rain. Cattle, driven from their accustomed feeding grounds, wandered aimlessly over the still-unburned range, and lowed often in the night as they drifted before the flame-heated wind.

Fifteen miles to the east of Cold Spring Coulee, the Wishbone outfit watched uneasily the deepening haze. Kent and Bob Royden were put to riding the range from the river north and west, and Polycarp Jenks, who had taken a claim where were good water and some shelter, and who never seemed to be there for more than a few hours at a time, because of his boundless curiosity, wandered about on his great, raw-boned sorrel with the white legs, and seemed always to have the latest fire news on the tip of his tongue, and always eager to impart it to somebody.

To the northwest there was the Double Diamond, also sleeping with both eyes open, so to speak. They also had two men out watching the range, though the fires were said to be all across the river. But there was the railroad seaming the country straight through the grassland, and though the company was prompt at plowing fire guards, contract work would always bear watching, said the stockmen, and with the high winds that prevailed there was no telling what might happen.

So Fred De Garmo and Bill Madison patrolled the country in rather desultory fashion, if the truth be known. They liked best to ride to the north and east — which, while following faithfully the railroad and the danger line, would bring them eventually to Hope, where they never failed to stop as long as they dared. For, although they never analyzed their feelings, they knew that as long as they kept their jobs and their pay was forthcoming, a few miles of blackened range concerned them personally not at all. Still, barring a fondness for the trail which led to town, they were not unfaithful to their trust.

One day Kent and Polycarp met on the brink of a deep coulee, and, as is the way of men who ride the dim trails, they stopped to talk a bit.

Polycarp, cracking his face across the middle with his habitual grin, straightened his right leg to its full length, slid his hand with difficulty into his pocket, brought up a dirty fragment of "plug" tobacco, looked it over inquiringly, and pried off the corner with his teeth. When he had rolled it comfortably into his cheek and had straightened his leg and replaced the tobacco in his pocket, he was "all set" and ready for conversation.

Kent had taken the opportunity to roll a cigarette, though smoking on the range was a weakness to be indulged in with much care. He pinched out the blaze of his match, as usual, and then spat upon it for added safety before throwing it away.

"If this heat does n't let up," he remarked, "the grass is going to blaze up from sunburn."

"It won't need to, if you ask me. I would n't be su'prised to see this hull range afire any time. Between you an' me, Kenneth, them Double Diamond fellers ain't watching it as close as they might. I was away over Dry Creek way yesterday, and I seen where there was two different fires got through the company's guards, and kited off across the country. It jest *happened* that the grass give out in that red clay soil, and starved 'em both out. They wa'n't *put* out. I looked close all around, and there was n't nary a track of man or horse. That 's their business — ridin' line on the railroad. The section men 's been workin' off down the other way, where a culvert got scorched up pretty bad. By granny, Fred 'n' Bill Madison spend might' nigh all their time ridin' the trail to town. They 're might' p'ticular about watchin' the railroad between the switches — *he-he!*"

"That's something for the Double Diamond to worry over," Kent rebuffed. He hated that sort of gossip which must speak ill of somebody. "Our winter range lays mostly south and east; we could stop a fire between here and the Double Diamond, even if they let one get past 'em."

Polycarp regarded him cunningly with his little, slitlike eyes. "Mebbe you could," he said doubtfully. "And then again, mebbe you could n't. Oncet it got past Cold Spring — " He shook his wizened head slowly, leaned, and expectorated gravely.

"Man Fleetwood's keeping tab pretty close over that way."

Polycarp gave a grunt that was half a chuckle. "Man Fleetwood's keeping tab on what runs down his gullet," he corrected. "I seen him an' his wife out burnin' guards t' other day — over on his west line — and, by granny, it would n't stop nothing! A toad could jump it — *he-he!*" He sent another stream of tobacco juice afar, with the grave air as before.

"And I told him so. 'Man,' I says, 'what you think you 're doing?'

"'Buildin' a fire guard,' he says. 'My wife, Mr. Jenks.'

"'Polycarp Jenks is my cognomen,' I says. 'And I don't want no misterin' in mine. Polycarp 's good enough

for me,' I says, and I took off my hat and bowed to 'is
wife. Funny kinda eyes, she 's got — ever take notice?
Yeller, by granny! First time I ever seen yeller eyes in
a human's face. Mebbe it was the sun in 'em, but they
sure was yeller. I dunno as they hurt her looks none,
either. Kinda queer lookin', but when you git used to
'em you kinda like 'em.

"'N' I says: ' 'Tain't half wide enough, nor a third' —
spoke right up to 'im! I was thinkin' of the hull blamed
country, and I did n't care how he took it. 'Any good,
able-bodied wind 'll jump a fire across that guard so quick
it won't reelize there was any there,' I says.

"Man did n't like it none too well, either. He says to
me: 'That guard 'll stop any fire I ever saw,' and I got
right back at him — *he-he!* 'Man,' I says, 'you ain't
never saw a prairie fire' — just like that. 'You wait,' I
says, 'till the real thing comes along. We ain't had any
fires since you come into the country,' I says, 'and you
don't know what they 're like. Now, you take my advice
and plow another four or five furrows — and plow 'em out,
seventy-five or a hundred feet from here,' I says, 'an'
make sure you git all the grass burned off between — and
do it on a still day,' I says. 'You 'll burn up the hull
country if you keep on this here way you 're doing,' I told
him — straight out, just like that. 'And when you do
it,' I says, 'you better let somebody know, so 's they can

come an' help,' I says. ''Tain't any job a man oughta tackle alone,' I says to him. 'Git help, Man, git help.'

"Well, by granny — *he-he!* Man's wife brustled up at me like a — a —" He searched his brain for a simile, and failed to find one. "'I have been helping Manley, Mr. Polycarp Jenks,' she says to me, 'and I flatter myself I have done as well as any *man* could do.' And, by granny! the way them yeller eyes of hern blazed at me — *he-he!* I had to laugh, jest to look at her. Dressed jest like a city girl, by granny! with ruffles on her skirts — to ketch afire if she was n't mighty keerful! — and a big straw hat tied down with a veil, and kid gloves on her hands, and her yeller hair kinda fallin' around her face — and them yeller eyes snappin' like flames — by granny! if she did n't make as purty a picture as I ever want to set eyes on! Slim and straight, jest like a storybook woman — *he-he!* 'Course, she was all smoke an' dirt; a big flake of burned grass was on her hair, I took notice, and them ruffles was black up to her knees — *he-he!* And she had a big smut on her cheek — but she was right there with her stack of blues, by granny! Settin' into the game like a — a —" He leaned and spat. "But burnin' guards ain't no work for a woman to do, an' I told Man so — straight out. 'You git help,' I says. 'I see you 're might' near through with this here strip,' I says, 'an' I 'm in a hurry, or I 'd stay, right now.' And, by granny! if that there wife of Man's did n't up an' hit me another biff — *he-he!*

"'Thank you very much,' she says to me, like ice water. 'When we need your help, we 'll be sure to let you know — but at present,' she says, 'we could n't think of troubling you.' And then, by granny! she turns right around and smiles up at me — *he-he!* Made me feel like somebody 'd tickled m' ear with a spear of hay when I was asleep, by granny! Never felt anything like it — not jest with somebody smilin' at me.

"'Polycarp Jenks,' she says to me, 'we do appreciate what you 've told us, and I believe you 're right,' she says. 'But don't insiniwate I 'm not as good a fighter as any man who ever breathed,' she says. 'Manley has another of his headaches to-day — going to town always gives him a sick headache,' she says, 'and I 've done nearly all of this my own, lone self,' she says. 'And I 'm horribly proud of it, and I 'll never forgive you for saying I — ' And then, by granny! if she did n't begin to blink them eyes, and I felt like a — a — " He put the usual period to his hesitation.

"Between you an' *me*, Kenneth," he added, looking at Kent slyly, "she ain't having none too easy a time. Man 's gone back to drinkin' — I knowed all the time he would n't stay braced up very long — lasted about six weeks, from all I c'n hear. Mebbe she reely thinks it 's

jest headaches ails him when he comes back from town —
I dunno. You can't never tell what idees a woman's got
tucked away under her hair — from all I c'n gether. I
don't p'tend to know nothing about 'em — don't want
to know — *he-he!* But I guess," he hinted cunningly,
"I know as much about 'em as you do — hey, Kenneth? You don't seem to chase after 'em none, yourself
— *he-he!*"

"Whereabouts did Man run his guards?" asked Kent,
passing over the invitation to personal confessions.

Polycarp gave a grunt of disdain. "Just on the west
rim of his coulee. About forty rod of six-foot guard, and
slanted so it 'll shoot a fire right into high grass at the
head of the coulee and send it kitin' over this way. That 's
supposin' it turns a fire, which it won't. Six feet — a fall
like this here! Why, I never see grass so thick on this
range — did you?"

"I wonder, did he burn that extra guard?" Kent was
keeping himself rigidly to the subject of real importance.

"No, by granny! he did n't — not unless he done it
since yest'day. He went to town for suthin, and he might'
nigh forgot to go home — *he-he!* He was there yest'day
about three o'clock, an' I says to him — "

"Well, so-long; I got to be moving." Kent gathered
up the reins and went his way, leaving Polycarp just in
the act of drawing his "plug" from his pocket, by his

usual laborious method, in mental preparation for another half hour of talk.

"If you 're ridin' over that way, Kenneth, you better take a look at Man's guard," he called after him. "A good mile of guard, along there, would help a lot if a fire got started beyond. The way he fixed it, it ain't no account at all."

Kent proved by a gesture that he heard him, and rode on without turning to look back. Already his form was blurred as Polycarp gazed after him, and in another minute or two he was blotted out completely by the smoke veil, though he rode upon the level. Polycarp watched him craftily, though there was no need, until he was completely hidden, then he went on, ruminating upon the faults of his acquaintances.

Kent had no intention of riding over to Cold Spring. He had not been there since Manley's marriage, though he had been a frequent visitor before, and unless necessity drove him there, it would be long before he faced again the antagonism of Mrs. Fleetwood. Still, he was mentally uncomfortable, and he felt much resentment against Polycarp Jenks because he had caused that discomfort. What was it to him, if Manley had gone back to drinking? He asked the question more than once, and he answered always that it was nothing to him, of course. Still, he wished futilely that he had not been quite so eager to cover up Manley's weakness and deceive the girl. He ought to have given her a chance —

A cinder like a huge black snowflake struck him suddenly upon the cheek. He looked up, startled, and tried to see farther into the haze which closed him round. It seemed to him, now that his mind was turned from his musings, that the smoke was thicker, the smell of burning grass stronger, and the breath of wind hotter upon his face. He turned, looked away to the west, fancied there a tumbled blackness new to his sight, and put his horse to a run. If there were fire close, then every second counted; and as he raced over the uneven prairie he fumbled with the saddle string that held a sodden sack tied fast to the saddle, that he might lose no time.

The cinders grew thicker, until the air was filled with them, like a snowstorm done in India ink. A little farther and he heard a faint crackling; topped a ridge and saw not far ahead, a dancing, yellow line. His horse was breathing heavily with the pace he was keeping, but Kent, swinging away from the onrush of flame and heat, spurred him to a greater speed. They neared the end of the crackling, red line, and as Kent swung in behind it upon the burned ground, he saw several men beating steadily at the flames.

He was hardly at work when Polycarp came running up and took his place beside him, but beyond that Kent paid no attention to the others, though he heard and recognized the voice of Fred De Garmo calling out to some one. The smoke which rolled up in uneven volumes as the wind lifted it and bore it away, or let it suck backward as it veered for an instant, blinded him while he fought. He heard other men gallop up, and after a little some one clattered up with a wagon filled with barrels of water. He ran to wet his sack, and saw that it was Blumenthall himself, foreman of the Double Diamond, who drove the team.

"Lucky it ain't as windy as it was yesterday and the day before," Blumenthall cried out, as Kent stepped upon the brake block to reach a barrel. "It 'd sweep the whole country if it was."

Kent nodded, and ran back to the fire, trailing the dripping sack after him. As he passed Polycarp and another, he heard Polycarp saying something about Man Fleetwood's fire guard; but he did not stop to hear what it was. Polycarp was always talking, and he did n't always keep too closely to facts.

Then, of a sudden, he saw men dimly when he glanced down the leaping fire line, and he knew that the fire was almost conquered. Another frenzied minute or two, and he was standing in a group of men, who dropped their charred, blackened fragments of blanket and bags, and began to feel for their smoking material, while they stamped upon stray embers which looked live enough to be dangerous.

"Well, she 's out," said a voice. "But it did look for a while as if it 'd get away in spite of us."

Kent turned away, wiping an eye which held a cinder fast under the lid. It was Fred De Garmo who spoke.

"If somebody 'd been watchin' the railroad a leetle might closer — " Polycarp began, in his thin, rasping voice.

Fred cut him short. "I thought you laid it to Man Fleetwood, burning fire guards," he retorted. "Keep on, and you 'll get it right pretty soon. This never come from the railroad; you can gamble on that."

Blumenthall had left his team and come among them. "If you want to know how it started, I can tell you. Somebody dropped a match, or a cigarette, or something, by the trail up here a ways. I saw where it started when I went to Cold Spring after the last load of water. And if I knew who it was — "

Polycarp launched his opinion first, as usual. "Well, I don't *know* who done it — but, by granny! I can might' nigh guess who it was. There 's jest one man that I know of been traveling that trail lately when he wa'n't in his sober senses — "

Here Manley Fleetwood rode up to them, coughing at the soot his horse kicked up. "Say! you fellows come on

over to the house and have something to eat — and," he
added significantly, "something *wet.* I told my wife,
when I saw the fire, to make plenty of coffee, for fighting
fire 's hungry work, let me tell you. Come on — no hanging back, you know. There 'll be lots of coffee, and I 've
got a quart of something better cached in the haystack!"

As he had said, fighting fire is hungry work, and none
save Blumenthall, who was dyspeptic and only ate twice
a day, and then of certain foods prepared by himself,
declined the invitation.

CHAPTER VII

TO Val the days of heat and smoke, and the isolation, had made life seem unreal, like a dream which holds one fast and yet is absurd and utterly improbable. Her past was pushed so far from her that she could not even long for it as she had done during the first few weeks. There were nights of utter desolation, when Manley was in town upon some errand which prevented his speedy return — nights when the coyotes howled much louder than usual, and she could not sleep for the mysterious snapping and creaking about the shack, but lay shivering with fear until dawn; but not for worlds would she have admitted to Manley her dread of staying alone. She believed it to be necessary, or he would not require it of her, and she wanted to be all that he expected her to be. She was very sensitive, in those days, about doing her whole duty as a wife — the wife of a Western rancher.

For that reason, when Manley shouted to her the news of the fire as he galloped past the shack, and told her to have something for the men to eat when the fire was out, she never thought of demurring, or explaining to him that there was scarcely any wood, and that she could not cook a meal without fuel. Instead, she waved her hand to him and let him go; and when he was quite out of sight she went up to the corrals to see if she could find another useless pole, or a broken board or two which her slight strength would be sufficient to break up with the axe. Till she came to Montana, Val had never taken an axe in her hands; but its use was only one of the many things she must learn, of which she had all her life been ignorant.

There was an old post there, lying beside a rusty, overturned plow. More than once she had stopped and eyed it speculatively, and the day before she had gone so far as to lift an end of it tentatively; but she had found it very heavy, and she had also disturbed a lot of black bugs that went scurrying here and there, so that she was forced to gather her skirts close about her and run for her life.

Where Manley had built his hayrack she had yesterday discovered some ends of planking hidden away in the rank, ripened weeds and grass. She went there now, but there were no more, look closely as she might. She circled the evil-smelling stable in discouragement, picked up one short piece of rotten board, and came back to the post. As she neared it she involuntarily caught her skirts and held them close, in terror of the black bugs.

She eyed it with extreme disfavor, and finally ventured

to poke it with her slipper toe; one lone bug scuttled out and away in the tall weeds. With the piece of board she turned it over, stared hard at the yellowed grass beneath, discovered nothing so very terrifying after all, and, in pure desperation, dragged the post laboriously down to the place where had been the woodpile. Then, lifting the heavy axe, she went awkwardly to work upon it, and actually succeeded, in the course of half an hour or so, in worrying an armful of splinters off it.

She started a fire, and then she had to take the big zinc pail and carry some water down from the spring before she could really begin to cook anything. Manley's work, every bit of it — but then Manley was so very busy, and he could n't remember all these little things, and Val hated to keep reminding him. Theoretically, Manley objected to her chopping wood or carrying water, and always seemed to feel a personal resentment when he discovered her doing it. Practically, however, he was more and more often making it necessary for her to do these things.

That is why he returned with the fire fighters and found Val just laying the cloth upon the table, which she had moved into the front room so that there would be space to seat her guests at all four sides. He frowned when he looked in and saw that they must wait indefinitely, and her cheeks took on a deeper shade of pink.

"Everything will be ready in ten minutes," she hurriedly assured him. "How many are there, dear?"

"Eight, counting myself," he answered gruffly. "Get some clean towels, and we 'll go up to the spring to wash; and try and have dinner ready when we get back — we 're half starved." With the towels over his arm, he led the way up to the spring. He must have taken the trail which led past the haystack, for he returned in much better humor, and introduced the men to his wife with the genial air of a host who loves to entertain largely.

Val stood back and watched them file in to the table and seat themselves with a noisy confusion. Unpolished they were, in clothes and manner, though she dimly appreciated the way in which they refrained from looking at her too intently, and the conscious lowering of their voices while they talked among themselves.

They did, however, glance at her surreptitiously while she was moving quietly about, with her flushed cheeks and her yellow-brown hair falling becomingly down at the temples because she had not found a spare minute in which to brush it smooth, and her dainty dress and crisp, white apron. She was not like the women they were accustomed to meet, and they paid her the high tribute of being embarrassed by her presence.

She poured coffee until all the cups were full, replenished the bread plate and brought more butter, and hunted the kitchen over for the can opener, to punch little holes in another can of condensed cream; and she rather astonished her guests by serving it in a beautiful cut-glass pitcher instead of the can in which it was bought.

They handled the pitcher awkwardly because of their mental uneasiness, and Val shared with them their fear of breaking it, and was guilty of an audible sigh of relief when at last it found safety upon the table.

So perturbed was she that even when she decided that she could do no more for their comfort and retreated to the kitchen, she failed to realize that the one extra plate meant an absent guest, and not a miscount in placing them, as she fancied.

She remembered that she would need plenty of hot water to wash all those dishes, and the zinc pail was empty; it always was, it seemed to her, no matter how often she filled it. She took the tin dipper out of it, so that it would not rattle and betray her purpose to Manley, sitting just inside the door with his back toward her, and tiptoed quite guiltily out of the kitchen. Once well away from the shack, she ran.

She reached the spring quite out of breath, and she actually bumped into a man who stood carefully rinsing a bloodstained handkerchief under the overflow from the horse trough. She gave a little scream, and the pail went rolling noisily down the steep bank and lay on its side in the mud.

Kent turned and looked at her, himself rather startled by the unexpected collision. Involuntarily he threw out his hand to steady her. "How do you do, Mrs. Fleetwood?" he said, with all the composure he could muster to his aid. "I'm afraid I scared you. My nose got to bleeding — with the heat, I guess. I just now managed to stop it." He did not consider it necessary to explain his presence, but he did feel that talking would help her recover her breath and her color. "It's a plumb nuisance to have the nosebleed so much," he added plaintively.

Val was still trembling and staring up at him with her odd, yellow-brown eyes. He glanced at her swiftly, and then bent to squeeze the water from his handkerchief; but his trained eyes saw her in all her dainty allurement; saw how the coppery sunlight gave a strange glint to her hair, and how her eyes almost matched it in color, and how the pupils had widened with fright. He saw, too, something wistful in her face, as though life was none too kind to her, and she had not yet abandoned her first sensation of pained surprise that it should treat her so.

"That's what I get for running," she said, still panting a little as she watched him. "I thought all the men were at the table, you see. Your dinner will be cold, Mr. Burnett."

Kent was a bit surprised at the absence of cold hauteur in her manner; his memory of her had been so different.

"Well, I'm used to cold grub," he smiled over his shoulder. "And, anyway, when your nose gets to acting up with you, it's like riding a pitching horse; you've got to pass up everything and give it all your time and attention." Then, with the daring that sometimes possessed him like a devil, he looked straight at her.

"Sure you intend to give me my dinner?" he quizzed, his lips lifting humorously at the corners. "I kinda thought, from the way you turned me down cold when we met before, you'd shut your door in my face if I came pestering around. How *about* that?"

Little flames of light flickered in her eyes. "You are the guest of my husband, here by his invitation," she answered him coldly. "Of course I shall give you your dinner, if you want any."

He inspected his handkerchief critically, decided that it was not quite clean, and held it again under the stream of water. "If I want it — yes," he drawled maliciously. "Maybe I'm not sure about that part. Are you a pretty fair cook?"

"Perhaps you'd better interview your friends," she retorted, "if you are so very fastidious. I —" She drew her brows together, as if she was in doubt as to the proper method of dealing with this impertinence. She suspected that he was teasing her purposely, but still —

"Oh, I can eat 'most any old thing," he assured her, with calm effrontery. "You look as if you'd learn easy, and Man ain't the worst cook I ever ate after. If he's trained you faithful, maybe it'll be safe to take a chance. How *about* that? Can you make sour-dough bread yet?"

"No!" she flung the word at him. "And I don't want to learn," she added, at the expense of her dignity.

Kent shook his head disapprovingly. "That sure ain't the proper spirit to show," he commented. "Man must have to beat you up a good deal, if you talk back to *him* that way." He eyed her sidelong. "You're a real little wolf, aren't you?" He shook his head again solemnly, and sighed. "A fellow sure must build himself lots of trouble when he annexes a wife — a wife that won't learn to make sour-dough bread, and that talks back. I'm plumb sorry for Man. We used to be pretty good friends —" He stopped short, his face contrite.

Val was looking away, and she was winking very fast. Also, her lips were quivering unmistakably, though she was biting them to keep them steady.

Kent stared at her helplessly. "Say! I never thought you'd mind a little joshing," he said gently, when the silence was growing awkward. "I ought to be killed! You — you must get awful lonesome —"

She turned her face toward him quickly, as if he were the first person who had understood her blank loneliness. "That," she told him, in an odd, hesitating manner, "atones for the — the 'joshing.' No one seems to realize —"

"Why don't you get out and ride around, or do something beside stick right here in this coulee like a — a cactus?" he demanded, with a roughness that somehow was grateful to her. "I'll bet you haven't been a mile from the ranch since Man brought you here. Why don't you go to town with him when he goes? It'd be a whole lot better for you — for both of you. Have you got acquainted with any of the women here yet? I'll gamble you haven't!" He was waving the handkerchief gently like a flag, to dry it.

Val watched him; she had never seen any one hold a handkerchief by the corners and wave it up and down like that for quick drying, and the expedient interested her, even while she was wondering if it was quite proper for him to lecture her in that manner. His scolding was even more confusing than his teasing.

"I've been down to the river twice," she defended weakly, and was angry with herself that she could not find words with which to quell him.

"Really?" He smiled down at her indulgently. "How did you ever manage to get so far? It must be all of half a mile!"

"Oh, you 're perfectly horrible!" she flashed suddenly. "I don't see how it can possibly concern you whether I go anywhere or not."

"It does, though. I 'm a lot public-spirited. I hate to see taxes go up, and every lunatic that goes to the asylum costs the State just that much more. I don't know an easier recipe for going crazy than just to stay off alone and think. It 's a fright the way it gets sheep-herders, and such."

"I 'm *such*, I suppose!"

Kent glanced at her, approved mentally of the color in her cheeks and the angry light in her eyes, and laughed at her quite openly.

"There 's nothing like getting good and mad once in a while, to take the kinks out of your brain," he observed. "And there 's nothing like lonesomeness to put 'em in. A good fighting mad is what you need, now and then; I 'll have to put Man next, I guess. He 's too mild."

"No one could accuse you of that," she retorted, laughing a little in spite of herself. "If I were a man I should want to blacken your eyes —" And she blushed hotly at being betrayed into a personality which seemed to her undignified, and, what was worse, unrefined. She turned her back squarely toward him, started down the path, and remembered that she had not filled the water bucket, and that without it she could not consistently return to the house.

Kent interpreted her glance, went sliding down the steep bank and recovered the pail; he was laughing to himself while he rinsed and filled it at the spring, but he made no effort to explain his amusement. When he came back to where she stood watching him, Val gave her head a slight downward tilt to indicate her thanks, turned, and led the way back to the house without a word. And he, following after, watched her slim figure swinging lightly down the hill before him, and wondered vaguely what sort of a hell her life was going to be, out here where everything was different from what she had been accustomed to, and where she did not seem to "fit into the scenery," as he put it.

"You ought to learn to ride horseback," he advised unexpectedly.

"Pardon me — you ought to learn to wait until your advice is wanted," she replied calmly, without turning her head. And she added, with a sort of defiance: "I do not feel the need of either society or diversion, I assure you; I am perfectly contented."

"That's real nice," he approved. "There's nothing

like being satisfied with what's handed out to you."
But, though he spoke with much unconcern, his tone
betrayed his skepticism.

The others had finished eating and were sitting upon
their heels in the shade of the house, smoking and talking
in that desultory fashion common to men just after a
good meal. Two or three glanced rather curiously at
Kent and his companion, and he detected the covert smile
on the scandal-hungry face of Polycarp Jenks, and also
the amused twist of Fred De Garmo's lips. He went
past them without a sign of understanding, set the water
pail down in its proper place upon a bench inside the
kitchen door, tilted his hat to Val, who happened to be
looking toward him at that moment, and went out again.

"What's the hurry, Kenneth?" quizzed Polycarp,
when Kent started toward the corral.

"Follow my trail long enough and you'll find out —
maybe," Kent snapped in reply. He felt that the whole
group was watching him, and he knew that if he looked
back and caught another glimpse of Fred De Garmo's
sneering face he would feel compelled to strike it a blow.
There would be no plausible explanation, of course, and
Kent was not by nature a trouble hunter; and so he
chose to ride away without his dinner.

While Polycarp was still wondering audibly what was
the matter, Kent passed the house on his gray, called

"So-long, Man," with scarcely a glance at his host, and speedily became a dim figure in the smoke haze.

"He must be runnin' away from you, Fred," Polycarp hinted, grinning cunningly. "What you done to him — hey?"

Fred answered him with an unsatisfactory scowl. "You sure would be wise, if you found out everything you wanted to know," he said contemptuously, after an appreciable wait. "I guess we better be moving along, Bill." He rose, brushed off his trousers with a downward sweep of his hands, and strolled toward the corrals, followed languidly by Bill Madison.

As if they had been waiting for a leader, the others rose also and prepared to depart. Polycarp proceeded, in his usual laborious manner, to draw his tobacco from his pocket, and pry off a corner.

"Why don't you burn them guards now, Manley, while you got plenty of help?" he suggested, turning his slit-lidded eyes toward the kitchen door, where Val appeared for an instant to reach the broom which stood outside.

"Because I don't want to," snapped Manley. "I 've got plenty to do without that."

"Well, they ain't wide enough, nor long enough, and they don't run in the right direction — if you ask me." Polycarp spat solemnly off to the right.

"I don't ask you, as it happens." Manley turned and went into the house.

Polycarp looked quizzically at the closed door. "He's mighty touchy about them guards, for a feller that thinks they're all right — *he-he!*" he remarked, to no one in particular. "Some of these days, by granny, he'll wisht he'd took my advice!"

Since no one gave him the slightest attention, Polycarp did not pursue the subject further. Instead, with both ears open to catch all that was said, he trailed after the others to the corral. It was a matter of instinct, as well as principle, with Polycarp Jenks, to let no sentence, however trivial, slip past his hearing and his memory.

CHAPTER VIII

A CALAMITY expected, feared, and guarded against by a whole community does sometimes occur, and with a suddenness which finds the victims unprepared in spite of all their elaborate precautions. Compared with the importance of saving the range from fire, it was but a trivial thing which took nearly every man who dwelt in Lonesome Land to town on a certain day when the wind blew free from out the west. They were weary of watching for the fire which did not come licking through the prairie grass, and a special campaign train bearing a prospective President of our United States was expected to pass through Hope that afternoon.

Since all trains watered at the red tank by the creek, there would be a five-minute stop, during which the prospective President would stand upon the rear platform and deliver a three-minute address — a few gracious words to tickle the self-esteem of his listeners — and would employ the other two minutes in shaking the hand of every man, woman, and child who could reach him before the train pulled out. There would be a cheer or

two given as he was borne away — and there would be
something to talk about afterward in the saloons. Scarce
a man of them had ever seen a President, and it was worth
riding far to look upon a man who even hoped for so
exalted a position.

Manley went because he intended to vote for the man,
and called it an act of loyalty to his party to greet the
candidate; also because it took very little, now that hay-
ing was over and work did not press, to start him down
the trail in the direction of Hope.

At the Blumenthall ranch no man save the cook remained at home, and he only because he had a boil on
his neck which sapped his interest in all things else. Polycarp Jenks was in town by nine o'clock, and only one
man remained at the Wishbone. That man was Kent,
and he stayed because, according to his outraged companions, he was an ornery cuss, and his bump of patriot-
ism was a hollow in his skull. Kent had told them, one
and all, that he would n't ride twenty-five miles to shake
hands with the Deity Himself — which, however, is not
a verbatim report of his statement. The prospective
President had not done anything so big, he said, that a
man should want to break his neck getting to town just
to watch him go by. He was dead sure he, for one, was n't
going to make a fool of himself over any swell-headed
politician.

Still, he saddled and rode with his fellows for a mile or two, and called them unseemly names in a facetious tone; and the men of the Wishbone answered his taunts with shrill yells of derision when he swung out of the trail and jogged away to the south, and finally passed out of sight in the haze which still hung depressingly over the land.

Oddly enough, while all the able-bodied men save Kent were waiting hilariously in Hope to greet, with enthusiasm, the brief presence of the man who would fain be their political chief, the train which bore him eastward scattered fiery destruction abroad as it sped across their range, four minutes late and straining to make up the time before the next stop.

They had thought the railroad safe at last, what with the guards and the numerous burned patches where the fire had jumped the plowed boundary and blackened the earth to the fence which marked the line of the right of way, and, in some places, had burned beyond. It took a flag-flying special train of that bitter Presidential campaign to find a weak spot in the guard, and to send a spark straight into the thickest bunch of wiry sand grass, where the wind could fan it to a blaze and then seize it and bend the tall flame tongues until they licked around the next tuft of grass, and the next, and the next — until the spark was grown to a long, leaping line of fire, sweeping eastward with the relentless rush of a tidal wave upon a low-lying beach.

Arline Hawley was, perhaps, the only citizen of Hope who had deliberately chosen to absent herself from the crowd standing, in perspiring expectation, upon the depot platform. She had permitted Minnie, the "breed" girl, to go, and had even grudgingly consented to her using a box of cornstarch as first aid to her complexion. Arline had not approved, however, of either the complexion or the occasion.

"What you want to go and plaster your face up with starch for, gits me," she had criticised frankly. "Seems to me you're homely enough without lookin' silly, into the bargain. Nobody's going to look at you, no matter what you do. They're out to rubber at a higher mark than you be. And what they expect to see so great, gits me. He ain't nothing but a man — and, land knows, men is common enough, and ornery enough, without runnin' like a band of sheep to see one. I don't see as he's anny better, jest because he's runnin' for President; if he gits beat, he'll want to hide his head in a hole in the ground. Look at my Walt. *He* was the biggest man in Hope, and so swell-headed he would n't so much as pack a bucket of water all fall, or chop up a tie for kindlin' — till the day after 'lection. And what was he then but a frazzled-out back number, that everybody give the laugh —

till he up and blowed his brains out! Any fool can *run*
for President — it 's the feller that gits there that counts.

"Say, that red-white-'n'-blue ribbon sure looks fierce
on that green dress — but I reckon blood will tell, even
if it 's Injun blood. G'wan, or you 'll be late and have
your trouble for your pay. But hurry back soon 's the
agony 's over; the bread 'll be ready to mix out."

Even after the girl was gone, her finery a-flutter in
the sweeping west wind, Arline muttered aloud her
opinion of men, and particularly of politicians who rode
about in special trains and expected the homage of their
fellows.

She was in the back yard, taking her "white clothes"
off the line, when the special came puffing slowly into
town. To emphasize her disapproval of the whole system
of politics, she turned her back square toward it, and
laid violent hold of a sheet. There was a smudge of
cinders upon its white surface, and it crushed crisply
under her thumb with the unmistakable feel of burned
grass.

"Now, what in time — " began Arline aloud, after the
manner of women whose tongues must keep pace with
their thoughts. "That there feels fresh and " — with a
sniff at the spot — "*smells* fresh."

With the wisdom of much experience she faced the hot
wind and sniffed again, while her eyes searched keenly

the sky line, which was the ragged top of the bluff mark-
ing the northern boundary of the great prairie land. A
trifle darker it was there, and there was a certain sullen
glow discernible only to eyes trained to read the sky for
warning signals of snow, fire, and flood.

"That's a fire, and it's this side of the river. And if
it is, then the railroad set it, and there ain't a livin' thing
to stop it. An' the wind's jest right — " A curdled roll
of smoke showed plainly for a moment in the haze. She
crammed her armful of sheets into the battered willow
basket, threw two clothespins hastily toward the same
receptacle, and ran.

The special had just come to a stop at the depot. The
cattlemen, cowboys, and townspeople were packed close
around the rear of the train, their backs to the wind and
the disaster sweeping down upon them, their browned
faces upturned to the sleek, carefully groomed man in the
light-gray suit, with a flaunting, prairie sunflower osten-
tatiously displayed in his buttonhole and with his campaign smile upon his lips and dull boredom looking out
of his eyes.

"Ladies and gentlemen," he was saying, as he smiled,
"you favoured ones whose happy lot it is to live in the
most glorious State of our glorious union, I greet you,
and I envy you — "

Arline, with her soiled kitchen apron, her ragged coil

of dust-brown hair, her work-drawn face and faded eyes which blazed with excitement, pushed unceremoniously through the crowd and confronted him undazzled.

"Mister Candidate, you better move on and give these men a chancet to save their prope'ty," she cried shrilly. "They got something to do besides stand around here and listen at you throwin' campaign loads. The hull country 's afire back of us, and the wind bringin' it down on a long lope."

She turned from the astounded candidate and glared at the startled crowd, every one of whom she knew personally.

"I must say I got my opinion of a bunch that 'll stand here swallowin' a lot of hot air, while their coat tails is most ready to ketch afire!" Her voice was rasping, and it carried to the farthest of them. "You make me *tired!* Political slush, all of it — and the hull darned country a-blazin' behind you!"

The crowd moved uneasily, then scattered away from the shelter of the depot to where they could snuff inquiringly the wind, like dogs in the leash.

"That 's right," yelled Blumenthall, of the Double Diamond. "There 's a fire, sure as hell!" He started to run.

The man behind him hesitated but a second, then gripped his hat against the push of the wind, and began running. Presently men, women, and children were running, all in one direction.

The prospective President stood agape upon the platform of his bunting-draped car, his chosen allies grouped foolishly around him. It was the first time men had turned from his presence with his gracious, flatteringly noncommittal speech unuttered, his hand unshaken, his smiling, bowing departure unmarked by cheers growing fainter as he receded. Only Arline tarried, her thin fingers gripping the arm of her "breed girl," lest she catch the panic and run with the others.

Arline tilted back her head upon her scrawny shoulders and eyed the prospective President with antagonism unconcealed.

"I got something to say to you before you go," she announced, in her rasping voice, with its querulous note. "I want to tell you that the chances are a hundred to one you set that fire yourself, with your engine that 's haulin' you around over the country, so you can jolly men into votin' for you. Your train 's the only one over the road since noon, and that fire started from the railroad. The hull town 's liable to burn, unless it can be stopped the other side the creek, to say nothing of the range, that feeds our stock, and the hay, and maybe houses — and maybe *people!*"

She caught her breath, and almost shrieked the last

three words, as a dreadful probability flashed into her mind.

"I know a woman — just a girl — and she 's back there twenty mile — *alone*, and her man 's here to look at you go by! I hope you git beat, just for that!

"If this town ketches afire and burns up, I hope you run into the ditch before you git ten mile! If you was a man, and them fellers with you was men, you 'd hold up your train and help save the town. Every feller counts, when it comes to fightin' fire."

She stopped and eyed the group keenly. "But you won't. I don't reckon you ever done anything with them hands in your life that would grind a little honest dirt into your knuckles and under them shiny nails!"

The prospective President turned red to his ears, and hastily removed his immaculate hands from where they had been resting upon the railing. And he did not hold up the train while he and his allies stopped to help save the town. The whistle gave a warning toot, the bell jangled, and the train slid away toward the next town, leaving Arline staring, tight-lipped, after it.

"The darned chump — he 'd 'a' made votes hand over fist if he 'd called my bluff; but I knew he would n't, soon as I seen his face. He ain't man enough."

"He 's real good-lookin'," sighed Minnie, feebly attempting to release her arm from the grasp of her mistress. "And did you notice the fellow with the big yellow mustache? He kept eyin' me — "

"Well, I don't wonder — but it ain't anything to your credit," snapped Arline, facing her toward the hotel. "You do look like sin a-flyin', in that green dress, and with all that starch on your face. You git along to the house and mix that bread, first thing you do, and start a fire. And if I ain't back by that time, you go ahead with the supper; you know what to git. We 're liable to have all the tables full, so you set all of 'em."

She was hurrying away, when the girl called to her.

"Did you mean Mis' Fleetwood, when you said that about the woman burning? And do you s'pose she 's really in the fire?"

"You shut up and go along!" cried Arline roughly, under the stress of her own fears. "How in time 's anybody going to tell, that 's twenty miles away?"

She left the street and went hurrying through back yards and across vacant lots, crawled through a wire fence, and so reached, without any roundabout method, the trail which led to the top of the bluff, where the whole town was breathlessly assembling. Her flat-chested, uncorseted figure merged into the haze as she half trotted up the steep road, swinging her arms like a man, her skirts flapping in the wind. As she went, she kept muttering to herself:

"If she really is caught by the fire — and her alone — and Man more 'n half drunk — " She whirled, and stood waiting for the horseman who was galloping up the trail behind her. "You going home, Man? You don't think it could git to your place, do you?" She shouted the questions at him as he pounded past.

Manley, sallow white with terror, shook his head vaguely and swung his heavy quirt down upon the flanks of his horse. Arline lowered her head against the dust kicked into her face as he went tearing past her, and kept doggedly on. Some one came rattling up behind her with empty barrels dancing erratically in a wagon, and she left the trail to make room. The hostler from their own stable it was who drove, and at the creek ahead of them he stopped to fill the barrels. Arline passed him by and kept on.

At the brow of the hill the women and children were gathered in a whimpering group. Arline joined them and gazed out over the prairie, where the smoke was rolling toward them, and, lifting here and there, let a flare of yellow through.

"It 'll show up fine at dark," a fat woman in a buggy remarked. "There 's nothing grander to look at than a prairie fire at night. I do hope," she added weakly, "it don't do no great damage!"

"Oh, it won't," Arline cut in, with savage sarcasm,

panting from her climb. "It's bound to sweep the hull country slick an' clean, and maybe burn us all out — but that won't matter, so long as it looks purty after dark!"

"They say it's a good ten mile away yet," another woman volunteered encouragingly. "They'll git it stopped, all right. There's lots of men here to fight it, thank goodness!"

Arline moved on to where a plow was being hurriedly unloaded from a wagon, the horses hitched to it, and a man already grasping the handles in an aggressive manner. As she came up he went off, yelling his opinions and turning a shallow, uneven furrow for a back fire. Within five minutes another plow was tearing up the sod in an opposite direction.

"If it jumps here, or they can't turn it, the creek 'll help a lot," some one was yelling.

The plowed furrows lengthened, the horses sweating and throwing their heads up and down with the discomfort of the pace they must keep. Whiplashes whistled and the drivers urged them on with much shouting. Blumenthall, cut off, with his men, from reaching his own ranch, was directing a group about to set a back fire. His voice boomed as if he were shouting across a milling herd. A roll of his eye brought his attention momentarily from the work, and he ran toward a horseman who was gesticulating wildly and seemed on the point of riding straight toward the fire.

"Hi! Fleetwood, we need you here!" he yelled. "You can't get home now, and you know it. The fire 's past your place already; you 'd have to ride through it, you fool! Hey? Your wife home alone — *alone?*"

He stood absolutely still and stared out to the southwest, where the smoke cloud was rolling closer with every breath. He drew his fingers across his forehead and glanced at the men around him, also stunned into inactivity by the tragedy behind the words.

"Well — get to work, men. We 've got to save the town. Fine time to burn guards — when a fire 's loping up on you! But that 's the way it goes, generally. This ought to 've been done a month ago. Put it off and put it off — while they haggle over bids — Brinberg, you and I 'll string the fire. The rest of you watch it don't jump back. And, say!" he shouted to the group around Manley. "Don't let that crazy fool start off now. Put him to work. Best thing for him. But — my God, that 's awful!" He did not shout the last sentence. He spoke so that only the nearest man heard him — heard, and nodded dumb assent.

Manley raged, sitting helpless there upon his horse. They would not let him ride out toward that sweeping wave of fire. He could not have gone five miles toward home before he met the flames. He stood in the stirrups and shook his fists impotently. He strained his eyes to see what it was impossible for him to see — his ranch and Val, and how they had fared. He pictured mentally the guard he had burned beyond the coulee to protect them from just this danger, and his heart squeezed tight at the realization of his own shiftlessness. That guard! A twelve-foot strip of half-burned sod, with tufts of grass left standing here and there — and he had meant to burn it wider, and had put it off from day to day, until now. *Now!*

His clenched fist dropped upon the saddle horn, and he stared dully at the rushing, rolling smoke and fire. It was not *that* he saw — it was Val, with cinder-blackened ruffles, grimy face, and yellow hair falling in loose locks upon her cheeks — locks which she must stop to push out of her eyes, so that she could see where to swing the sodden sack while she helped him — him, Manley, who had permitted her to do work fit for none but a man's hard muscles, so that he might finish the sooner and ride to town upon some flimsy pretext. And he could not even reach her now — or the place where she had been!

The group had thinned around him, for there was something to do besides give sympathy to a man bereaved. Unless they bestirred themselves, they might all be in need of sympathy before the day was done. Manley took his eyes from the coming fire and glanced around him, saw that he was alone, and, with a despairing oath, wheeled his horse and raced back down the hill to town, as if fiends rode behind the saddle.

At the saloon opposite the Hawley Hotel he drew up; rather, his horse stopped there of his own accord, as if he were quite at home at that particular hitching pole. Manley dismounted heavily and lurched inside. The place was deserted save for Jim, who was paid to watch the wares of his employer, and was now standing upon a chair at the window, that he might see over the top of Hawley's coal shed and glimpse the hilltop beyond. Jim stepped down and came toward him.

"How 's the fire?" he demanded anxiously. "Think she 'll swing over this way?"

But Manley had sunk into a chair and buried his face in his arms, folded upon a whisky-spotted card table.

"Val — my Val!" he wailed. "Back there alone — get me a drink," he added thickly, "or I 'll go crazy!"

Jim hastily poured a full glass, and stood over him anxiously.

"Here it is. Drink 'er down, and brace up. What you mean? Is your wife — "

Manley lifted his head long enough to gulp the whisky, then dropped it again upon his arms and groaned.

CHAPTER IX

THE fire had been burning a possible half-hour when Kent, jogging aimlessly toward a long ridge with the lazy notion of riding to the top and taking a look at the country to the west before returning to the ranch, first smelled the stronger tang of burned grass and swung instinctively into the wind. He galloped to higher ground, and, trained by long watching of the prairie to detect the smoke of a nearer fire in the haze of those long distant, saw at once what must have happened, and knew also the danger. His horse was fresh, and he raced him over the uneven prairie toward the blaze.

It was tearing straight across the high ground between Dry Creek and Cold Spring Coulee when he first saw it plainly, and he altered his course a trifle. The roar of it came faintly on the wind, like the sound of storm-beaten surf pounding heavily upon a sand bar when the tide is out, except that this roar was continuous, and was full of sharp cracklings and sputterings; and there was also the red line of flame to visualize the sound.

When his eyes first swept the mile-long blaze, he felt his helplessness, and cursed aloud the man who had drawn all the fighting force from the prairie that day. They might at least have been able to harry it and hamper it and turn the savage sweep of it into barren ground upon some rock-bound coulee's rim. If they could have caught it at the start, or even in the first mile of its burning — or, even now, if Blumenthall's outfit were on the spot — or if Manley Fleetwood's fire guards held it back — He hoped some of them had stayed at home, so that they could help fight it.

In that brief glimpse before he rode down into a hollow and so lost sight of it, he knew that the fire they had fought and vanquished before had been a puny blaze compared with this one. The ground it had burned was not broad enough to do more than check this fire temporarily. It would simply burn around the blackened area and rush on and on, until the bend of the river turned it back to the north, where the river's first tributary stream would stop it for good and all. But before that happened it would have done its worst — and its worst was enough to pale the face of every prairie dweller.

Once more he caught sight of the fire as he was riding swiftly across the level land to the east of Cold Spring Coulee. He was going to see if Manley's fire guards were any good, and if anyone was there ready to fight it when it came up; they could set a back fire from the guards, he thought, even if the guards themselves were not wide enough to hold the main fire.

He pounded heavily down the long trail into the coulee, passed close by the house with a glance sidelong to see if anybody was in sight there, rounded the corral to follow the trail which wound zigzag up the farther coulee wall, and overtook Val, running bareheaded up the hill, dragging a wet sack after her. She was panting already from the climb, and she had on thin slippers with high heels, he noticed, that impeded her progress and promised a sprained ankle before she reached the top. Kent laughed grimly when he overtook her; he thought it was like a five-year-old child running with a cup of water to put out a burning house.

"Where do you think you 're going with that sack?" he called out, by way of greeting.

She turned a pale, terrified face toward him, and reached up a hand mechanically to push her fair hair out of her eyes. "So much smoke was rolling into the coulee," she panted, "and I knew there must be a fire. And I 've never felt quite easy about our guards since Polycarp Jenks said — Do you know where it is — the fire?"

"It 's between here and the railroad. Give me that sack, and you go on back to the house. You can't do any good." And when she handed the sack up to him and then kept on up the hill, he became autocratic in his tone. "Go on back to the house, I tell you!"

"I shall not do anything of the kind," she retorted indignantly, and Kent gave a snort of disapproval, kicked his horse into a lunging gallop, and left her.

"You 'll spoil your complexion," he cried over his shoulder, "and that 's about all you will do. You better go back and get a parasol."

Val did not attempt to reply, but she refused to let his taunts turn her back, and kept stubbornly climbing, though tears of pure rage filled her eyes and even slipped over the lids to her cheeks. Before she had reached the top, he was charging down upon her again, and the pallor of his face told her much.

"All hell could n't stop that fire!" he cried, before he was near her, and the words were barely distinguishable in the roar which was growing louder and more terrifying. "*Get back!* You want to stand there till it comes down on you?" Then, just as he was passing, he saw how white and trembling she was, and he pulled up, with Michael sliding his front feet in the loose soil that he might stop on that steep slope.

"You don't want to go and faint," he remonstrated in a more kindly tone, vaguely conscious that he had perhaps seemed brutal. "Here, give me your hand, and stick your toe in the stirrup. Ah, don't waste time trying to make up your mind — up you come! Don't you want to save the house and corrals — and the haystacks? We 've got our work cut out, let me tell you, if we do it."

He had leaned and lifted her up bodily, helped her to put her foot in the stirrup from which he had drawn his own, and held her beside him while he sent Michael down the trail as fast as he dared. It was a good deal of a nuisance, having to look after her when seconds were so precious, but he could n't go on and leave her, though she might easily have reached the bottom as soon as he if she had not been so frightened. He was afraid to trust her; she looked, to him, as if she were going to faint in his arms.

"You don't want to get scared," he said, as calmly as he could. "It 's back two or three miles on the bench yet, and I guess we can easy stop it from burning anything but the grass. It 's this wind, you see. Manley went to town, I suppose?"

"Yes," she answered weakly. "He went yesterday, and stayed over. I 'm all alone, and I did n't know what to do, only to go up and try — "

"No use, up there."

They were at the corral gate then, and he set her down carefully, then dismounted and turned Michael into the corral and shut the gate.

"If we can't stop it, and I ain't close by, I wish you 'd

let Michael out," he said hurriedly, his eyes taking in the immediate surroundings and measuring the danger which lurked in weeds, grass, and scattered hay. "A horse don't have much show when he's shut up, and — Out there where that dry ditch runs, we'll back-fire. You take this sack and come and watch out my fire don't jump the ditch. We'll carry it around the house, just the other side the trail." He was pulling a handful of grass for a torch, and while he was twisting it and feeling in his pocket for a match, he looked at her keenly. "You are n't going to get hysterics and leave me to fight it alone, are you?" he challenged.

"I hope I'm not quite such a silly," she answered stiffly, and he smiled to himself as he ran along the far side of the ditch with his blazing tuft of grass, setting fire to the tangled, brown mat which covered the coulee bottom.

Val followed slowly behind him, watching that the blaze did not blow back across the ditch, and beating it out when it seemed likely to do so. Now that she could actually do something, she was no more excited than he, if one could judge by her manner. She did look sulky, however, at his way of treating her.

To back-fire on short notice, with no fresh-turned furrow of moist earth, but only a shallow little dry ditch with the grass almost meeting over its top in places, is ticklish business at best. Kent went slowly, stamping out incipient blazes that seemed likely to turn unruly, and not trusting to Val any more than he was compelled to do. She was a woman, and Kent's experience with women of her particular type had not been extensive enough to breed confidence in an emergency like this.

He had no more than finished stringing his line of fire in the irregular half circle which enclosed house, corral, stables, and haystacks, and had for its eastern half the muddy depression which, in seasons less dry, was a fair-sized creek fed by the spring, when a jagged line of fire with an upper wall of tumbling, brown smoke, leaped into view at the top of the bluff.

One thing was in his favor: The grass upon the hillside was scantier than on the level upland, and here and there were patches of yellow soil absolutely bare of vegetation, where a fire would be compelled to halt and creep slowly around. Also, fire usually burns slower down a hill than over a level. On the other hand, the long, seamlike depressions which ran to the top were filled with dry brush, and even the coulee bottom had clumps of rosebushes and wild currant, where the flames would revel briefly.

But already the black, smoking line which curved around the haystacks to the north, and around the house toward the south, was widening with every passing second.

Val had a tub half filled with water at the house, and that

helped amazingly by making it possible to keep the sacks wet, so that every blow counted as they beat out the ragged tongues of flame which, in that wind, would jump here and there the ditch and the road, and go creeping back toward the stacks and the buildings. For it was a long line they were guarding, and there was a good deal of running up and down in their endeavor to be in two places at once.

Then Val, in turning to strike a new-born flame behind her, swept her skirt across a tuft of smoldering grass and set herself afire. With the excitement of watching all points at once, and with the smoke and smell of fire all about her, she did not see what had happened, and must have paid a frightful penalty if Kent had not, at that moment, been running past her to reach a point where a blaze had jumped the ditch.

He swerved, and swung a newly wet sack around her with a force which would have knocked her down if he had not at the same time caught and held her. Val screamed, and struggled in his arms, and Kent knew that it was of him she was afraid. As soon as he dared, he released her and backed away sullenly.

"Sorry I did n't have time to say please — you were just ready to go up in smoke," he flung savagely over his shoulder. But he found himself shaking and weak, so that when he reached the blaze he must beat out, the sack was heavy as lead. "Afraid of *me* — women sure do beat hell!" he told himself, when he was a bit steadier. He glanced back at her resentfully. Val was stooping, inspecting the damage done to her dress. She stood up, looked at him, and he saw that her face was white again, as it had been upon the hillside.

A moment later he was near her again.

"Mr. Burnett, I 'm — ashamed — but I did n't know, and you — you startled me," she stopped him long enough to confess, though she did not meet his eyes. "You saved —"

"You 'll be startled worse, if you let the fire hang there in that bunch of grass," he interrupted coolly. "Behind you, there."

She turned obediently, and swung her sack down several times upon a smoldering spot, and the incident was closed.

Speedily it was forgotten, also. For with the meeting of the fires, which they stood still to watch, a patch of wild rosebushes was caught fairly upon both sides, and flared high, with a great snapping and crackling. The wind seized upon the blaze, flung it toward them like a great, yellow banner, and swept cinders and burning twigs far out over the blackened path of the back fire. Kent watched it and hardly breathed, but Val was shielding her face from the searing heat with her arms, and so did not see what happened then. A burning branch like a long, flaming dagger flew straight with the wind and lighted true as if flung by the hand of an enemy. A long, neatly tapered stack received it fairly, and Kent's cry brought Val's arms down, and her scared eyes staring at him.

"That settles the hay," he exclaimed, and raced for the stacks knowing all the while that he could do nothing, and yet panting in his hurry to reach the spot.

Michael, trampling uneasily in the corral, lifted his head and neighed shrilly as Kent passed him on the run. Michael had watched fearfully the fire sweeping down upon him, and his fear had troubled Val not a little. When she saw Kent pass the gate, she hurried up and threw it open, wondering a little that Kent should forget his horse. He had told her to see that he was turned loose if the fire could not be stopped — and now he seemed to have forgotten it.

Michael, with a snort and an upward toss of his head to throw the dragging reins away from his feet, left the corral with one jump, and clattered away, past the house and up the hill, on the trail which led toward home. Val stood for a moment watching him. Could he out-run the fire? He was holding his head turned to one side now, so that the reins dangled away from his pounding feet; once he stumbled to his knees, but he was up in a flash, and running faster than ever. He passed out of sight over the hill, and Val, with eyes smarting and cheeks burning from the heat, drew a long breath and started after Kent.

Kent was backing, step by step, away from the heat of the burning stacks. The roar, and the crackle, and the heat were terrific; it was as if the whole world was burning around them, and they only were left. A brand flew low over Val's head as she ran staggeringly, with a bewildered sense that she must hurry somewhere and do something immediately, to save something which positively must be saved. A spark from the brand fell upon her hand, and she looked up stupidly. The heat and the smoke were choking her so that she could scarcely breathe.

A new crackle was added to the uproar of flames. Kent, still backing from the furnace of blazing hay, turned, and saw that the stable, with its roof of musty hay, was afire. And, just beyond, Val, her face covered with her sooty hands, was staggering drunkenly. He reached her as she fell to her knees.

"I — can't — fight — any more," she whispered faintly.

He picked her up in his arms and hesitated, his face toward the house; then ran straight away from it, stumbled across the dry ditch and out across the blackened strip which their own back fire had swept clean of grass. The hot earth burned his feet through the soles of his riding boots, but the wind carried the heat and the smoke away, behind them. Clumps of bushes were still burning at the roots, but he avoided them and kept on to the far side hill, where a barren, yellow patch, with jutting sandstone rocks, offered a resting place. He set Val down upon a rock, placed himself beside her so that she was leaning against him, and began fanning her vigorously with his hat.

"Thank the Lord, we 're behind that smoke, anyhow," he observed, when he could get his breath. He felt that silence was not good for the woman beside him, though he doubted much whether she was in a condition to understand him. She was gasping irregularly, and her body was a dead weight against him. "It was sure fierce, there, for a few minutes."

He looked out across the coulee at the burning stables, and waited for the house to catch. He could not hope that it would escape, but he did not mention the probability of its burning.

"Keep your eyes shut," he said. "That 'll help some, and soon as we can we 'll go to the spring and give our faces and hands a good bath." He untied his silk neckerchief, shook out the cinders, and pressed it against her closed eyes. "Keep that over 'em," he commanded, "till we can do better. My eyes are more used to smoke than yours, I guess. Working around branding fires toughens 'em some."

Still she did not attempt to speak, and she did not seem to have energy enough left to keep the silk over her eyes. The wind blew it off without her stirring a finger to prevent, and Kent caught it just in time to save it from sailing away toward the fire. After that he held it in place himself, and he did not try to keep talking. He sat quietly, with his arm around her, as impersonal in the embrace as if he were holding a strange partner in a dance, and watched the stacks burn, and the stables. He saw the corral take fire, rail by rail, until it was all ablaze. He saw hens and roosters running heavily, with wings dragging, until the heat toppled them over. He saw a cat, with white spots upon its sides, leave the bushes down by the creek and go bounding in terror to the house.

And still the house stood there, the curtains flapping in and out through the open windows, the kitchen door banging open and shut as the gusts of wind caught it. The fire licked as close as burned ground and rocky creek bed would let it, and the flames which had stayed behind to eat the spare gleanings died, while the main line raged on up the hillside and disappeared in a huge, curling wave of smoke. The stacks burned down to blackened, smoldering butts. The willows next the spring, and the choke-cherries and wild currants withered in the heat and waved charred, naked arms impotently in the wind. The stable crumpled up, flared, and became a heap of embers. The corral was but a ragged line of smoking, half-burned sticks and ashes. Spirals of smoke, like dying camp fires, blew thin ribbons out over the desolation.

Kent drew a long breath and glanced down at the limp figure in his arms. She lay so very still that in spite of a quivering breath now and then he had a swift, unreasoning fear she might be dead. Her hair was a tangled mass of gold upon her head, and spilled over his arm. He carefully picked a flake or two of charred grass from the locks on her temples, and discovered how fine and soft was the hair. He lifted the grimy neckerchief from her eyes and looked down at her face, smoke-soiled and reddened from the heat. Her lips were drooped pitifully, like a hurt child. Her lashes, he noticed for the first time, were at least four shades darker than her hair. His gaze traveled on down her slim figure to her ringed fingers lying loosely in her lap, a long, dry-looking blister upon one hand near the thumb; down to her slippers, showing beneath her scorched skirt. And he drew another long breath. He did not know why, but he had a strange, fleeting sense of possession, and it startled him into action.

"You gone to sleep?" he called gently, and gave her a little shake. "We can get to the spring now, if you feel like walking that far; if you don't, I reckon I 'll have to carry you — for I sure do want a drink!"

She half lifted her lashes and let them drop again, as if life were not worth the effort of living. Kent hesitated, set his lips tightly together, and lifted her up straighter. His eyes were intent and stern, as though some great issue was at stake, and he must rouse her at once, in spite of everything.

"Here, this won't do at all," he said — but he was speaking to himself and his quivering nerves, more than to her.

She sighed, made a conscious effort, and half opened her eyes again. But she seemed not to share his anxiety for action, and her mental and physical apathy were not to be mistaken. The girl was utterly exhausted with fire-fighting and nervous strain.

"You seem to be all in," he observed, his voice softly complaining. "Well, I packed you over here, and I reckon I better pack you back again — if you *won't* try to walk."

She muttered something, of which Kent only distinguished "a minute." But she was still limp, and absolutely without interest in anything, and so, after a moment of hesitation, he gathered her up in his arms and carried her back to the house, kicked the door savagely open, took her in through the kitchen, and laid her down upon the couch, with a sigh of relief that he was rid of her.

The couch was gay with a bright, silk spread of "crazy" patchwork, and piled generously with dainty cushions, too evidently made for ornamental purposes than for use. But Kent piled the cushions recklessly around her, tucked her smudgy skirts close, went and got a towel, which he immersed recklessly in the water pail, and bathed her face and hands with clumsy gentleness, and pushed back her tangled hair. The burn upon her hand showed an angry red around the white of the blister, and he laid the wet towel carefully upon it. She did not move.

He was a man, and he had lived all his life among men. He could fight anything that was fightable. He could save her life, but after this slight attention to her comfort he had reached the limitations set by his purely masculine training. He lowered the shades so that the room was dusky and as cool as any other place in that fire-tortured land, and felt that he could no do more for her.

He stood for a moment looking down at the inert, grimy little figure stretched out straight, like a corpse, upon the bright-hued couch, her eyes closed and sunken, with blue shadows beneath, her lips pale and still with that tired, pitiful droop. He stooped and rearranged the wet towel on her burned hand, held his face close above hers for a second, sighed, frowned, and tiptoed out into the kitchen, closing the door carefully behind him.

CHAPTER X

DESOLATION

FOR more than two hours Kent sat outside in the shade of the house, and stared out over the black desolation of the coulee. His horse was gone, so that he could not ride anywhere — and there was nowhere in particular to ride. For twenty miles around there was no woman whom he could bring to Val's assistance, even if he had been sure that she needed assistance. Several times he tiptoed into the kitchen, opened the door into the front room an inch or so, and peered in at her. The third time, she had relaxed from the corpselike position, and had thrown an arm up over her face, as if she were shielding her eyes from something. He took heart at that, and went out and foraged for firewood.

There was a hard-beaten zone around the corral and stables, which had kept the fire from spreading toward the house, and the wind had borne the sparks and embers back toward the spring, so that the house stood in a brown oasis of unburned grass and weeds, scanty enough, it is true, but yet a relief from the dead black surroundings.

The woodpile had not suffered. A chopping block, a decrepit sawhorse, an axe, and a rusty bucksaw marked the spot; also three ties, hacked eloquently in places, and just five sticks of wood, evidently chopped from a tie by a man in haste. Kent looked at that woodpile, and swore. He had always known that Manley had an aversion to laboring with his hands, but he was unprepared for such an exhibition of shiftlessness.

He savagely attacked the three ties, chopped them into firewood, and piled them neatly, and then, walking upon his toes, he made a fire in the kitchen stove, filled the woodbox, the teakettle, and the water pail, sat out in the shade until he heard the kettle boiling over on the stove, took another peep in at Val, and then, moving as quietly as he could, proceeded to cook supper for them both.

He had been perfectly familiar with the kitchen arrangements in the days when Manley was a bachelor, and it interested him and filled him with a respectful admiration for woman in the abstract and for Val in particular, to see how changed everything was, and how daintily clean and orderly. Val's smooth, white hands, with their two sparkly rings and the broad wedding band, did not suggest a familiarity with actual work about a house, but the effect of her labor and thought confronted him at every turn.

"You can see your face in everything you pick up that was made to shine," he commented, standing for a moment while he surveyed the bottom of a stewpan. "She don't look it, but that yellow-eyed little dame sure knows how to keep house." Then he heard her cough, and set down the stewpan hurriedly and went to see if she wanted anything.

Val was sitting upon the couch, her two hands pushing back her hair, gazing stupidly around her.

"Everything's all ready but the tea," Kent announced, in a perfectly matter-of-fact tone. "I was just waiting to see how strong you want it."

Val turned her yellow-brown eyes upon him in bewilderment. "Why, Mr. Burnett — maybe I wasn't dreaming, then. I thought there was a fire. Was there?"

Kent grinned. "Kinda. You worked like a son of a gun, too — till there wasn't any more to do, and then you laid 'em down for fair. You were all in, so I packed you in and put you there where you could be comfortable. And supper's ready — but how strong do you want your tea? I kinda had an idea," he added lamely, "that women drink tea, mostly. I made coffee for myself."

Val let herself drop back among the pretty pillows. "I don't want any. If there was a fire," she said dully, "then it's true. Everything's all burned up. I don't want any tea. I want to die!"

Kent studied her for a moment. "Well, in that case — shall I get the axe?"

Val had closed her eyes, but she opened them again. "I don't care what you do," she said.

"Well, I aim to please," he told her calmly. "What *I'd* do, in your place, would be to go and put on something that ain't all smoked and scorched like a — a ham, and then I'd sit up and drink some tea, and be nice about it. But, of course, if you want to cash in —"

Val gave a sob. "I can't help it — I'd just as soon be dead as alive. It was bad enough before — and now everything's burned up — and all Manley's nice — ha-ay —"

"Well," Kent interrupted mercilessly, "I've heard of women doing all kinds of fool things — but this is the first time I ever knew one to commit suicide over a couple of measly haystacks!" He went out and slammed the door so that the house shook, and tramped three times across the kitchen floor. "That 'll make her so mad at me she won't think about anything else for a while," he reasoned shrewdly. But all the while his eyes were shiny, and when he winked, his lashes became unaccountably moist. He stopped and looked out at the blackened coulee. "Shut into this hole, week after week, without a woman to speak to — it must be — damned tough!" he muttered.

He tiptoed up and laid his ear against the inner door, and heard a smothered sobbing inside. That did not sound as if she were "mad," and he promptly cursed himself for a fool and a brute. With his own judgment to guide him, he brewed some very creditable tea, sugared and creamed it lavishly, browned a slice of bread on top of the stove — blowing off the dust beforehand — after Arline's recipe for making toast, buttered it until it dripped oil, and carried it in to her with the air of a man who will have peace even though he must fight for it. The forlorn picture she made, lying there with her face buried in a pink-and-blue cushion, and with her shoulders shaking with sobs, almost made him retreat, quite unnerved. As it was, he merely spilled a third of the tea and just missed letting the toast slide from the plate to the floor; when he had righted his burden he had recovered his composure to a degree.

"Here, this won't do at all," he reproved, pulling a chair to the couch by the simple method of hooking his toe under a round and dragging it toward him. "You don't want Man to come and catch you acting like this. He's liable to feel pretty blue himself, and he'll need some cheering up — don't you think? I don't know for sure — but I've always been kinda under the impression that's what a man gets a wife for. Ain't it? You don't want to throw down your cards now. You sit up and drink this tea, and eat this toast, and I 'll gamble you 'll feel about two hundred per cent. better.

"Come," he urged gently, after a minute. "I never thought a nervy little woman like you would give up so easy. I was plumb ashamed of myself, the way you worked on that back fire. You had me going, for a while. You 're just tired out, is all ails you. You want to hurry up and drink this, before it gets cold. Come on. I 'm liable to feel insulted if you pass up my cooking this way."

Val choked back the tears, and, without taking her face from the pillow, put out the burned hand gropingly until it touched his knee.

"Oh, you — you 're good," she said brokenly. "I used to think you were — horrid, and I 'm a—ashamed. You 're good, and I —"

"Well, I ain't going to be good much longer, if you don't get your head outa that pillow and drink this tea!" His tone was amused and half impatient. But his face — more particularly his eyes — told another story, which perhaps it was as well she did not read. "I 'll be dropping the blamed stuff in another minute. My elbow 's plumb getting a cramp in it," he added complainingly.

Val made a sound half-way between a sob and a laugh, and sat up. With more haste than the occasion warranted, Kent put the tea and toast on the chair and started for the kitchen.

"I was bound you 'd eat before I did," he explained, "and I could stand a cup of coffee myself. And, say! If there 's anything more you want, just holler, and I 'll come on the long lope."

Val took up the teaspoon, tasted the tea, and then regarded the cup doubtfully. She never drank sugar in her tea. She wondered how much of it he had put in. Her head ached frightfully, and she felt weak and utterly hopeless of ever feeling different.

"Everything all right?" came Kent 's voice from the kitchen.

"Yes," Val answered hastily, trying hard to speak with some life and cheer in her tone. "It 's lovely — all of it."

"Want more tea?" It sounded, out there, as though he was pushing back his chair to rise from the table.

"No, no, this is plenty." Val glanced fearfully toward the kitchen door, lifted the teacup, and heroically drank every drop. It was, she considered, the least that she could do.

When he had finished eating he came in, and found her nibbling apathetically at the toast. She looked up at him with an apology in her eyes.

"Mr. Burnett, don't think I am always so silly," she

began, leaning back against the piled pillows with a sigh. "I have always thought that I could bear anything. But last night I did n't sleep much. I dreamed about fires, and that Manley was — dead — and I woke up in a perfect horror. It was only ten o'clock. So then I sat up and tried to read, and every five minutes I would go out and look at the sky, to see if there was a glow anywhere. It was foolish, of course. And I did n't sleep at all to-day, either. The minute I would lie down I 'd imagine I heard a fire roaring. And then it came. But I was all used up before that, so I was n't really — I must have fainted, for I don't remember getting into the house — and I do think fainting is the silliest thing! I never did such a thing before," she finished abjectly.

"Oh, well — I guess you had a license to faint if you felt that way," he comforted awkwardly. "It was the smoke and the heat, I reckon; they were enough to put a crimp in anybody. Did Man say about when he would be back? Because I ought to be moving along; it 's quite a walk to the Wishbone."

"Oh — you won't go till Manley comes! Please! I — I 'd go crazy, here alone, and — and he might not come — he 's frequently detained. I — I 've such a horror of fires — " She certainly looked as if she had. She was sitting up straight, her hands held out appealingly to him, her eyes big and bright.

"Sure I won't go if you feel that way about it." Kent was half frightened at her wild manner. "I guess Man will be along pretty soon, anyway. He 'll hit the trail as soon as he can get behind the fire, that 's a cinch. He 'll be worried to death about you. And you don't need to be afraid of prairie fires any more, Mrs. Fleetwood; you 're safe. There can't be any more fires till next year, anyway; there 's nothing left to burn." He turned his face to the window and stared out somberly at the ravaged hillside. "Yes — you 're dead safe, now!"

"I 'm such a fool," Val confessed, her eyes also turning to the window. "If you want to go, I — " Her mouth was quivering, and she did not finish the sentence.

"Oh, I 'll stay till Man comes. He 's liable to be along any time, now." He glanced at her scorched, smoke-stained dress. "He 'll sure think you made a hand, all right!"

Val took the hint, and blushed with true feminine shame that she was not looking her best. "I 'll go and change," she murmured, and rose wearily. "But I feel as if the world had been ' rolled up in a scroll and burned,' as the Bible puts it, and as if nothing matters any more."

"It does, though. We 'll all go right along living the same as ever, and the first snow will make this fire seem as old as the war — except to the cattle; they 're the ones to get it in the neck this winter."

He went out and walked aimlessly around in the yard, and went over to the smoking remains of the stable, and to the heap of black ashes where the stacks had been. Manley would be hard hit, he knew. He wished he would hurry and come, and relieve him of the responsibility of keeping Val company. He wondered a little, in his masculine way, that women should always be afraid when there was no cause for fear. For instance, she had stayed alone a good many times, evidently, when there was real danger of a fire sweeping down upon her at any hour of the day or night; but now, when there was no longer a possibility of anything happening, she had turned white and begged him to stay — and Val, he judged shrewdly, was not the sort of woman who finds it easy to beg favors of anybody.

There came a sound of galloping, up on the hill, and he turned quickly. Dull dusk was settling bleakly down upon the land, but he could see three or four horsemen just making the first descent from the top. He shouted a wordless greeting, and heard their answering yells. In another minute or two they were pulling up at the house, where he had hurried to meet them. Val, tucking a side comb hastily into her freshly coiled hair, her pretty self clothed all in white linen, appeared eagerly in the doorway.

"Why — where 's Manley?" she demanded anxiously.

Blumenthall was dismounting near her, and he touched his hat before he answered. "We were on the way home, and we thought we 'd better ride around this way and see how you came out," he evaded. "I see you lost your hay and buildings — pretty close call for the house, too, I should judge. You must have got here in time to do something, Kent."

"But where 's Manley?" Val was growing pale again. "Has anything happened? Is he hurt? Tell me!"

"Oh, he 's all right, Mrs. Fleetwood." Blumenthall glanced meaningly at Kent — and Fred De Garmo, sitting to one side of his saddle, looked at Polycarp Jenks and smiled slightly. "We left town ahead of him, and knocked right along."

Val regarded the group suspiciously. "He 's coming, then, is he?"

"Oh, certainly. Glad you 're all right, Mrs. Fleetwood. That was an awful fire — it swept the whole country clean between the two rivers, I 'm afraid. This wind made it bad." He was tightening his cinch, and now he unhooked the stirrup from the horn and mounted again. "We 'll have to be getting along — don't know, yet, how we came out of it over to the ranch. But our guards ought to have stopped it there." He looked at Kent. "How did the Wishbone make it?" he inquired.

"I was just going to ask you if you knew," Kent replied, scowling because he saw Fred looking at Val in what he considered an impertinent manner. "My horse ran off while I was fighting fire here, so I'm afoot. I was waiting for Man to show up."

"You'll git all of that you want — *he-he!*" Polycarp cut in tactlessly. "Man won't git home t'-night — not unless — "

"Aw, come on." Fred started along the charred trail which led across the coulee and up the farther side. Blumenthall spoke a last, commonplace sentence or two, just to round off the conversation and make the termination not too abrupt, and they rode away, with Polycarp glancing curiously back, now and then, as though he was tempted to stay and gossip, and yet was anxious to know all that had happened at the Double Diamond.

"What did Polycarp Jenks mean — about Manley not coming to-night?" Val was standing in the doorway, staring after the group of horsemen.

"Nothing, I guess. Polycarp never does mean anything half the time; he just talks to hear his head roar. Man'll come, all right. This bunch happened to beat him out, is all."

"Oh, do you think so? Mr. Blumenthall acted as if there was something — "

"Well, what can you expect of a man that lives on oatmeal mush and toast and hot water?" Kent demanded aggressively. "And Fred De Garmo is always grinning and winking at somebody; and that other fellow is a Swede and got about as much sense as a prairie dog — and Polycarp is an old granny gossip that nobody ever pays any attention to. Man won't stay in town — he 'll be too anxious."

"It 's terrible," sighed Val, "about the hay and the stables. Manley will be so discouraged — he worked so hard to cut and stack that hay. And he was just going to gather the calves together and put them in the river field, in a couple of weeks — and now there is n't anything to feed them!"

"I guess he 's coming; I hear somebody." Kent was straining his eyes to see the top of the hill, where the dismal night shadows lay heavily upon the dismal black earth. "Sounds to me like a rig, though. Maybe he drove out." He left her, went to the wire gate which gave egress from the tiny, unkempt yard, and walked along the trail to meet the newcomer.

"You stay there," he called back, when he thought he heard Val following him. "I 'm just going to tell him you 're all right. You 'll get that white dress all smudged up in these ashes."

In the narrow little gully where the trail crossed the half-dry channel from the spring he met the rig. The driver pulled up when he caught sight of Kent.

"Who's that? Did she git out of it?" cried Arline Hawley, in a breathless undertone. "Oh — it's you, is it, Kent? I could n't stand it — I just had to come and see if she's alive. So I made Hank hitch right up — as soon as we knew the fire was n't going to git into all that brush along the creek, and run down to the town — and bring me over. And the way — "

"But where's Man?" Kent laid a hand upon the wheel and shot the question into the stream of Arline's talk.

"Man! I dunno what devil gits into men sometimes. Man went and got drunk as a fool soon as he seen the fire and knew what coulda happened out here. Started right in to drownd his sorrows before he made sure whether he had any to drown! If that ain't like a man, every time! Time we all got back to town, and the fire was kiting away from us instead of coming up toward us, he was too drunk to do anything. He must of poured it down him by the quart. He — "

"Manley! Is that you, dear?" It was Val, a slim, white figure against the blackness all around her, coming down the trail to see what delayed them. "Why don't you come to the house? There *is* a house, you know. We are n't quite burned out. And I'm all right, so there's no need to worry any more."

"Now, ain't that a darned shame?" muttered Arline

wrathfully to Kent. "A feller that 'll drink when he 's got a wife like that had oughta be hung!

"It 's me, Arline Hawley!" She raised her voice to its ordinary shrill level. "It ain't just the proper time to make a call, I guess, but it 's better late than never. Man, he was took with one of his spells, so I told him I 'd come on out and take you back to town. How are you, anyhow? Scared plumb to death, I 'll bet, when that fire come over the hill. You need n't 'a' tramped clear down here — we was coming on to the house in a minute. I got to chewin' the rag with Kent. Git in; you might as well ride back to the house, now you 're here."

"Manley did n't come?" Val was standing beside the rig, near Kent. Her white-clothed figure was indistinct, and her face obscured in the dark. Her voice was quiet — lifelessly quiet. "Is he sick?"

"Well — of course his nerves was all upset — "

"Oh! Then he *is* sick?"

"Well — nothing dangerous, but — he was n't feelin' well, so I thought I 'd come out and take you back with me."

"Oh!"

"Man was awful worried; you must n't think he was n't. He was pretty near crazy, for a while."

"Oh, yes, certainly."

"Get in and ride. And you must n't worry none about Man, nor feel hurt that he did n't come. He felt so bad —"

"I 'll walk, thank you; it 's only a few steps. And I 'm not worried at all. I quite understand."

The team started on slowly, and Mrs. Hawley turned in the seat so that she could continue talking without interruption to the two who walked behind. But it was Kent who answered her at intervals, when she asked a direct question or appeared to be waiting for some comment. Betweenwhiles he was wondering if Val did, after all, understand. She knew so little of the West and its ways, and her faith in Manley was so firm and unquestioning, that he felt sure she was only hurt at what looked very much like an indifference to her welfare. He suspected shrewdly that she was thinking what she would have done in Manley's place, and was trying to reconcile Mrs. Hawley's assurances that Manley was not actually sick or disabled with the blunt fact that he had stayed in town and permitted others to come out to see if she were alive or dead.

And Kent had another problem to solve. Should he tell her the truth? He had never ceased to feel, in some measure, responsible for her position. And she was sure to discover the truth before long; not even her innocence and her ignorance of life could shield her from that knowledge. He let a question or two of Arline's go unanswered while he struggled for a decision, but when they reached the house, only one point was clearly settled in his mind. Instead of riding as far as he might, and then walking across the prairie to the Wishbone, he intended to go on to town with them — "to see her through with it."

CHAPTER XI

VAL stood just inside the door of the hotel parlor and glanced swiftly around at the place of unpleasant memory.

"No, I must see Manley before I can tell you whether we shall want to stay or not," she replied to Arline's insistence that she "go right up to a room" and lie down. "I feel quite well, and you must not bother about me at all. If Mr. Burnett will be good enough to send Manley to me — I must see him first of all." It was Val in her most unapproachable mood, and Arline subsided before it.

"Well, then, I'll go and send word to Man, and see about some supper for us. I feel as if *I* could eat tenpenny nails!" She went out into the hall, hesitated a moment, and then boldly invaded the "office."

"Say! have you got Man rounded up yit?" she demanded of her husband. "And how is he, anyhow? That girl ain't got the first idea of what ails him — how anybody with the brains and edecation she's got can be so thick-headed gits me. Jim told me Man 's been packing a bottle or two home with him every trip he 's made for the last month — and she don't know a thing about it. I 'd like to know what 'n time they learn folks back East, anyhow; to put their eyes and their sense in their pockets, I guess, and go along blind as bats. Where 's Kent at? Did he go after him? She won't do nothing till she sees Man —"

At that moment Kent came in, and his disgust needed no words. He answered Mrs. Hawley's inquiring look with a shake of the head.

"I can't do anything with him," he said morosely. "He 's so full he don't know he 's got a wife, hardly. You better go and tell her, Mrs. Hawley. Somebody 's got to."

"Oh, my heavens!" Arline clutched at the doorknob for moral support. "I could no more face them yellow eyes of hern when they blaze up — you go tell her yourself, if you want her told. I 've got to see about some supper for us. I ain't had a bite since dinner, and Min 's off gadding somewheres —" She hurried away, mentally washing her hands of the affair. "Women 's got to learn some time what men is," she soliloquized, "and I guess she ain't no better than any of the rest of us, that she can't learn to take her medicine — but *I* ain't goin' to be the one to tell her what kinda fellow she 's tied to.

My stunt 'll be helpin' her pick up the pieces and make the best of it after she 's told."

She stopped, just inside the dining room, and listened until she heard Kent cross the hall from the office and open the parlor door. "Gee! It 's like a hangin'," she sighed. "If she was n't so plumb innocent —" She started for the door which opened into the parlor from the dining room, strongly tempted to eavesdrop. She did yield so far as to put her ear to the keyhole, but the silence within impressed her strangely, and she retreated to the kitchen and closed the door tightly behind her as the most practical method of bidding Satan begone.

The silence in the parlor lasted while Kent, standing with his back against the door, faced Val and meditated swiftly upon the manner of his telling.

"Well?" she demanded at last. "I am still waiting to see Manley. I am not quite a child, Mr. Burnett. I know something is the matter, and you — if you have any pity, or any feeling of friendship, you will tell me the truth. Don't you suppose I know that Arline was — *lying* to me all the time about Manley? You helped her to lie. So did that other man. I waited until I reached town, where I could do something, and now you must tell me the truth. Manley is badly hurt, or he is dead. Tell me which it is, and take me to him." She spoke fast, as if she was afraid she might not be able to finish, and, though her voice was even and low, it was also flat and toneless with her effort to seem perfectly calm and self-controlled.

Kent looked at her, forgot all about leading up to the truth by easy stages, as he had intended to do, and gave it to her straight. "He ain't either one," he said. "He's drunk!"

Val stared at him. "Drunk!" He could see how even her lips shrank from the word. She threw up her head. "That," she declared icily, "I know to be impossible!"

"Oh, do you? Let me tell you that's *never* impossible with a man, not when there's whisky handy."

"Manley is not that sort of a man. When he left me, three years ago, he promised me never to frequent places where liquor is sold. He never had touched liquor; he never was tempted to touch it. But, just to be doubly sure, he promised me, on his honor. He has never broken that promise; I know, because he told me so." She made the explanation scornfully, as if her pride and her belief in Manley almost forbade the indignity of explaining. "I don't know why you should come here and insult me," she added, with a lofty charity for his sin.

"I don't see how it can insult you," he contended. "You've got a different way of looking at things, but that won't help you to dodge facts. Man's drunk. I said it, and I mean it. It ain't the first time, nor the second. He was drunk the day you came, and could n't meet the train. That 's why I met you. I ought to 've told you, I guess, but I hated to make you feel bad. So I went to work and sobered him up, and sent him over to get married. I 've always been kinda sorry for that. It was a low-down trick to play on you, and that 's a fact. You ought to 've had a chance to draw outa the game, but I did n't think about it at the time. Man and I have always been pretty good friends, and I was thinking of *his* side of the case. I thought he 'd straighten up after he got married; he was n't such a hard drinker — only he 'd go on a toot when he got into town, like lots of men. I did n't think it had such a strong hold on him. And I knew he thought a lot of you, and if you went back on him it 'd hit him pretty hard. Man ain't a bad fellow, only for that. And he 's liable to do better when he finds out you know about it. A man will do 'most anything for a woman he thinks a lot of."

"Indeed!" Val was sitting now upon the red plush chair. Her face was perfectly colorless, her manner frozen. The word seemed to speak itself, without having any relation whatever to her thoughts and her emotions.

Kent waited. It seemed to him that she took it harder than she would have taken the news that Manley was dead. He had no means of gauging the horror of a young woman who has all her life been familiar with such terms as "the demon rum," and who has been taught that "intemperance is the doorway to perdition"; a young woman whose life has been sheltered jealously from all contact with the ugly things of the world, and who believes that she might better die than marry a drunkard. He watched her unobtrusively.

"Anyway, it was worrying over you that made him get off wrong to-day," he ventured at last, as a sort of palliative. "They say he was going to start home right in the face of the fire, and when they would n't let him, he headed straight for a saloon and commenced to pour whisky down him. He thought sure you — he thought the fire would —"

"I see," Val interrupted stonily. "For the very doubtful honor of shaking the hand of a politician, he left me alone to face as best I might the possibility of burning alive; and when it seemed likely that the possibility had become a certainty, he must celebrate his bereavement by becoming a beast. Is that what you would have me believe of my husband?"

"That 's about the size of it," Kent admitted reluctantly. "Only I would n't have put it just that way, maybe."

"Indeed! And how would you put it, then?"

Kent leaned harder against the door, and looked at

her curiously. Women, it seemed to him, were always going to extremes; they were either too soft and meek, or else they were too hard and unmerciful.

"How would you put it? I am rather curious to know your point of view."

"Well, I know men better than you do, Mrs. Fleetwood. I know they can do some things that look pretty rotten on the surface, and yet be fairly decent underneath. You don't know how a habit like that gets a fellow just where he's weakest. Man ain't a beast. He's selfish and careless, and he gives way too easy, but he thinks the world of you. Jim says he cried like a baby when he came into the saloon, and acted like a crazy man. You don't want to be too hard on him. I've an idea this will learn him a lesson. If you take him the right way, Mrs. Fleetwood, the chances are he'll quit drinking."

Val smiled. Kent thought he had never before seen a smile like that, and hoped he never would see another. There was in it neither mercy nor mirth, but only the hard judgment of a woman who does not understand.

"Will you bring him to me here, Mr. Burnett? I do not feel quite equal to invading a saloon and begging him, on my knees, to come — after the conventional manner of drunkards' wives. But I should like to see him."

Kent stared. "He ain't in any shape to argue with," he remonstrated. "You better wait a while."

She rested her chin upon her hands, folded upon the high chair back, and gazed at him with her tawny eyes, that somehow reminded Kent of a lioness in a cage. He thought swiftly that a lioness would have as much mercy as she had in that mood.

"Mr. Burnett," she began quietly, when Kent's nerves were beginning to feel the strain of her silent stare, "I want to see Manley *as he is now*. I will tell you why. You are n't a woman, and you never will understand, but I shall tell you; I want to tell *somebody*.

"I was raised well — that sounds queer, but modesty forbids more. At any rate, my mother was very careful about me. She believed in a girl marrying and becoming a good wife to a good man, and to that end she taught me and trained me. A woman must give her all — her life, her past, present, and future — to the man she marries. For three years I thought how unworthy I was to be Manley's wife. *Unworthy*, do you hear? I slept with his letters under my pillow." The self-contempt in her tone! "I studied the things I thought would make me a better companion out here in the wilderness. I practiced hours and hours every day upon my violin, because Manley had admired my playing, and I thought it would please him to have me play in the firelight on winter evenings, when the blizzards were howling about the house! I learned to cook, to wash clothes, to iron, to sweep, and to scrub, and to make my own clothes, because Manley's wife would live where she could not hire servants to do these things. I lived a beautiful, picturesque dream of domestic happiness.

"I left my friends, my home, all the things I had been accustomed to all my life, and I came out here to live that dream!" She laughed bitterly.

"You can easily guess how much of it has come true, Mr. Burnett. But you don't know what it costs a girl to come down from the clouds and find that reality is hard and ugly — from dreaming of a cozy little nest of a home, and the love and care of — of Manley, to the reality — to carrying water and chopping wood and being left alone, day after day, and to find that his love only meant — Oh, you don't know how a woman clings to her ideals! You don't know how I have clung to mine. They have become rather tattered, and I have had to mend them often, but I have clung to them, even though they do not resemble much the dreams I brought with me to this horrible country.

"But if it's true, what you tell me — if Manley himself is another disillusionment — if beyond his selfishness and his carelessness he is a drunken brute whom I can't even respect, then I'm done with my ideals. I want to

see him just as he is. I want to see him once without the
halo I have kept shining all these months. I 've got my
life to live — but I want to face facts and live facts. I
can't go on dreaming and making believe, after this."
She stopped and looked at him speculatively, absolutely
without emotion.

"Just before I left home," she went on in the same calm
quiet, "a girl showed me some verses written by a very
wicked man. At least, they say he is very wicked — at
any rate, he is in jail. I thought the verses horrible and
brutal; but now I think the man must be very wise. I
remember a few lines, and they seem to me to mean
Manley.

> "For each man kills the thing he loves —
> Some do it with a bitter look,
> Some with a flattering word;
> The coward does it with a kiss,
> The brave man with a sword.

"I don't remember all of it, but there was another line
or two:

> "The kindest use a knife, because
> The dead so soon grow cold.

"I wish I had that poem now — I think I could understand it. I think — "

"I think you 've got talking hysterics, if there is such
a thing," Kent interrupted harshly. "You don't know
half what you 're saying. You 've had a hard day, and
you 're all tired out, and everything looks outa focus. I

know — I 've seen men like that sometimes when some
trouble hit 'em hard and unexpected. What you want is
sleep; not poetry about killing people. A man, in the
shape you are in, takes to whisky. You 're taking to
graveyard poetry — and, if you ask *me*, that 's worse than
whisky. You ain't normal. What you want to do is go
straight to bed. When you wake up in the morning you
won't feel so bad. You won't have half as many troubles
as you 've got now."

"I knew you would n't understand it," Val remarked
coldly, still staring at him with her chin on her hands.

"You won't yourself, to-morrow morning," Kent declared unsympathetically, and called Mrs. Hawley from
the kitchen. "You better put Mrs. Fleetwood to bed,"
he advised gruffly. "And if you 've got anything that 'll
make her sleep, give her a dose of it. She 's so tired
she can't see straight." He was nearly to the outside
door when Val recovered her speech.

"You men are all alike," she said contemptuously.
"You give orders and you consider yourselves above all
the laws of morality or decency; in reality you are beneath
them. We should n't expect anything of the lower ani-
mals! How I *despise* men!"

"Now you 're *talking*," grinned Kent, quite unmoved.
"Whack us in a bunch all you like — but don't make one
poor devil take it all. Men as a class are used to it and

can stand it." He was laughing as he left the room, but his amusement lasted only until the door was closed behind him. "Lord!" he exclaimed, and drew a deep breath. "I'd sure hate to have that little woman say all them things about *me!*" and glanced involuntarily over his shoulder to where a crack of light showed under the faded green shade of one of the parlor windows.

He crossed the street and entered the saloon where Manley was still drinking heavily, his face crimson and blear-eyed and brutalized, his speech thickened disgustingly. He was sprawled in an armchair, waving an empty glass in an erratic attempt to mark the time of a college ditty six or seven years out of date, which he was trying to sing. He leered up at Kent.

"Wife 'sall righ'," he informed him solemnly. "Knew she would be — fine guards 's got out there. 'Sall righ' — somebody shaid sho. Have a drink."

Kent glowered down at him, made a swift, mental decision, and gripped him by the shoulder. "You come with me," he commanded. "I've got something important I want to tell you. Come on — if you can walk."

"'Course I c'n walk all righ'. Shertainly I can walk. Wha's makes you think I can't walk? Want to inshult me? 'Sall my friends here — no secrets from my friends. Wha's want tell me? Shay it here."

Kent was a big man; that is to say, he was tall, well-muscled and active. But so was Manley. Kent tried the power of persuasion, leaving force as a last, doubtful result. In fifteen minutes or thereabouts he had succeeded in getting Manley outside the door, and there he balked.

"Wha's matter wish you?" he complained, pulling back. "C'm on back 'n' have drink. Wha's wanna tell me?"

"You wait. I 'll tell you all about it in a minute. I 've got something to show you, and I don't want the bunch to get next. Savvy?"

He had a sickening sense that the subterfuge would not have deceived a five-year-old child, but it was accepted without question.

He led Manley stumbling up the street, evading a direct statement as to his destination, pulled him off the board walk, and took him across a vacant lot well sprinkled with old shoes and tin cans. Here Manley fell down, and Kent's patience was well tested before he got him up and going again.

"Where y' goin'?" Manley inquired pettishly, as often as he could bring his tongue to the labor of articulation.

"You wait and I 'll show you," was Kent's unvaried reply.

At last he pushed open a door and led his victim into the darkness of a small, windowless building. "It 's in here — back against the wall, there," he said, pulling Manley after him. By feeling, and by a good sense of location, he arrived at a rough bunk built against the farther wall, with a blanket or two upon it.

"There you are," he announced grimly. "You 'll have a sweet time getting anything to drink here, old boy. When you 're sober enough to face your wife and have some show of squaring yourself with her, I 'll come and let you out." He had pushed Manley down upon the bunk, and had reached the door before the other could get up and come at him. He pulled the door shut with a slam, slipped a padlock into the staple, and snapped it just before Manley lurched heavily against it. He was cursing as well as he could — was Manley, and he began kicking like an unruly child shut into a closet.

"Aw, let up," Kent advised him, through a crack in the wall. "Want to know where you are? Well, you 're in Hawley's ice house; you know it 's a fine place for drunks to sober up in; it 's awful popular for that purpose. Aw, you can't do any business kicking — that 's been tried lots of times. This is sure well built, for an ice house. No, I can't let you out. Could n't possibly, you know. I have n't got the key — old lady Hawley has got it, and she 's gone to bed hours ago. You go to sleep and forget about it. I 'll talk to you in the morning. Good night, and pleasant dreams!"

The last thing Kent heard as he walked away was Manley's profane promise to cut Kent's heart out very early the next day.

"The darned fool," Kent commented, as he stopped in the first patch of lamplight to roll a cigarette. "He ain't got another friend in town that 'd go to the trouble I 've gone to for him. He 'll realize it, too, when all that whisky quits stewing inside him."

CHAPTER XII

A LESSON IN FORGIVENESS

"WELL, old-timer, how you coming? You sure do sleep sound — this is the third time I 've come to tell you breakfast is ready and then some. You 'll get the bottom of the coffeepot, for fair, if you don't hustle." Kent left the door of the ice house wide open behind him, so that the warmth of mid-morning swept in to do battle with the chill and damp of wet sawdust and buried ice.

Manley rolled over so that he faced his visitor, and his reply was abusive in the extreme. Kent waited, with an air of impersonal interest, until he was done and had turned his face away as though the subject was quite exhausted.

"Well, now you 've got that load off your mind, come on over and get a cup of coffee. But while you 're thinking about whether you want anything but my heart's blood, I 'm going to speak right up and tell you a few things that commonly ain't none of my business.

"Do you know your wife came within an ace of burning to death yesterday?" Manley sat up with a jerk and glared at him. "Do you know you 're burned out, slick and clean — all except the shack? Hay, stables, corral, wagons, chickens — " Kent spread his hands in a gesture including all minor details. "I rode over there when I saw the fire coming, and it 's lucky I did, old-timer. I back-fired and saved the house — and your wife — from going up in smoke. But everything else went. Let that sink into your system, will you? And just see if you can draw a picture of what woulda happened if nobody had showed up — if that fire had hit the coulee with nobody there but your wife. Why, I run onto her half-way up the bluff, packing a wet sack, to fight it at the fire guards! Now, Man, it ain't any credit to *you* that the worst did n't happen. I 'd sure like to tell you what I think of a fellow that will leave a woman out there, twenty miles from town and ten from the nearest neighbor — and them not at home — to take a chance on a thing like that; but I can't. I never learned words enough.

"There 's another thing. Old lady Hawley took more interest in her than you did; she drove out there to see how about it, as soon as the fire had burned on past and left the trail safe. And it did n't look good to her — that little woman stuck out there all by herself. She made her pack up some clothes, and brought her to town with her. She did n't want to come; she had an idea that she ought to stay with it till you showed up. But the only original Hawley is sure all right! She talked your wife plumb outa the house and into the rig, and brought her to town. She 's over to the hotel now."

"Val at the hotel? How long has she been there?" Manley began smoothing his hair and his crumpled clothes with his hands. "Good heavens! You told her I 'd gone on out, and had missed her on the trail, did n't you, Kent? She does n't know I 'm in town, does she? You always were a good fellow — I have n't forgotten how you —"

"Well, you can forget it now. I did n't tell her anything like that. I did n't think of it, for one thing. She knew all the time that you were in town. I 'm tired of lying to her. I told her the truth. I told her you were drunk."

Manley's jaw dropped. "You — you told her —"

"Ex-actly. I told her you were drunk." Kent nodded gravely, and his lips curled as he watched the other cringe. "She called me a liar," he added, with a certain reminiscent amusement.

Manley brightened. "That 's Val — once she believes in a person she 's loyal as —"

"She ain't now," Kent interposed dryly. "When I let up she was plumb convinced. She knows now what ailed you the day she came and you did n't meet her."

"You dirty cur! And I thought you were a friend. You —"

"You thought right — until you got to rooting a little too deep in the mud, old-timer. And let me tell you something. I was your friend when I told her. She's got to know — you could n't go on like this much longer without having her get wise; she ain't a fool. The thing for you to do now is to buck up and let her reform you. I 've always heard that women are tickled plumb to death when they can reform a man. You go on over there and make your little talk, and then buckle down and live up to it. Savvy? That 's your only chance now. It 'll work, too.

"You *ought* to straighten up, Man, and act white! Not just to square yourself with her, but because you 're going downhill pretty fast, if you only knew it. You ain't anything like you were two years ago, when we bached together. You 've got to brace up pretty sudden, or you 'll be so far gone you can't climb back. And when a man has got a wife to look after, it seems to me he ought to be the best it 's in him to be. You were a fine fellow when you first hit the country — and she thought she was getting that same fine fellow when she came away out here to marry you. It ain't any of my business — but do you think you 're giving her a square deal?" He waited a minute, and spoke the next sentence with a certain diffidence. "I 'll gamble you have n't been disappointed in *her*."

"She 's an angel — and I 'm a beast!" groaned Manley, with the exaggerated self-abasement which so frequently follows close upon the heels of intoxication. "She 'll never forgive a thing like that — the best thing I can do is to blow my brains out!"

"Like Walt. And have your picture enlarged and put in a gold frame, and hubby number two learning his morals from your awful example," elaborated Kent, in much the same tone he had employed when Val, only the day before, had rashly expressed a wish for a speedy death.

Manley sat up straighter, and sent a look of resentment toward the man who bantered when he should have sympathized. "It 's all a big joke with you, of course," he flared weakly. "You 're not married — to a perfect woman; a woman who never did anything wrong in her life, and can't understand how anybody should want to, and can't forgive him when he does. She expects a man to be a saint. Why, I don't even smoke in the house — and she does n't dream I 'd ever swear, under any circumstances.

"Why, Kent, a fellow 's *got* to go to town and turn himself loose sometimes, when he lives in a rarified atmosphere of refined morality, and listens to Songs Without Words and weepy classics on the violin, and never a thing to make your feet tingle. She does n't

believe in public dances, either. Nor cards. She reads
'The Ring and the Book' evenings, and wants to discuss
it and read passages of it to me. I used to take some
interest in those things, and she does n't seem to see I 've
changed. Why, hang it, Kent, Cold Spring Coulee 's
no place for Browning — he does n't fit in. All that sort
of thing is a thousand miles behind me — and I 've got
to —" He stopped short and brooded, his eyes upon
the dank sawdust at his feet.

"I 'm a beast," he repeated rather lugubriously. "She 's
an angel — an Eastern-bred angel. And let me tell you,
Kent, all that 's pretty hard to live up to!"

Kent looked down at him meditatively, wondering if
there was not a good deal of truth and justice in Manley's
argument. But his sympathies had already gone to the
other side, and Kent was not the man to make an emotional
pendulum of himself.

"Well, what you going to do about it?" he asked, after
a short silence.

For answer Manley rose to his feet with a certain air
of determination, which flamed up oddly above his general
weakness, like the last sputter of a candle burned down.
"I 'm going over and take my medicine — face the music,"
he said almost sullenly. "She 's too good for me — I
always knew it. And I have n't treated her right — I 've
left her out there alone too much. But she would n't

come to town with me — she said she could n't endure the sight of it. What could I do? *I* could n't stay out there all the time; there were times when I had to come. She did n't seem to mind staying alone. She never objected. She was always sweet and good-natured — and shut up inside of herself. She just gives you what she pleases of her mind, and the rest she hides —"

Kent laughed suddenly. "You married men sure do have all kinds of trouble," he remarked. "A fellow like me can go on a jamboree any time he likes, and as long as he likes, and it don't concern anybody but himself — and maybe the man he 's working for; and look at you, scared plumb silly thinking of what your wife 's going to say about it. If you ask me, I 'm going to trot alone; I 'd rather be lonesome than good, any old time."

That, however, did not tend to raise Manley's spirits any. He entered the hotel with visible reluctance, looked into the parlor, and heaved a sigh of relief when he saw that it was empty, wavered at the foot of the steep, narrow stairs, and retreated to the dining room, with Kent at his heels knowing that the matter had passed quite beyond his help or hindrance and had entered that mysterious realm of matrimony where no unwedded man or woman may follow and yet is curious enough to linger.

Just inside the door Manley stopped so suddenly that

Kent bumped against him. Val, sweet and calm and cool, was sitting just where the smoke-dimmed sunlight poured in through a window upon her, and a breeze came with it and stirred her hair. She had those purple shadows under her eyes which betray us after long, sleepless hours when we live with our troubles and the world dreams around us; she had no color at all in her cheeks, and she had that aloofness of manner which Manley, in his outburst, had described as being shut up inside herself. She glanced up at them, just as she would have done had they both been strangers, and went on sugaring her coffee with a dainty exactness which, under the circumstances, seemed altogether too elaborate to be unconscious.

"Good morning," she greeted them quietly. "I think we must be the laziest people in town; at any rate, we seem to be the latest risers."

Kent stared at her frankly, so that she flushed a little under the scrutiny. Manley consciously avoided looking at her, and muttered something unintelligible while he pulled out a chair three places distant from her.

Val stole a sidelong, measuring look at her husband while she took a sip of coffee, and then her eyes turned upon Kent. More than ever, it seemed to him, they resembled the eyes of a lioness watching you quietly from the corner of her cage. You could look at them, but you could not look into them. Always they met your gaze with a baffling veil of inscrutability. But they were darker than the eyes of a lioness; they were human eyes; woman eyes — alluring eyes. She did not say a word, and, after a brief stare which might have meant almost anything, she turned to her plate of toast and broke away the burned edges of a slice and nibbled at the passable center as if she had no trouble beyond a rather unsatisfactory breakfast.

It was foolish, it was childish for three people who knew one another very well, to sit and pretend to eat, and to speak no word; so Kent thought, and tried to break the silence with some remark which would not sound constrained.

"It's going to storm," he flung into the silence, like chucking a rock into a pond.

"Do you think so?" Val asked languidly, just grazing him with a glance, in that inattentive way she sometimes had. "Are you going out home — or to what's left of it — to-day, Manley?" She did not look at him at all, Kent observed.

"I don't know — I'll have to hire a team — I'll see what —"

"Mrs. Hawley thinks we ought to stay here for a few days — or that I ought — while you make arrangements for building a new stable, and all that."

"If you want to stay," Manley agreed rather eagerly,

"why, of course, you can. There's nothing out there to —"

" Oh, it does n't matter in the slightest degree where I stay. I only mentioned it because I promised her I would speak to you about it." There was more than languor in her tone.

"They're going to start the fireworks pretty quick," Kent mentally diagnosed the situation and rose hurriedly. "Well, I 've got to hunt a horse, myself, and pull out for the Wishbone," he explained gratuitously. "Ought to 've gone last night. Good-bye." He closed the door behind him and shrugged his shoulders. "Now they can fight it out," he told himself. "Glad *I* ain't a married man!"

However, they did not fight it out then. Kent had no more than reached the office when Val rose, hoped that Manley would please excuse her, and left the room also. Manley heard her go up-stairs, found out from Arline what was the number of Val's room, and followed her. The door was locked, but when he rapped upon it Val opened it an inch and held it so.

"Val, let me in. I want to talk with you. I — God knows how sorry I am —"

"If He does, that ought to be sufficient," she answered coldly. "I don't feel like talking now — especially upon the subject you would choose. You 're a man, supposedly.

You must know what it is your duty to do. Please let us not discuss it — now or ever."

"But, Val —"

"I don't want to talk about it, I tell you! I won't — I *can't*. You must do without the conventional confession and absolution. You must have some sort of conscience — let that receive your penitence." She started to close the door, but he caught it with his hand.

"Val — do you hate me?"

She looked at him for a moment, as if she were trying to decide. "No," she said at last, "I don't think I do; I 'm quite sure that I do not. But I 'm terribly hurt and disappointed." She closed the door then and turned the key.

Manley stood for a moment rather blankly before it, then put his hands as deep in his pockets as they would go, and went slowly down the stairs. At that moment he did not feel particularly penitent. She would not listen to "the conventional confession!"

"That girl can be hard as nails!" he muttered, under his breath.

He went into the office, got a cigar, and lighted it moodily. He glanced at the bottles ranged upon the shelves behind the bar, drew in his breath for speech, let it go in a sigh, and walked out. He knew perfectly well what Val had meant. She had deliberately thrown him back upon his own strength. He had fallen by himself, he must pick himself up; and she would stand back and watch the struggle, and judge him according to his failure or his success. He had a dim sense that it was a dangerous experiment.

He looked for Kent, found him just as he was mounting at the stables, and let him go almost without a word. After all, no one could help him. He stood there smoking after Kent had gone, and when his cigar was finished he wandered back to the hotel. As was always the case after hard drinking, he had a splitting headache. He got a room as close to Val's as he could, shut himself into it, and gave himself up to his headache and to gloomy meditation. All day he lay upon the bed, and part of the time he slept. At supper time he rapped upon Val's door, got no answer, and went down alone, to find her in the dining room. There was an empty chair beside her, and he took it as his right. She talked a little —about the fire and the damage it had done. She said she was worried because she had forgotten to bring the cat, and what would it find to eat out there?

"Everything 's burned perfectly black for miles and miles, you know," she reminded him.

They left the room together, and he followed her upstairs and to her door. This time she did not shut him out, and he went in and sat down by the window, and looked out upon the meager little street. Never, in the years he had known her, had she been so far from him. He watched her covertly while she searched for something in her suit case.

"I 'm afraid I did n't bring enough clothes to last more than a day or two," she remarked. "I could n't seem to think of anything that night. Arline did most of the packing for me. I 'm afraid I misjudged that woman, Manley; there 's a good deal to her, after all. But she *is* funny."

"Val, I want to tell you I 'm going to — to be different. I 've been a beast, but I 'm going to —" So much he had rushed out before she could freeze him to silence again.

"I hope so," she cut in, as he hesitated. "That is something you must judge for yourself, and do by yourself. Do you think you will be able to get a team tomorrow?"

"Oh — to hell with a team!" Manley exploded.

Val dropped her hairbrush upon the floor. "Manley Fleetwood! Has it come to that, also? Is n't it enough to —" She choked. "Manley, you can be a — a drunken sot, if you choose — I 've no power to prevent you; but you shall not swear in my presence. I thought you had some of the instincts of a gentleman, but — " She set her teeth hard together. She was white around the mouth, and her whole, slim body was aquiver with outraged dignity.

There was something queer in Manley's eyes as he looked at her, the length of the tiny room between them.

"Oh, I beg your pardon. I remember, now, your Fern Hill ethics. I may *go* to hell, for all of you — you will simply hold back your immaculate, moral skirts so that I may pass without smirching them; but I must not mention my destination — that is so unrefined!" He got up from the chair, with a laugh that was almost a snort. "You refuse to discuss a certain subject, though it's almost a matter of life and death with me; at least, it was. Your happiness and my own was at stake, I thought. But it's all right — I need n't have worried about it. I still have some of the instincts of a gentleman, and your pure ears shall not be offended by any profanity or any disagreeable 'conventional confessions.' The absolution, let me say, I expected to do without." He started, full of some secret intent, for the door.

Val humanized suddenly. By the time his fingers touched the door knob she had read his purpose, had reached his side, and was clutching his arm with both her hands.

"Manley Fleetwood, what are you going to do?" She was actually panting with the jump of her heart.

He turned the knob, so that the latch clicked. "Get

drunk. Be the drunken sot you expect me to be. Go
to that vulgar place which I must not mention in your
presence. Let go my arm, Val."

She was all woman, then. She pulled him away from
the door and the unnamed horror which lay outside. She
was not the crying sort, but she cried, just the same —
heartbrokenly, her head against his shoulder, as if she
herself were the sinner. She clung to him, she begged
him to forgive her hardness.

She learned something which every woman must learn
if she would keep a little happiness in her life: she learned
how to forgive the man she loved, and to trust him afterward.

CHAPTER XIII

A HOUSE, it would seem, is almost the least important part of a ranch; one can camp, with frying pan and blankets, in the shade of a bush or the shelter of canvas. But to do anything upon a ranch, one must have many things — burnable things, for the most part, as Manley was to learn by experience when he left Val at the hotel and rode out, the next day, to Cold Spring Coulee.

To ride over twenty miles of blackness is depressing enough in itself, but to find, at the end of the journey, that one's work has all gone for nothing, and one's money and one's plans and hopes, is worse than depressing. Manley sat upon his horse and gazed rather blankly at the heap of black cinders that had been his haystacks, and at the cold embers where had stood his stables, and at the warped bits of iron that had been his buckboard, his wagon, his rake and mower — all the things he had gathered around him in the three years he had spent upon the place.

The house merely emphasized his loss. He got down

and picked up the cat, which was mewing plaintively beside his horse, snuggled it into his arm, and remounted. Val had told him to be sure and find the cat, and bring it back with him. His horses and his cattle — not many, to be sure, in that land of large holdings — were scattered, and it would take the round-up to gather them together again. So the cat, and the horse he rode, the bleak coulee, and the unattractive little house with its three rooms and its meager porch, were all that he could visualize as his worldly possessions. And when he thought of his bank account he winced mentally. Before snow fell he would be debt-ridden, the best he could do. For he must have a stable, and corral, and hay, and a wagon, and — he refused to remind himself of all the things he must have if he would stay on the ranch.

His was not a strong nature at best, and now he shrank from facing his misfortune and wanted only to get away from the place. He loped his horse half-way up the hill, which was not merciful riding. The half-starved cat yowled in his arms, and struck her claws through his coat till he felt the prick of them, and he swore; at the cat, nominally, but really at the trick fate had played upon him.

For a week he dallied in town, without heart or courage, though Val urged him to buy lumber and build, and cheered him as best she could. He did make a half-hearted attempt to get lumber to the place, but there seemed to be no team in town which he could hire. Every one was busy, and put him off. He tried to buy hay of Blumenthall, of the Wishbone, of every man he met who had hay. No one had any hay to sell, however. Blumenthall complained that he was short, himself, and would buy if he could, rather than sell. The Wishbone foreman declared profanely that hay was going to be worth a dollar a pound to *them*, before spring. They were all sorry for Manley, and told him he was "sure playing tough luck," but they could n't sell any hay, that was certain.

"But we must manage somehow to fix the place so we can live on it this winter," Val would insist, when he told her how every move seemed blocked. "You 're very brave, dear, and I 'm proud of the way you are holding out — but Hope is not a good place for you. It would be foolish to stay in town. Can't you buy enough hay here in town — baled hay from the store — to keep our horses through the winter?"

"Well, I tried," Manley responded gloomily. "But Brinberg is nearly out. He 's expecting a carload in, but it has n't come yet. He said he 'd let me know when it gets here."

Meanwhile the days slipped away, and imperceptibly the heat and haze of the fires gave place to bright sun-

light and chill winds, and then to the chill winds without
the sunshine.   One morning the ground was frozen hard,
and all the roofs gleamed white with the heavy frost.
Arline bestirred herself, and had a heating stove set up
in the parlor, and Val went down to the dry heat and
the peculiar odor of a rusted stove in the flush of its first
fire since spring.

The next day, as she sat by her window up-stairs, she
looked out at the first nip of winter.   A few great snow-
flakes drifted down from the slaty sky; a puff of wind
sent them dancing down the street, shook more down,
and whirled them giddily.   Then the storm came and
swept through the little street and whined lonesomely
around the hotel.

Over at the saloon — " Pop's Place," it proclaimed itself
in washed-out lettering — three tied horses circled uneasily until they were standing back to the storm, their
bodies hunched together with the chill of it, their tails
whipping between their legs.   They accentuated the
blank dreariness of the empty street.   The snow was
whitening their rumps and clinging, in tiny drifts, upon
the saddle skirts behind the cantles.

All the little hollows of the rough, frozen ground were
filling slowly, making white patches against the brown
of the earth — patches which widened and widened until
they met, and the whole street was blanketed with fresh,

untrodden snow. Val shivered suddenly, and hurried down-stairs where the air was warm and all a-steam with cooking, and the odor of frying onions smote the nostrils like a blow in the face.

"I suppose we must stay here, now, till the storm is over," she sighed, when she met Manley at dinner. "But as soon as it clears we must go back to the ranch. I simply cannot endure another week of it."

"You 're gitting uneasy — I seen that, two or three days ago," said Arline, who had come into the dining room with a tray of meat and vegetables, and overheard her. "You want to stay, now, till after the dance. There 's going to be a dance Friday night, you know — everybody 's coming. You got to wait for that."

"I don't attend public dances," Val stated calmly. "I am going home as soon as the storm clears — if Manley can buy a little hay, and find our horses, and get some sort of a driving vehicle."

"Well, if he can't, maybe he can round up a *ridin'* vee-hicle," Arline remarked dryly, placing the meat before Manley, the potatoes before Val, and the gravy exactly between the two, with mathematical precision. "I 'm givin' that dance myself. You 'll have to go — I 'm givin' it in your honor."

"In — my — why, the *idea!* It 's good of you, but — "

"And you 're goin', and you 're goin' to take your

vi'lin over and play us some pieces. I tucked it into the
rig and brought it in, on purpose. I planned out the hull
thing, driving out to your place. In case you was n't all
burned up, I made up my mind I was going to give you a
dance, and git you acquainted with folks. You need n't to
hang back — I 've told everybody it was in your honor,
and that you played the vi'lin swell, and we 'd have some
real music. And I 've sent to Chinook for the dance
music — harp, two fiddles, and a coronet — and you ain't
going to stall the hull thing now. I did n't mean to tell
you till the last minute, but you 've got to have time to
make up your mind you 'll go to a public dance for oncet
in your life. It ain't going to hurt you none. I 've went,
ever sence I was big enough to reach up and grab holt of
my pardner — and I 'm every bit as virtuous as you be.
You 're going, and you 'n Man are going to head the
grand march."

Val's face was flushed, her lips pursed, and her eyes
wide. Plainly she was not quite sure whether she was
angry, amused, or insulted. She descended straight to a
purely feminine objection.

"But I have n't a thing to wear, and — "

"Oh, yes, you have. While you was dillydallying out
in the front room, that night, wondering whether you 'd
have hysterics, or faint, or what all, I dug deep in that
biggest trunk of yourn, and fished up one of your party

dresses — white satin, it is, with embroid'ry all up 'n' down the front, and slimpsy lace; it 's kinda low-'n'-behold — one of them — "

"My white satin — why, Mrs. Hawley! That — you must have brought the gown I wore to my farewell club reception. It has a train, and — why, the *idea!*"

"You can cut off the trail — you got plenty of time — or you can pin it up. I did n't have time that night to see how the thing was made, and I took it because I found white skirts and stockin's, and white satin slippers to go with it, right handy. You 're a bride, and white 'll be suitable, and the dance is in your honor. Wear it just as it is, fer all me. Show the folks what real clothes look like. I never seen a woman dressed up that way in my hull life. You wear it, Val, trail 'n' all. I 'll back you up in it, and tell folks it 's my idee, and not yourn."

"I 'm not in the habit of apologizing to people for the clothes I wear." Val lifted her chin haughtily. "I am not at all sure that I shall go. In fact, I — "

"Oh, you 'll go!" Arline rested her arms upon her bony hips and snapped her meager jaws together. "You 'll go, if I have to carry you over. I 've sent for fifteen yards of buntin' to decorate the hall with. I ain't going to all that trouble for nothing. I ain't giving a dance in honor of a certain person, and then let that person stay away. You — why, you 'd queer yourself with the hull country,

Val Fleetwood! You ain't got the least sign of an excuse.
You got the clothes, and you ain't sick. There's a reason
why you got to show up. I ain't going into no details at
present, but under the circumstances, it's *advisable*."
She smelled something burning then, and bolted for the
kitchen, where her sharp, rather nasal voice was heard
upbraiding Minnie for some neglect.

Polycarp Jenks came in, eyed Val and Manley from
under one lifted eyebrow, smiled skinnily, and pulled out
a chair with a rasping noise, and sat down facing them.
Instinctively Val refrained from speaking her mind about
Arline and her dance before Polycarp, but afterward, in
their own room, she grew rather eloquent upon the subject. She would not go. She would not permit that
woman to browbeat her into doing what she did not want
to do, she said. In her honor, indeed! The impertinence
of going to the bottom of her trunk, and meddling with
her clothes — with that reception gown, of all others!
The idea of wearing that gown to a frontier dance — even
if she consented to go to such a dance! And expecting her to amuse the company by playing "pieces" on the
violin!

"Well, why not?" Manley was sitting rather apathetically upon the edge of the bed, his arms resting upon his
knees, his eyes moodily studying the intricate rose pattern
in the faded Brussels carpet. They were the first words

he had spoken; one might easily have doubted whether he had heard all Val said.

"Why not? Manley Fleetwood, do you mean to tell me — "

"Why not go, and get acquainted, and quit feeling that you 're a pearl cast among swine? It strikes me the Hawley person is pretty level-headed on the subject. If you 're going to live in this country, why not quit thinking how out of place you are, and how superior, and meet us all on a level? It won't hurt you to go to that dance, and it won't hurt you to play for them, if they want you to. You *can* play, you know; you used to play at all the musical doings in Fern Hill, and even in the city sometimes. And, let me tell you, Val, we are n't quite savages, out here. I 've even suspected, sometimes, that we 're just as good as Fern Hill."

"We?" Val looked at him steadiiy. "So you wish to identify yourself with these people — with Polycarp Jenks, and Arline Hawley, and — "

"Why not? They 're shaky on grammar, and their manners could stand a little polish, but aside from that they 're exactly like the people you 've lived among all your life. Sure, I wish to identify myself with them. I 'm just a rancher — pretty small punkins, too, among all these big outfits, and you 're a rancher's wife. The Haw-ley person could buy us out for cash to-morrow, if she wanted to, and never miss the money. And, Val, she's giving that dance in your honor; you ought to appreciate that. The Hawley does n't take a fancy to every woman she sees — and, let me tell you, she stands ace-high in this country. If she did n't like you, she could make you wish she did."

"Well, upon my word! I begin to suspect you of being a humorist, Manley. And even if you mean that seriously — why, it's all the funnier." To prove it, she laughed.

Manley hesitated, then left the room with a snort, a scowl, and a slam of the door; and the sound of Val's laughter followed him down the stairs.

Arline came up, her arms full of white satin, white lace, white cambric, and the toes of two white satin slippers showing just above the top of her apron pockets. She walked briskly in and deposited her burden upon the bed.

"My! them's the nicest smellin' things I ever had a hold of," she observed. "And still they don't seem to smell, either. Must be a dandy perfumery you 've got. I brought up the things, seein' you know they 're here. I thought you could take your time about cuttin' off the trail and fillin' in the neck and sleeves."

She sat down upon the foot of the bed, carefully tucking her gingham apron close about her so that it might not come in contact with the other.

"I never did see such clothes," she sighed. "I dunno how you'll ever git a chancet to wear 'em out in this country — seems to me they're most too pretty to wear, anyhow. I can git Marthy Winters to come over and help you — she does sewin' — and you can use my machine any time you want to. I'd take a hold myself if I did n't have all the baking to do for the dance. That Min can't learn nothing, seems like. I can't trust her to do a thing, hardly, unless I stand right over her. Breed girls ain't much account ever; but they're all that'll work out, in this country, seems like. Sometimes I swear I'll git a Chink and be done with it — only I got to have somebody I can talk to oncet in a while. I could n't never talk to a Chink — they don't seem hardly human to me. Do they to you?

"And say! I've got some allover lace — it's eecrue — that you can fill in the neck with; you're welcome to use it — there's most a yard of it, and I won't never find a use for it. Or I was thinkin', there'll be enough cut off 'n the trail to make a gamp of the satin, sleeves and all." She lifted the shining stuff with manifest awe. "It does seem a shame to put the shears to it — but you never'll git any wear out of it the way it is, and I don't believe — "

"Mis' *Hawley!*" shrilled the voice of Minnie at the foot of the stairs. "There's a couple of *drummers* off 'n the *train*, 'n' they want *supper*, 'n' what'll I *give* 'em?"

"My heavens! That girl 'll drive me crazy, sure!"
Arline hurried to the door. "Don't take the roof off 'n
the house," she cried querulously down the stairway.
"I 'm comin'."

Val had not spoken a word. She went over to the bed,
lifted a fold of satin, and smiled down at it ironically.
"Mamma and I spent a whole month planning and sewing and gloating over you," she said aloud. "You were
almost as important as a wedding gown; the club's farewell reception — 'To what base uses we do — '"

"Oh, here 's your slippers!" Arline thrust half her
body into the room and held the slippers out to Val.
"I stuck 'em into my pockets to bring up, and forgot all
about 'em, mind you, till I was handin' the drummers
their tea. And one of 'em happened to notice 'em, and
raised right up outa his chair, an' said: 'Cind'*rilla*, sure
as I live! Say, if there 's a foot in this town that 'll go
into them slippers, for God's sake introduce me to the
owner!' I told him to mind his own business. Drummers
do get awful fresh when they think they can get away
with it." She departed in a hurry, as usual.

Every day after that Arline talked about altering the
satin gown. Every day Val was noncommittal and un-
enthusiastic. Occasionally she told Arline that she was
not going to the dance, but Arline declined to take seriously
so preposterous a declaration.

"You want to break a leg, then," she told Val grimly on Thursday. "That's the only excuse that'll go down with this bunch. And you better git a move on — it comes off to-morrer night, remember."

"I won't go, Manley!" Val consoled herself by declaring, again and again. "The idea of Arline Hawley ordering me about like a child! Why should I go if I don't care to go?"

"Search me." Manley shrugged his shoulders. "It isn't so long, though, since you were just as determined to stay and have the shivaree, you remember."

"Well, you and Mr. Burnett tried to do exactly what Arline is doing. You seemed to think I was a child, to be ordered about."

At the very last minute — to be explicit, an hour before the hall was lighted, several hours after smoke first began to rise from the chimney, Val suddenly swerved to a reckless mood. Arline had gone to her own room to dress, too angry to speak what was in her mind. She had worked since five o'clock that morning. She had bullied Val, she had argued, she had begged, she had wheedled. Val would not go. Arline had appealed to Manley, and Manley had assured her, with a suspicious slurring of his *esses*, that he was out of it, and had nothing to say. Val, he said, could not be driven.

It was after Arline had gone to her room and Manley had returned to the "office" that Val suddenly picked up her hairbrush and, with an impish light in her eyes, began to pile her hair high upon her head. With her lips curved to match the mockery of her eyes, she began hurriedly to dress. Later, she went down to the parlor, where four women from the neighboring ranches were sitting stiffly and in constrained silence, waiting to be escorted to the hall. She swept in upon them, a glorious, shimmery creature all in white and gold. The women stared, wavered, and looked away — at the wall, the floor, at anything but Val's bare, white shoulders and arms as white. Arline had forgotten to look for gloves.

Val read the consternation in their weather-tanned faces, and smiled in wicked enjoyment. She would shock all of Hope; she would shock even Arline, who had insisted upon this. Like a child in mischief, she turned and went rustling down the hall to the dining room. She wanted to show Arline. She had not thought of the possibility of finding any one but Arline and Minnie there, so that she was taken slightly aback when she discovered Kent and another man eating a belated supper.

Kent looked up, eyed her sharply for just an instant, and smiled.

"Good evening, Mrs. Fleetwood," he said calmly. "Ready for the ball, I see. We got in late." He went on spreading butter upon his bread, evidently quite un-impressed by her magnificence.

The other man stared fixedly at his plate. It was a trifle, but Val suddenly felt foolish and ashamed. She took a step or two toward the kitchen, then retreated; down the hall she went, up the stairs and into her own room, the door of which she shut and locked.

"Such a fool!" she whispered vehemently, and stamped her white-shod foot upon the carpet. "He looked per-fectly disgusted — and so did that other man. And no wonder. Such — it 's *vulgar*, Val Fleetwood! It 's just ill-bred, and coarse, and horrid!" She threw herself upon the bed and put her face in the pillow.

Some one — she thought it sounded like Manley — came up and tried the door, stood a moment before it, and went away again. Arline's voice, sharpened with displeasure, she heard speaking to Minnie upon the stairs. They went down, and there was a confusion of voices below. In the street beneath her window footsteps sounded intermittently, coming and going with a certain eagerness of tread. After a time there came, from a dis-tance, the sound of violins and the "coronet" of which Arline had been so proud; and mingled with it was an undercurrent of shuffling feet, a mere whisper of sound, cut sharply now and then by the sharp commands of the floor manager. They were dancing — in her honor.

And she was a fool; a proud, ill-tempered, selfish fool.

With one of her quick changes of mood she rose, patted her hair smooth, caught up a wrap oddly inharmonious with the gown and slippers, looped her train over her arm, took her violin, and ran lightly down-stairs. The parlor, the dining room, the kitchen were deserted and the lights turned low. She braced herself mentally, and, flushing at the unaccustomed act, rapped timidly upon the door which opened into the office — which by that time she knew was really a saloon. Hawley himself opened the door, and his eyes bulged at sight of her.

"Is Mr. Fleetwood here? I — I thought, after all, I 'd go to the dance," she said, in rather a timid voice, shrinking back into the shadow.

"Fleetwood? Why, I guess he 's gone on over. He said you was n't going. You wait a minute. I — here, Kent! You take Mrs. Fleetwood over to the hall. Man 's gone."

"Oh, no! I — really, it does n't matter —"

But Kent had already thrown away his cigarette and come out to her, closing the door immediately after him.

"I 'll take you over — I was just going, anyway," he assured her, his eyes dwelling upon her rather intently.

"Oh — I wanted Manley. I — I hate to go — like this, it seems so — so queer, in this place. At first I—

I thought it would be a joke, but it is n't; it 's silly and
— and ill-bred. You — everybody will be shocked, and—"

Kent took a step toward her, where she was shrinking
against the stairway. Once before she had lost her calm
composure and had let him peep into her mind. Then
it had been on account of Manley; now, womanlike, it
was her clothes.

"You could n't be anything but all right, if you tried,"
he told her, speaking softly. "It is n't silly to look the
way the Lord meant you to look. You — you — oh, you
need n't worry — nobody 's going to be shocked very
hard." He reached out and took the violin from her;
took also her arm and opened the outer door. "You 're
late," he said, speaking in a more commonplace tone.
"You ought to have overshoes, or something — those
white slippers won't be so white time you get there.
Maybe I ought to carry you."

"The idea!" she stepped out daintily upon the slushy
walk.

"Well, I can take you a block or two around, and have
sidewalk all the way; that 'll help some. Women sure
are a lot of bother — I 'm plumb sorry for the poor devils
that get inveigled into marrying one."

"Why, Mr. Burnett! Do you always talk like that?
Because if you do, I don't wonder —"

"No," Kent interrupted, looking down at her and

smiling grimly, "as it happens, I don't. I 'm real nice, generally speaking. Say! this is going to be a good deal of trouble, do you know? After you dance with hubby, you 've got to waltz with me."

"*Got* to?" Val raised her eyebrows, though the expression was lost upon him.

"Sure. Look at the way I worked like a horse, saving your life — and the cat's — and now leading you all over town to keep those nice white slippers clean! By rights, you ought n't to dance with anybody else. But I ain't looking for real gratitude. Four or five waltzes is all I 'll insist on, but —" His tone was lugubrious in the extreme.

"Well, I 'll waltz with you once — for saving the cat; and once for saving the slippers. For saving me, I 'm not sure that I thank you." Val stepped carefully over a muddy spot on the walk. "Mr. Burnett, you — really, you 're an awfully queer man."

Kent walked to the next crossing and helped her over it before he answered her. "Yes," he admitted soberly then, "I reckon you 're right. I am — queer."

CHAPTER XIV

SUNDAY it was, and Val had insisted stubbornly upon going back to the ranch; somewhat to her surprise, if one might judge by her face, Arline Hawley no longer demurred, but put up lunch enough for a week almost, and announced that she was going along. Hank would have to drive out, to bring back the team, and she said she needed a rest, after all the work and worry of that dance. Manley, upon whose account it was that Val was so anxious, seemed to have nothing whatever to say about it. He was sullenly acquiescent — as was perhaps to be expected of a man who had slipped into his old habits and despised himself for doing so, and almost hated his wife because she had discovered it and said nothing. Val was thankful, during that long, bleak ride over the prairie, for Arline's incessant chatter. It was better than silence, when the silence means bitter thoughts.

"Now," said Arline, moving excitedly in her seat when they neared Cold Spring Coulee, "maybe I better tell you that the folks round here has kinda planned a little

su'prise for you. They don't make much of a showin'
about bein' neighborly — not when things go smooth —
but they 're right there when trouble comes. It 's jest
a little weddin' present — and if it comes kinda late in
the day, why, you don't want to mind that. My dance
that I gave was a weddin' party, too, if you care to call
it that. Anyway, it was to raise the money to pay for
our present, as far as it went — and I want to tell you
right now, Val, that you was sure the queen of the ball;
everybody said you looked jest like a queen in a picture,
and I never heard a word ag'inst your low-neck dress.
It looked all right on *you*, don't you see? On me, for
instance, it woulda been something fierce. And I 'm real
glad you took a hold and danced like you did, and never
passed nobody up, like some woulda done. You 'll be
glad you did, now you know what it was for. Even
danced with Polycarp Jenks — and there ain't hardly
any woman but what 'll turn *him* down; I 'll bet he
tromped all over your toes, did n't he?"

"Sometimes," Val admitted. "What about the surprise you were speaking of, Mrs. Hawley?"

"It does seem as if you might call me Arline," she
complained irrelevantly. "We 're comin' to that —
don't you worry."

"Is it — a piano?"

"My lands, no! You don't need a fiddle and a piano

both, do you? Man, what 'd you ruther have for a weddin' present?"

Manley, upon the front seat beside Hank, gave his shoulders an impatient twitch. "Fifty thousand dollars," he replied glumly.

"I 'm glad you 're real modest about it," Arline retorted sharply. She was beginning to tell herself quite frequently that she "did n't have no time for Man Fleetwood, seeing he would n't brace up and quit drinkin'."

Val's lips curled as she looked at Manley's back. "What I should like," she said distinctly, "is a great, big pile of wood, all cut and ready for the stove, and water pails that never would go empty. It 's astonishing how one's desires eventually narrow down to bare essentials, is n't it? But as we near the place, I find those two things more desirable than a piano!" Then she bit her lip angrily because she had permitted herself to give the thrust.

"Why, you poor thing! Man Fleetwood, do you —"

Val impulsively caught her by the arm. "Oh, hush! I was only joking," she said hastily. "I was trying to balance Manley's wish for fifty thousand dollars, don't you see? It was stupid of me, I know." She laughed unconvincingly. "Let me guess what the surprise is. First, is it large or small?"

"Kinda big," tittered Arline, falling into the spirit of the joke.

"Bigger than a — wait, now. A sewing machine?"

Arline covered her mouth with her hand and nodded dumbly.

"You say all the neighbors gave it and the dance helped pay for it — let me see. Could it possibly be — what in the world could it be? Manley, help me guess! Is it something useful, or just something nice?"

"Useful," said Arline, and snapped her jaws together as if she feared to let another word loose.

"Larger than a sewing machine, and useful." Val puckered her brows over the puzzle. "And all the neighbors gave it. Do you know, I 've been thinking all sorts of nasty things about our poor neighbors, because they refused to sell Manley any hay. And all the while they were planning this sur — " She never finished that sentence, or the word, even.

With a jolt over a rock, and a sharp turn to the right, Hank had brought them to the very brow of the hill, where they could look down into the coulee, and upon the house standing in its tiny, unkempt yard, just beyond the sparse growth of bushes which marked the spring creek. Involuntarily every head turned that way, and every pair of eyes looked downward. Hank chirped to the horses, threw all his weight upon the brake, and they rattled down the grade, the brake block squealing against the rear wheels. They were half-way down before any one spoke. It was Val, and she almost whispered one word:

"Manley!"

Arline's eyes were wet, and there was a croak in her voice when she cried jubilantly: "Well, ain't that better 'n a sewin' machine — or a piano?"

But Val did not attempt an answer. She was staring — staring as if she could not convince herself of the reality. Even Manley was jarred out of his gloomy meditations, and half rose in the seat that he might see over Hank's shoulder.

"That's what your neighbors have done," Arline began eagerly, "and they nearly busted tryin' to git through in time, and to keep it a dead secret. They worked like whiteheads, lemme tell you, and never even stopped for the storm. The night of the dance I heard all about how they had to hurry. And I guess Kent's there an' got a fire started, like I told him to. I was afraid it might be colder 'n what it is. I asked him if he would n't ride over an' warm up the house t'-day — and I see there's a smoke, all right." She looked at Manley, and then turned to Val. "Well, ain't you goin' to say anything? You dumb, both of you?"

Val took a deep breath. "We should be dumb," she said contritely. "We should go down on our knees and beg their pardon and yours — I especially. I think I've

never in my life felt quite so humbled — so overwhelmed
with the goodness of my fellows, and my own unworthiness. I — I can't put it into words — all the resentment
I have felt against the country and the people in it — as
if — oh, tell them all how I want them to forgive me for
— for the way I have felt. And — *Arline* — "

"There, now — I did n't bargain for you to make it so
serious," Arline expostulated, herself near to crying. "It
ain't nothing much — us folks believe in helpin' when
help 's needed, that 's all. For Heaven's sake, don't go
'n' *cry* about it!"

Hank pulled up at the gate with a loud *whoa* and a
grip of the brake. From the kitchen stovepipe a blue
ribbon of smoke waved high in the clear air. Kent appeared, grinning amiably, in the doorway, but Val was
looking beyond, and scarcely saw him — beyond, where
stood a new stable upon the ashes of the old; a new corral,
the posts standing solidly in the holes dug for those
burned away; a new haystack — when hay was almost
priceless! A few chickens wandered about near the
stable, and Val recognized them as Arline's prized Ply-
mouth Rocks. Small wonder that she and Manley were
stunned to silence. Manley still looked as if some one
had dealt him an unexpected blow in the face. Val was
white and wide-eyed.

Together they walked out to the stable. When they

stopped, she put her hand timidly upon his arm. "Dear," she said softly, "there is only one way to thank them for this, and that is to be the very best it is in us to be. We will, won't we? We — we have n't been our best, but we 'll start in right now. Shall we, Manley?"

Manley looked down at her for a moment, saying nothing.

"Shall we, Manley? Let us start now, and try again. Let 's play the fire burned up our old selves, and we 're all new, and strong — shall we? And we won't feel any resentment for what is past, but we 'll work together, and think together, and talk together, without any hidden thing we can't discuss freely. Please, Manley!"

He knew what she meant, well enough. For the last two days he had been drinking again. On the night of the dance he had barely kept within the limit of decent behavior. He had read Val's complete understanding and her disgust the morning after — and since then they had barely spoken except when speech was necessary. Oh, he knew what she meant! He stood for another minute, and she let go his arm and stood apart, watching his face.

A good deal depended upon the next minute, and they both knew it, and hardly breathed. His hand went slowly into a deep pocket of his overcoat, his fingers closed over something, and drew it reluctantly to the light. Shamefaced, he held it up for her to see — a flat bottle of generous size, full to within an inch of the cork with a pale, yellow liquid.

"There — take it, and break it into a million pieces," he said huskily. "I 'll try again."

Her yellow-brown eyes darkened perceptibly. "Manley Fleetwood, *you* must throw it away. This is your fight — be a man and *fight*."

"Well — there! May God damn me forever if I touch liquor again! I 'm through with the stuff for keeps!" He held the bottle high, without looking at it, and sent it crashing against the stable door.

"Manley!" She stopped her ears, aghast at his words, but for all that her eyes were ashine. She went up to him and put her arms around him. "Now we can start all over again," she said. "We 'll count our lives from this minute, dear, and we 'll keep them clean and happy. Oh, I 'm so glad! So glad and so proud, dear!"

Kent had got half-way down the path from the house; he stopped when Manley threw the bottle, and waited. Now he turned abruptly and retraced his steps, and he did not look particularly happy, though he had been smiling when he left the kitchen.

Arline turned from the window as he entered.

"Looks like Man has swore off ag'in," she observed dryly. "Well, let 's hope 'n' pray he stays swore off."

CHAPTER XV

A COMPACT

THE blackened prairie was fast hiding the mark of its fire torture under a cloak of tender new grass, vividly green as a freshly watered, well-kept lawn. Meadow larks hopped here and there, searching long for a sheltered nesting place, and missing the weeds where they were wont to sway and swell their yellow breasts and sing at the sun. They sang just as happily, however, on their short, low flights over the levels, or sitting upon gray, half-buried boulders upon some barren hilltop. Spring had come with lavish warmth. The smoke of burning ranges, the bleak winter with its sweeping storms of snow and wind, were pushed into the past, half forgotten in this new heaven and new earth, when men were glad simply because they were alive.

On a still, Sunday morning — that day which, when work does not press, is set apart in the range land for slight errands, attention to one's personal affairs, and to the pursuit of pleasure — Kent jogged placidly down the long hill into Cold Spring Coulee and pulled up at the familiar little unpainted house of rough boards, with its incongruously dainty curtains at the windows and its tiny yard, green and scrupulously clean.

The cat with white spots on its sides was washing its face on the kitchen doorstep. Val was kneeling beside the front porch, painstakingly stringing white grocery twine upon nails, which she drove into the rough posts with a small rock. The primitive trellis which resulted was obviously intended for the future encouragement of the sweet-pea plants just unfolding their second clusters of leaves an inch above ground. She did not see Kent at first, and he sat quiet in the saddle, watching her with a flicker of amusement in his eyes; but in a moment she struck her finger and sprang up with a sharp little cry, throwing the rock from her.

"Did n't you know that was going to happen, sooner or later?" Kent inquired, and so made known his presence.

"Oh — how do you do?" She came smiling down to the gate, holding the hurt finger tightly clasped in the other hand. "How comes it you are riding this way? Our trail is all growing up to grass, so few ever travel it."

"We 're all hard-working folks these days. Where 's Man?"

"Manley is down to the river, I think." She rested both arms upon the gatepost and regarded him with her steady eyes. "If you can wait, he will be back soon. He only went to see if the river is fordable. He thinks two or three of our horses are on the other side, and he'd like to get them. The river has been too high, but it's lowering rather fast. Won't you come in?" She was pleasant, she was unusually friendly, but Kent felt vaguely that, somehow, she was different.

He had not seen her for three months. Just after Christmas he had met her and Manley in town, when he was about to leave for a visit to his people in Nebraska. He had returned only a week or so before, and, if the truth were known, he was not displeased at the errand which brought him this way. He dismounted, and when she moved away from the gate he opened it and went in.

"Well," he began lightly, when he was seated upon the floor of the porch and she was back at her trellis, "and how's the world been using you? Had any more calamities while I've been gone?"

She busied herself with tying together two pieces of string, so that the whole would reach to a certain nail driven higher than her head. She stood with both hands uplifted, and her face, and her eyes; she did not reply for so long that Kent began to wonder if she had heard him. There was no reason why he should watch her so intently, or why he should want to get up and push back the one lock of hair which seemed always in rebellion and always falling across her temple by itself.

He was drifting into a dreamy wonder that all women with yellow-brown hair should not be given yellow-brown eyes also, and to wishing vaguely that it might be his luck to meet one some time — one who was not married — when she looked down at him quite unexpectedly. He was startled, and half ashamed, and afraid that she might not like what he had been thinking.

She was staring straight into his eyes, and he knew that she was thinking of something that affected her a good deal.

"Unless it's a calamity to discover that the world is — what it is, and people in it are — what they are, and that you have been a blind idiot. Is that a calamity, Mr. Cowboy? Or is it a blessing? I've been wondering."

Kent discovered, when he started to speak, that he had run short of breath. "I reckon that depends on how the discovery pans out," he ventured, after a moment. He was not looking at her then. For some reason, unexplained to himself, he felt that it was n't right for him to look at her; nor wise; nor quite pleasant in its effect. He did not know exactly what she meant, but he knew very well that she meant something more than to make conversation.

"That," she said, and gave a little sigh — "that takes so long — don't you know? The panning out, as you call it. It's hard to see things very clearly, and to make a decision that you know is going to stand the test, and then — just sit down and fold your hands, because some sordid, petty little reason absolutely prevents your doing anything. I hate waiting for anything. Don't you? When I want to do a thing, I want to do it immediately. These sweet-peas — now I've fixed the trellis for them to climb upon, I resent it because they don't take hold right now. Nasty little things — two inches high, when they should be two yards, and all covered with beautiful blossoms."

"Not the last of April," he qualified. "Give 'em a fair chance, can't you? They'll make it, all right; things take time."

She laughed surrenderingly, and came and sat down upon the porch near him, and tapped a slipper toe nervously upon the soft, green sod.

"Time! Yes —" She threw back her head and smiled at him brightly — and appealingly, it seemed to Kent. "You remember what you told me once — about sheepherders and *such* going crazy out here? The *such* is sometimes ready to agree with you." She turned her head with a quick impatience. "Such is learning to ride a horse," she informed him airily. "Such does it on the sly — and she fell off once and skinned her elbow, and she — well, Such has n't any sidesaddle — but she's learning, 'by granny!'"

Kent laughed unsteadily, and looked sidelong at her with eyes alight. She matched the glance for just about one second, and turned her eyes away with a certain consciousness that gave Kent a savage delight. Of a truth, she was different! She was human, she was intolerably alluring. She was not the prim, perfectly well-bred young woman he had met at the train. Lonesome Land was doing its work. She was beginning to think as an individual — as a woman; not merely as a member of conventional society.

"Such is beginning to be the proper stuff — 'by granny,'" he told her softly.

He was afraid his tone had offended her. She rose, and her color flared and faded. She leaned slightly against the post beside her, and, with a hand thrown up and half shielding her face, she stared out across the coulee to the hill beyond.

"Did you — I feel like a fool for talking like this, but one sometimes clutches at the least glimmer of sympathy and — and understanding, and speaks what should be kept bottled up inside, I suppose. But I 've been bottled up for so *long* —" She struck her free hand suddenly against her lips, as if she would apply physical force to keep them from losing all self-control. When she spoke again, her voice was calmer. "Did you ever get to the point, Mr. Cowboy, where you — you dug right down to the bottom of things, and found that you must do something or go mad — and there was n't a thing you could do? Did you ever?" She did not turn toward him, but kept her eyes to the hills. When he did not answer, however, she swung her head slowly and looked down at him, where he sat almost at her feet.

Kent was leaning forward, studying the gashes he had cut in the sod with his spurs. His brows were knitted close.

"I kinda think I 'm getting there pretty fast," he owned gravely when he felt her gaze upon him. "Why?"

"Oh — because you can understand how one must speak sometimes. Ever since I came, you have been — I don't know — different. At first I did n't like you at all; but I could see you were different. Since then — well, you have now and then said something that made me see one could speak to you, and you would understand. So I —" She broke off suddenly and laughed an apology. "Am I boring you dreadfully? One grows so self-centered living alone. If you are n't interested —"

"I am." Kent was obliged to clear his throat to get those two words out. "Go on. Say all you want to say."

She laughed again wearily. "Lately," she confessed nervously, "I 've taken to telling my thoughts to the cat. It 's perfectly safe, but, after all, it is n't quite satisfying." She stopped again, and stood silent for a moment.

"It 's because I am alone, day after day, week in and week out," she went on. "In a way, I don't mind it — under the circumstances I prefer to be alone, really. I mean, I would n't want any of my people near me. But one has too much time to think. I tell you this because I feel I ought to let you know that you were right that time; I don't suppose you even remember it! But I do. Once last fall — the first time you came to the ranch — you know, the time I met you at the spring, you seemed to see that this big, lonesome country was a little too much for me. I resented it then. I did n't want any one to tell me what I refused to admit to myself. I was trying so hard to like it — it seemed my only hope, you see. But now I 'll tell you you were right.

"Sometimes I feel very wicked about it. Sometimes I don't care. And sometimes I — I feel I shall go crazy if I can't talk to some one. Nobody comes here, except Polycarp Jenks. The only woman I know really well in the country is Arline Hawley. She 's good as gold, but — she 's intensely practical; you can't tell her your troubles — not unless they 're concrete and have to do with your physical well-being. Arline lacks imagination." She laughed again shortly.

"I don't know why I 'm taking it for granted you don't," she said. "You think I 'm talking pure nonsense, don't you, Mr. Cowboy?" She turned full toward him, and her yellow-brown eyes challenged him, begged him for sympathy and understanding, held him at bay — but most of all they set his blood pounding sullenly in his veins. He got unsteadily to his feet.

"You seem to pass up a lot of things that count, or you would n't say that," he reminded her huskily. "That night in town, just after the fire, for instance. And here, that same afternoon. I tried to jolly you out of feeling bad, both those times; but you know I understood. You know damn' *well* I understood! And you know I was sorry. And if you don't know, I 'd do anything on God's green earth —" He turned sharply away from her and stood kicking savagely backward at a clod with his rowel. Then he felt her hand touch his arm, and started. After that he stood perfectly still, except that he quivered like a frightened horse.

"Oh, it does n't mean much to you — you have your life, and you 're a man, and can do things when you want to. But I do so need a friend! Just somebody who understands, to whom I can talk when that is the only thing will keep me sane. You saved my life once, so I feel — no, I don't mean that. It is n't because of anything you did; it 's just that I feel I can talk to you more freely than to any one I know. I don't mean whine. I hope I 'm not a whiner. If I 've blundered, I 'm willing to — to take my medicine, as you would say. But if I can feel that somewhere in this big, empty country just one person will always feel kindly toward me, and wish me well, and be sorry for me when I — when I 'm miserable, and —" She could not go on. She pressed her lips together tightly, and winked back the tears.

Kent faced about and laid both his hands upon her shoulders. His face was very tender and rather sad, and if she had only understood as well as he did — But she did not.

"Little woman, listen here," he said. "You 're playing hard luck, and I know it; maybe I don't know just how hard — but maybe I can kinda give a guess. If you 'll think of me as your friend — your pal, and if you 'll always tell yourself that your pal is going to stand by you, no matter what comes, why — all right." He caught his breath.

She smiled up at him, honestly pleased, wholly without guile — and wholly blind. "I 'd rather have such a friend, just now, than anything I know, except — But if your sweetheart should object — could you —"

His fingers gripped her shoulders tighter for just a second, and he let her go. "I guess that part 'll be all right," he rejoined in a tone she could not quite fathom. "I never had one in m' life."

"Why, you poor thing!" She stood back and tilted her head at him. "You poor — *pal*. I 'll have to see

"Little woman, listen here," he said. "You're playing hard
luck, and I know it." *Page 214.*

about that immediately. Every young man wants a sweetheart — at least, all the young men I ever knew wanted one, and —"

"And I 'll gamble they all wanted the same one," he hinted wickedly, feeling himself unreasonably happy over something he could not quite put into words, even if he had dared.

"Oh, no. Hardly ever the same one, luckily. Do you know — pal, I 've quite forgotten what it was all about — the unburdening of my soul, I mean. After all, I think I must have been just lonesome. The country is just as big, but it is n't quite so — so *empty*, you see. Are n't you awfully vain, to see how you have peopled it with your friendship?" She clasped her hands behind her and regarded him speculatively. "I hope, Mr. Cowboy, you 're in earnest about this," she observed doubtfully. "I hope you have imagination enough to see it is n't silly, because if I suspected you were n't playing fair, and would go away and laugh at me, I 'd — scratch — you." She nodded her head slowly at him. "I 've always been told that, with tiger eyes, you find the disposition of a tiger. So if you don't mean it, you 'd better let me know at once."

Kent brought the color into her cheeks with his steady gaze. "I was just getting scared *you* did n't mean it," he averred. "If my pal goes back on me — why, Lord help her!"

She took a slow, deep breath. "How is it you men ratify a solemn agreement?" she puzzled. "Oh, yes." With a pretty impulse she held out her right hand, half grave, half playful. "Shake on it, pal!"

Kent took her hand and pressed it as hard as he dared. "You 're going to be a dandy little chum," he predicted gamely. "But let me tell you right now, if you ever get up on your stilts with me, there 's going to be all kinds of trouble. You call me Kent — that is," he qualified, with a little, unsteady laugh, "when there ain't any one around to get shocked."

"I suppose this *is n't* quite conventional," she conceded, as if the thought had just then occurred to her. "But, thank goodness, out here there are n't any conventions. Every one lives as every one sees fit. It is n't the best thing for some people," she added drearily. "Some people have to be bolstered up by conventions, or they can't help miring in their own weaknesses. But we don't; and as long as we understand —" She looked to him for confirmation.

"As long as we understand, why, it ain't anybody's business but our own," he declared steadily.

She seemed relieved of some lingering doubt. "That 's exactly it. I don't know why I should deny myself a friend, just because that friend happens to be a man, and I happen to be — married. I never did have much patience with the rule that a man must either be perfectly indifferent, or else make love. I'm so glad you — understand. So that's all settled," she finished briskly, "and I find that, as I said, it is n't at all necessary for me to unburden my soul."

They stood quiet for a moment, their thoughts too intangible for speech.

"Come inside, won't you?" she invited at last, coming back to everyday matters. "Of course you 're hungry — or you ought to be. You dare n't run away from my cooking this time, Mr. Cowboy. Manley will be back soon, I think. I must get some lunch ready."

Kent replied that he would stay outside and smoke, so she left him with a fleeting smile, infinitely friendly and confiding and glad. He turned and looked after her soberly, gave a great sigh, and reached mechanically for his tobacco and papers; thoughtfully rolled a cigarette, lighted it, and held the match until it burned quite down to his thumb and fingers. "Pals!" he said just under his breath, for the mere sound of the word. "All right — pals it is, then."

He smoked slowly, listening to her moving about in the house. Her steps came nearer. He turned to look.

"What was it you wanted to see Manley about?" she asked him from the doorway. "I just happened to wonder what it could be."

"Well, the Wishbone needs men, and sent me over to tell him he can go to work. The wagons are going to start to-morrow. He'll want to gather his cattle up, and of course we know about how he's fixed — for saddle horses and the like. He can work for the outfit and draw wages, and get his cattle thrown back on this range and his calves branded besides. Get paid for doing what he'll have to do anyhow, you see."

"I see." Val pushed back the rebellious lock of hair. "Of course you suggested the idea to the Wishbone. You're always doing something —"

"The outfit is short-handed," he reiterated. "They need him. They ain't straining a point to do Man a favor — don't you ever think it! Well — he's coming," he broke off, and started to the gate.

Manley clattered up, vociferously glad to greet him. Kent, at his urgent invitation, led his horse to the stable and turned him into the corral, unsaddled and unbridled him so that he could eat. Also, he told his errand. Manley interrupted the conversation to produce a bottle of whisky from a cunningly concealed hole in the depleted haystack, and insisted that Kent should take a drink. Kent waved it off, and Manley drew the cork and held the bottle to his own lips.

As he stood there, with his face uplifted while the yellow liquor gurgled down his throat, Kent watched him with a curiously detached interest. So that's how Manley had kept his vow! he was thinking, with an impersonal contempt. Four good swallows — Kent counted them.

"You're hitting it pretty strong, Man, for a fellow that swore off last fall," he commented aloud.

Manley took down the bottle, gave a sigh of pure, animal satisfaction, and pushed the cork in with an unconsciously regretful movement.

"A fellow's got to get something out of life," he defended peevishly. "I've had pretty hard luck — it's enough to drive a fellow to most any kind of relief. Burnt out, last fall — cattle scattered and calves running the range all winter — I haven't got stock enough to stand that sort of a deal, Kent. No telling where I stand now on the cattle question. I did have close to a hundred head — and three of my best geldings are missing — a poor man can't stand luck like that. I'm in debt too — and when you've got an iceberg in the house — when a man's own wife don't stand by him — when he can't get any sympathy from the very one that ought to — but, then, I hope I'm a gentleman; I don't make any kick against *her* — my domestic affairs are my own affairs. Sure. But when your wife freezes up solid —" He held the bottle up and looked at it. "Best friend I've got," he finished, with a whining note in his voice.

Kent turned away disgusted. Manley had coarsened.

He had "slopped down" just when he should have braced up and caught the fighting spirit — the spirit that fights and overcomes obstacles. With a tightening of his chest, he thought of his "pal," tied for life to this whining drunkard. No wonder she felt the need of a friend!

"Well, are you going out with the Wishbone?" he asked tersely, jerking his thoughts back to his errand. "If you are, you'll need to go over there to-night — the wagons start out to-morrow. Maybe you better ride around by Polly's place and have him come over here, once in a while, to look after things. You can't leave your wife alone without somebody to kinda keep an eye out for her, you know. Polycarp ain't going to ride this spring; he's got rheumatism, or some darned thing. But he can chop what wood she'll need, and go to town for her once in a while, and make sure she's all right. You better leave your gentlest horse here for her to use, too. She can't be left afoot out here."

Manley was taking another long swallow from the bottle, but he heard.

"Why, sure — I never thought about that. I guess maybe I *had* better get Polycarp. But Val could make out all right alone. Why, she's held it down here for a week at a time — last winter, when I'd forget to come home" — he winked shamelessly — "or a storm would come up so I couldn't get home. Val isn't like some fool women, I'll say that much for her. She don't care whether I'm around or not; fact is, sometimes I think she's better pleased when I'm gone. But you're right — I'll see Polycarp and have him come over once in a while. Sure. Glad you spoke of it. You always had a great head for thinking about other people, Kent. You ought to get married."

"No, thanks," Kent scowled. "I have n't got any grudge against women. The world's full of men ready and willing to give 'em a taste of pure, unadulterated hell."

Manley stared at him stupidly, and then laughed doubtfully, as if he felt certain of having, by his dullness, missed the point of a very good joke.

After that the time was filled with the preparations for Manley's absence. Kent did what he could to help, and Val went calmly about the house, packing the few necessary personal belongings which might be stuffed into a "war bag" and used during round-up. Beyond an occasional glance of friendly understanding, she seemed to have forgotten the compact she had made with Kent.

But when they were ready to ride away, Kent purposely left his gloves lying upon the couch, and remembered them only after Manley was in the saddle. So he went back, and Val followed him into the room. He wanted to say something — he did not quite know what — something that would bring them a little closer together, and keep them so; something that would make her think of him often and kindly. He picked up his gloves and held out his hand to her — and then a diffidence seized his tongue. There was nothing he dared say. All the eloquence, all the tenderness, was in his eyes.

"Well — good-by, pal. Be good to yourself," he said simply.

Val smiled up at him tremulously. "Good-by, my one friend. Don't — don't get hurt!"

Their clasp tightened, their hands dropped apart rather limply. Kent went out and got upon his horse, and rode away beside Manley, and talked of the range and of the round-up and of cattle and a dozen other things which interest men. But all the while one exultant thought kept reiterating itself in his mind: "She never said that much to *him !* She never said that much to *him !*"

CHAPTER XVI

TO the east, to the south, to the north went the riders of the Wishbone, gathering the cattle which the fires had driven afar. No rivers stopped them, nor mountains, nor the deep-scarred coulees, nor the plains. It was Manley's first experience in real round-up work, for his own little herd he had managed to keep close at home, and what few strayed afar were turned back, when opportunity afforded, by his neighbors, who wished him well. Now he tasted the pride of ownership to the full, when a VP cow and her calf mingled with the milling Wishbones and Double Diamonds. He was proud of his brand, and proud of the sentiment which had made him choose Val's initials. More than once he explained to his fellows that VP meant Val Peyson, and that he had got it recorded just after he and Val were engaged. He was not sentimental about her now, but he liked to dwell upon the fact that he had been; it showed that he was capable of fine feeling.

More dominant, however, as the weeks passed and the branding went on, became the desire to accumulate property — cattle. The Wishbone brand went scorching through the hair of hundreds of calves, while the VP seared tens. It was not right. He felt, somehow, cheated by fate. He mentally figured the increase of his herd, and it seemed to him that it took a long while, much longer than it should, to gain a respectable number in that manner. He cast about in his mind for some rich acquaintance in the East who might be prevailed upon to lend him capital enough to buy, say, five hundred cows. He began to talk about it occasionally when the boys lay around in the evenings.

"You want to ride with a long rope," suggested Bob Royden, grinning openly at the others. "That's the way to work up in the cow business. Capital nothing! You don't get enough excitement buying cattle; you want to steal 'em. That's what I'd do if I had a brand of my own and all your ambitions to get rich."

"And get sent up," Manley rounded out the situation. "No, thanks." He laughed. "It's a better way to get to the pen than it is to get rich, from all accounts."

Sandy Moran remembered a fellow who worked a brand and kept it up for seven or eight years before they caught him, and he recounted the tale between puffs at his cigarette. "Only they didn't catch him," he finished. "A puncher put him wise to what was in the wind, and he sold out cheap to a tenderfoot and pulled his freight.

They never did locate him." Then, with a pointed rock which he picked up beside him, he drew a rude diagram or two in the dirt. "That's how he done it," he explained. "Pretty smooth, too."

So the talk went on, as such things will, idly, without purpose save to pass the time. Shop talk of the range it was. Tales of stealing, of working brands, and of branding unmarked yearlings at weaning time. Of this big cattleman and that, who practically stole whole herds, and thereby took long strides toward wealth. Range scandals grown old; range gossip all of it, of men who had changed a brand or made one, using a cinch ring at a tiny fire in a secluded hollow, or a spur, or a jackknife; who were caught in the act, after the act, or merely suspected of the crime. Of "sweat" brands, blotched brands, brands added to and altered, of trials, of shootings, of hangings, even, and "getaways" spectacular and humorous and pathetic.

Manley, being in a measure a pilgrim, and having no experience to draw upon, and not much imagination, took no part in the talk, except that he listened and was intensely interested. Two months of mingling with men who talked little else had its influence.

That fall, when Manley had his hay up, and his cattle once more ranging close, toward the river and in the broken country bounded upon the west by the fenced-in railroad, three calves bore the VP brand — three husky heifers that never had suckled a VP mother. So had the range gossip, sown by chance in the soil of his greed of gain and his weakening moral fiber, borne fruit.

The deed scared him sober for a month. For a month his color changed and his blood quickened whenever a horseman showed upon the rim of Cold Spring Coulee. For a month he never left the ranch unless business compelled him to do so, and his return was speedy, his eyes anxious until he knew that all was well. After that his confidence returned. He grew more secretive, more self-assured, more at ease with his guilt. He looked the Wishbone men squarely in the eye, and it seldom occurred to him that he was a thief; or if it did, the word was but a synonym for luck, with shrewdness behind. Sometimes he regretted his timidity. Why three calves only? In a deep little coulee next the river — a coulee which the round-up had missed — had been more than three. He might have doubled the number and risked no more than for the three. The longer he dwelt upon that the more inclined he was to feel that he had cheated himself.

That fall there were no fires. It would be long before men grew careless when the grass was ripened and the winds blew hot and dry from out the west. The big prairie which lay high between the river and Hope was dotted with feeding cattle. Wishbones and Double Diamonds, mostly, with here and there a stray.

Manley grew wily, and began to plan far in advance. He rode here and there, quietly keeping his own cattle well down toward the river.   There was shelter there, and feed, and the idea was a good one. Just before the river broke up he saw to it that a few of his own cattle, and with them some Wishbone cows and a steer or two, were ranging in a deep, bushy coulee, isolated and easily passed by.   He had driven them there, and he left them there. That spring he worked again with the Wishbone.

When the round-up swept the home range, gathering and branding, it chanced that his part of the circle took him and Sandy Moran down that way. It was hot, and they had thirty or forty head of cattle before them when they neared that particular place.

"No need going down into the breaks here," he told Sandy easily. "I 've been hazing out everything I came across lately. They were mostly my own, anyway.   I believe I 've got it pretty well cleaned up along here."

Sandy was not the man to hunt hard riding.   He went to the rim of the coulee and looked down for a minute. He saw nothing moving, and took Manley's word for it with no stirring of his easy-going conscience.   He said all right, and rode on.

CHAPTER XVII

VAL BECOMES AN AUTHOR

QUITE as marked had been the change in Val that year. Every time Kent saw her, he recognized the fact that she was a little different; a little less superior in her attitude, a little more independent in her views of life. Her standards seemed slowly changing, and her way of thinking. He did not see her often, but when he did the mockery of their friendship struck him more keenly, his inward rebellion against circumstances grew more bitter. He wondered how she could be so blind as to think they were just pals, and no more. She did think so. All the little confidences, all the glances, all the smiles, she gave and received frankly, in the name of friendship.

"You know, Kent, this is my ideal of how people should be," she told him once, with a perfectly honest enthusiasm. "I 've always dreamed of such a friendship, and I 've always believed that some day the right man would come along and make it possible. Not one in a thousand could understand and meet one half-way — "

"They'd be liable to go farther," Kent assented dryly.

"Yes. That's just the trouble. They'd spoil an ideal friendship by falling in love."

"Darned chumps," Kent classed them sweepingly.

"Exactly. Pal, your vocabulary excites my envy. It's so forcible sometimes."

Kent grinned reminiscently. "It sure is, old girl."

"Oh, I don't mean necessarily profane. I wonder what your vocabulary will do to the secret I'm going to tell you." The sweet-peas had reached the desired height and profusion of blossoms, thanks to the pails and pails of water Val had carried and lavished upon them, and she was gathering a handful of the prettiest blooms for him. Her cheeks turned a bit pinker as she spoke, and her hesitation raised a wild hope briefly in Kent's heart.

"What is it?" He had to force the words out.

"I — I hate to tell, but I want you to — to help me."

"Well?" To Kent, at that moment, she was not Manley's wife; she was not any man's wife; she was the girl he loved — loved with the primitive, absorbing passion of the man who lives naturally and does not borrow his morals from his next-door neighbor. His code of ethics was his own, thought out by himself. Val hated her husband, and her husband did not seem to care much for her. They were tied together legally. And a mere legality could not hold back the emotions and the desires of Kent Burnett. With him, it was not a question of morals: it was a question of Val's feeling in the matter.

Val looked up at him, found something strange in his eyes, and immediately looked away again.

"Your eyes are always saying things I can't hear," she observed irrelevantly.

"Are they? Do you want me to act as interpreter?"

"No. I just want you to listen. Have you noticed anything different about me lately, Kent?" She tilted her head, while she passed judgment upon a cluster of speckled blossoms, odd but not particularly pretty.

"What do you mean, anyway? I'm liable to get off wrong if I tell you — "

"Oh, you're so horribly cautious! Have I seemed any more content — any happier lately?"

Kent picked a spray of flowers and pulled them ruthlessly to pieces. "Maybe I've kinda hoped so," he said, almost in a whisper.

"Well, I've a new interest in life. I just discovered it by accident, almost — "

Kent lifted his head and looked keenly at her, and his face was a lighter shade of brown than it had been.

"It seems to change everything. Pal, I — I've been writing things."

Kent discovered he had been holding his breath, and let it go in a long sigh.

"Oh!" After a minute he smiled philosophically. "What kinda things?" he drawled.

"Well, verses, but mostly stories. You see," she explained impulsively, "I want to earn some money — of my own. I have n't said much, because I hate whining; but really, things are growing pretty bad — between Manley and me. I hope it is n't my fault. I have tried every way I know to keep my faith in him, and to — to help him. But he 's not the same as he was. You know that. And I have a good deal of pride. I can't — oh, it 's intolerable having to ask a man for money! Especially when he does n't want to give you any," she added naïvely. "At first it was n't necessary; I had a little of my own, and all my things were new. But one must eventually buy things — for the house, you know, and for one's personal needs — and he seems to resent it dreadfully. I never would have believed that Manley could be stingy — actually stingy; but he is, unfortunately.

"I hate to speak of his faults, even to you. But I 've got to be honest with you. It is n't nice to say that I 'm writing, not for any particularly burning desire to express my thoughts, nor for the sentiment of it, but to earn money. It 's terribly sordid, is n't it?" She smiled wistfully up at him. "But there seems to be money in it, for those who succeed, and it 's work that I can do here. I have oceans of time, and I 'm not disturbed!" Her lips curved into bitter lines. "I do so much thinking, I might as well put my brain to some use." With one of her sudden changes of mood, she turned to Kent and clasped both hands upon his arm.

"Now you see, pal, how much our friendship means to me," she said softly. "I could n't have told this to another living soul! It seems awfully treacherous, saying it even to you — I mean about him. But you 're so good — you always understand, don't you, pal?"

"I guess so." Kent forced the words out naturally, and kept his breath even, and his arms from clasping her. He considered that he performed quite a feat of endurance.

"You 're modest!" She gave his arm a little shake. "Of course you do. You know I 'm not treacherous, really. You know I 'd do anything I could for him. But this is something that does n't concern him at all. He does n't know it, but that is because he would only sneer. When I have really sold something, and received the money for it, then it won't matter to me who knows. But now it 's a solemn secret, just between me and my pal." Her yellow-brown eyes dwelt upon his face.

Kent, stealing a glance at her from under his drooped lids, wondered if she had ever given any time to analyzing herself. He would have given much to know if, down deep in her heart, she really believed in this pal business; if she was really a friend, and no more. She puzzled him a good deal, sometimes.

"Well — if anybody can make good at that business, you sure ought to; you 've got brains enough to write a dictionary." He permitted himself the indulgence of saying that much, and he was perfectly sincere. He honestly considered Val the cleverest woman in the world.

She laughed with gratification. "Your sublime confidence, while it is undoubtedly mistaken, is nevertheless appreciated," she told him primly, moving away with her hands full of flowers. "If you 've got the nerve, come inside and read some of my stuff; I want to know if it 's any good at all."

Presently he was seated upon the couch in the little, pathetically bright front room, and he was knitting his eyebrows over Val's beautifully regular handwriting, — pages and pages of it, so that there seemed no end to the task, — and was trying to give his mind to what he was reading instead of to the author, sitting near him with her hands folded demurely in her lap and her eyes fixed expectantly upon his face, trying to read his decision even as it was forming.

Some verses she had tried on him first. Kent, by using all his determination of character, read them all, every word of them.

"That 's sure all right," he said, though, beyond a telling phrase or two, — one line in particular which would stick in his memory:

"Men live and love and die in that lonely land," —

he had no very clear idea of what it was all about. Certain lines seemed to go bumping along, and one had to mispronounce some of the final words to make them rhyme with others gone before, but it was all right — Val wrote it.

"I think I do better at stories," she ventured modestly. "I wrote one — a little story about university life — and sent it to a magazine. They wrote a lovely letter about it, but it seems that field is overdone, or something. The editor asked me why, living out here in the very heart of the West, I don't try Western stories. I think I shall — and that 's why I said I should need your help. I thought we might work together, you know. You 've lived here so long, and ought to have some splendid ideas — things that have happened, or that you 've heard — and you could tell me, and I 'd write them up. Would n't you like to collaborate — 'go in cahoots' on it?"

"Sure." Kent regarded her thoughtfully. She really was looking brighter and happier, and her enthusiasm was not to be mistaken. Her world had changed. "Anything I can do to help, you know —"

"Of course I know. I think it's perfectly splendid, don't you? We'll divide the money — when there *is* any, and —"

"Will we?" His tone was noncommittal in the extreme.

"Of course. Now, don't let's quarrel about that till we come to it. I have a good idea of my own, I think, for the first story. A man comes out here and disappears, you know, and after a while his sister comes to find him. She gets into all kinds of trouble — is kidnapped by a gang of robbers, and kept in a cave. When the leader of the gang comes back — he has been away on some depredation — you see, I have only the bare outline of the story yet — and, well, it's her brother! He kills the one who kidnapped her, and she reforms him. Of course, there ought to be some love interest. I think, perhaps, one member of the gang ought to fall in love with her, don't you know? And after a while he wins her —"

"She'll reform him, too, I reckon."

"Oh, yes. She couldn't love a man she couldn't respect — no woman could."

"Oh!" Kent took a minute to apply that personally. It was of value to him, because it was an indication of Val's own code. "Maybe," he suggested tentatively, "she'd get busy and reform the whole bunch."

"Oh, say — that would be great! She's an awfully

sweet little thing — perfectly lovely, you know — and they 'd all be in love with her, so it would n't be improbable. Don't you remember, Kent, you told me once that a man would do *anything* for a woman, if he cared enough for her?"

"Sure. He would, too." Kent fought back a momentary temptation to prove the truth of it by his own acquiescence in this pal business. He was saved from disaster by a suspicion that Val would not be able to see it from his point of view, and by the fact that he would much rather be pals than nothing.

She would have gone on, talking and planning and discussing, indefinitely. But the sun slid lower and lower, and Kent was not his own master. The time came when he had to go, regardless of his own wishes, or hers.

When he came again, the story was finished, and Val was waiting, with extreme impatience, to read it to him and hear his opinion before she sent it away. Kent was not so impatient to hear it, but he did not tell her so. He had not seen her for a month, and he wanted to talk; not about anything in particular — just talk about little things, and see her eyes light up once in a while, and her lips purse primly when he said something daring, and maybe have her play something on the violin, while he smoked and watched her slim wrist bend and rise and fall with the movement of the bow. He could imagine no single thing more fascinating than that — that, and the way she cuddled the violin under her chin, in the hollow of her neck.

But Val would not play — she had been too busy to practice, all spring and summer; she scarcely ever touched the violin, she said. And she did not want to talk — or if she did, it was plain that she had only one theme. So Kent, perforce, listened to the story. Afterward, he assured her that it was "outa sight." As a matter of fact, half the time he had not heard a word of what she was reading; he had been too busy just looking at her and being glad he was there. He had, however, a dim impression that it was a story with people in it whom one does not try to imagine as ever being alive, and with a West which, beyond its evident scarcity of inhabitants, was not the West he knew anything about. One paragraph of description had caught his attention, because it seemed a fairly accurate picture of the bench land which surrounded Cold Spring Coulee; but it had not seemed to have anything to do with the story itself. Of course, it must be good — Val wrote it. He began to admire her intensely, quite apart from his own personal subjugation.

Val was pleased with his praise. For two solid hours she talked of nothing but that story, and she gave him some fresh chocolate cake and a pitcher of lemonade, and urged him to come again in about three weeks, when she expected to hear from the magazine she thought would be glad to take the story; the one whose editor had suggested that she write of the West.

In the fall, and in the winter, their discussions were frequently hampered by Manley's presence. But Val's enthusiasm, though nipped here and there by unappreciative editors, managed, somehow, to live; or perhaps it had developed into a dogged determination to succeed in spite of everything. She still wrote things, and she still read them to Kent when there was time and opportunity; sometimes he was bold enough to criticize the worst places, and to tell her how she might, in his opinion, remedy them. Occasionally Val would take his advice.

So the months passed. The winds blew and brought storm and heat and sunshine and cloud. Nothing, in that big land, appreciably changed, except the people; and they so imperceptibly that they failed to realize it until afterward.

CHAPTER XVIII

WITH a blood-red sun at his back and a rosy tinge upon all the hills before him, Manley rode slowly down the western rim of Cold Spring Coulee, driving five rebellious calves that had escaped the branding iron in the spring. Though they were not easily driven in any given direction, he was singularly patient with them, and refrained from bellowing epithets and admonitions, as might have been expected. When he was almost down the hill, he saw Val standing in the kitchen door, shading her eyes with her hands that she might watch his approach.

"Open the corral gate!" he shouted to her, in the tone of command. "And stand back where you can head 'em off if they start up the coulee!"

Val replied by doing as she was told; she was not in the habit of wasting words upon Manley; they seemed always to precipitate an unpleasant discussion of some sort, as if he took it for granted she disapproved of all he did or said, and was always upon the defensive.

The calves came on, lumbering awkwardly in a half-hearted gallop, as if they had very little energy left. Their tongues protruded, their mouths dribbled a lathery foam, and their rough, sweaty hides told Val of the long chase — for she was wiser in the ways of the range land than she had been. She stood back, gently waving her ruffled white apron at them, and when they dodged into the corral, rolling eyes at her, she ran up and slammed the gate shut upon them, looped the chain around the post, and dropped the iron hook into a link to fasten it. Manley galloped up, threw himself off his panting horse, and began to unsaddle.

"Get some wood and start a fire, and put the iron in, Val," he told her brusquely.

Val looked at him quickly. "Now? Supper's all ready, Manley. There's no hurry about branding them, is there?" And she added: "Dear me! The round-up must have just skimmed the top off this range last spring. You've had to brand a lot of calves that were missed."

"What the devil is it to you?" he demanded roughly. "I want that fire, madam, and I want it *now*. I rather think I know when I want to brand without asking your advice."

Val curved her lips scornfully, shrugged and obeyed. She was used to that sort of thing, and she did not mind very much. He had brutalized by degrees, and by degrees she had hardened. He could rouse no feeling now but contempt.

"If you 'll kindly wait until I put back the supper," she said coldly. "I suppose in your zeal one need not sacrifice your food; you 're still rather particular about that, I observe."

Manley was leading his horse to the stable, and, though he answered something, the words were no more than a surly mumble.

"He 's been drinking again," Val decided dispassionately, on the way to the house. "I suppose he carried a bottle in his pocket — and emptied it."

She was not long; there was a penalty of profane reproach attached to delay, however slight, when Manley was in that mood. She had the fire going and the VP iron heating by the time he had stabled and fed his horse, and had driven the calves into the smaller pen. He drove a big, line-backed heifer into a corner, roped and tied her down with surprising dexterity, and turned impatiently.

"Come! Is n't that iron ready yet?"

Val, on the other side of the fence, drew it out and inspected it indifferently.

"It is not, Mr. Fleetwood. If you are in a very great hurry, why not apply your temper to it — and a few choice remarks?"

"Oh, don't try to be sarcastic — it's too pathetic. Kick a little life into that fire."

"Yes, sir — thank you, sir." Val could be rather exasperating when she chose. She always could be sure of making Manley silently furious when she adopted that tone of respectful servility — as employed by butlers and footmen upon the stage. Her mimicry, be it said, was very good.

"'Ere it is, sir — thank you, sir — 'ope I 'ave n't kept you wyting, sir," she announced, after he had fumed for two minutes inside the corral, and she had cynically hummed her way quite through the hymn which begins "Blest be the tie that binds." She passed the white-hot iron deftly through the rails to him, and fixed the fire for another heating.

Really, she was not thinking of Manley at all, nor of his mood, nor of his brutal coarseness. She was thinking of the rebuilt typewriter, advertised as being exactly as good as a new one, and scandalously cheap, for which she had sold her watch to Arline Hawley to get money to buy. She was counting mentally the days since she had sent the money order, and was thinking it should come that week surely.

She was also planning to seize upon the opportunity afforded by Manley's next absence for a day from the ranch, and drive to Hope on the chance of getting the machine. Only — she wished she could be sure whether

Kent would be coming soon. She did not want to miss seeing him; she decided to sound Polycarp Jenks the next time he came. Polycarp would know, of course, whether the Wishbone outfit was in from round-up. Polycarp always knew everything that had been done, or was intended, among the neighbors.

Manley passed the ill-smelling iron back to her, and she put it in the fire, quite mechanically. It was not the first time, nor the second, that she had been called upon to help brand. She could heat an iron as quickly and evenly as most men, though Manley had never troubled to tell her so.

Five times she heated the iron, and heard, with an inward quiver of pity and disgust, the spasmodic blat of the calf in the pen when the VP went searing into the hide on its ribs. She did not see why they must be branded that evening, in particular, but it was as well to have it done with. Also, if Manley meant to wean them, she would have to see that they were fed and watered, she supposed. That would make her trip to town a hurried one, if she went at all; she would have to go and come the same day, and Arline Hawley would scold and beg her to stay, and call her a fool.

"Now, how about that supper?" asked Manley, when they were through, and the air was clearing a little from the smoke and the smell of burned hair.

"I really don't know — I smelled the potatoes burning some time ago. I 'll see, however." She brushed her hands with her handkerchief, pushed back the lock of hair that was always falling across her temple, and, because she was really offended by Manley's attitude and tone, she sang softly all the way to the house, merely to conceal from him the fact that he could move her even to irritation. Her best weapon, she had discovered long ago, was absolute indifference — the indifference which overlooked his presence and was deaf to his recriminations.

She completed her preparations for his supper, made sure that nothing was lacking and that the tea was just right, placed his chair in position, filled the water glass beside his plate, set the tea-pot where he could reach it handily, and went into the living room and closed the door between. In the past year, filled as it had been with her literary ambitions and endeavors, she had neglected her music; but she took her violin from the box, hunted the cake of resin, tuned the strings, and, when she heard him come into the kitchen and sit down at the table, seated herself upon the front doorstep and began to play.

There was one bit of music which Manley thoroughly detested. That was the "Traumerei." Therefore, she played the "Traumerei" slowly — as it should, of course, be played — with full value given to all the pensive, long-drawn notes, and with a finale positively creepy in its dreamy wistfulness. Val, as has been stated, could be very exasperating when she chose.

In the kitchen there was the subdued rattle of dishes, unbroken and unhurried. Val went on playing, but she forgot that she had begun in a half-conscious desire to annoy her husband. She stared dreamily at the hill which shut out the world to the east, and yielded to a mood of loneliness; of longing, in the abstract, for all the pleasant things she was missing in this life which she had chosen in her ignorance.

When Manley flung open the inner door, she gave a stifled exclamation; she had forgotten all about Manley.

"By all the big and little gods of Greece!" he swore angrily. "Calves bawling their heads off in the corral, and you squalling that whiny stuff you call music in the house — home's sure a hell of a happy place! I'm going to town. You don't want to leave the place till I come back — I want those calves looked after." He seemed to consider something mentally, and then added:

"If I'm not back before they quit bawling, you can turn 'em down in the river field with the rest. You know when they're weaned and ready to settle down. Don't feed 'em too much hay, like you did that other bunch; just give 'em what they need; you don't have to pile the corral full. And don't keep 'em shut up an hour longer than necessary."

Val nodded her head to show that she heard, and went on playing. There was seldom any pretense of good feeling between them now. She tuned the violin to minor, and poised the bow over the strings, in some doubt as to her memory of a serenade she wanted to try next.

"Shall I have Polycarp take the team and haul up some wood from the river?" she asked carelessly. "We 're nearly out again."

"Oh, *I* don't care — if he happens along." He turned and went out, his mind turning eagerly to the town and what it could give him in the way of pleasure.

Val, still sitting in the doorway, saw him ride away up the grade and disappear over the brow of the hill. The dusk was settling softly upon the land, so that his figure was but a vague shape. She was alone again; she rather liked being alone, now that she had no longer a blind, unreasoning terror of the empty land. She had her thoughts and her work; the presence of Manley was merely an unpleasant interruption to both.

Some time in the night she heard the lowing of a cow somewhere near. She wondered dreamily what it could be doing in the coulee, and went to sleep again. The five calves were all bawling in a chorus of complaint against their forced separation from their mothers, and the deeper, throaty tones of the cow mingled not inharmoniously with the sound.

Range cattle were not permitted in the coulee, and when by chance they found a broken panel in the fence and strayed down there, Val drove them out; afoot, usually, with shouts and badly aimed stones to accelerate their lumbering pace.

After she had eaten her breakfast in the morning she went out to investigate. Beyond the corral, her nose thrust close against the rails, a cow was bawling dismally. Inside, in much the same position, its tail waving a violent signal of its owner's distress, a calf was clamoring hysterically for its mother and its mother's milk.

Val sympathized with them both; but the cow did not belong in the coulee, and she gathered two or three small stones and went around where she could frighten her away from the fence without, however, exposing herself too recklessly to her uncertain temper. Cows at weaning time did sometimes object to being driven from their calves.

"Shoo! Go on away from there!" Val raised a stone and poised it threateningly.

The cow turned and regarded her, wild-eyed. It backed a step or two, evidently uncertain of its next move.

"Go on away!" Val was just on the point of throwing the rock, when she dropped it unheeded to the ground and stared. "Why, you — you — why — the *idea!* " She turned slowly white. Certain things must filter to the understanding through amazement and disbelief; it took Val a minute or two to grasp the significance of what she saw. By the time she did grasp it, her knees were bending weakly beneath the weight of her body. She put out a groping hand and caught at the corner of the corral to keep herself from falling. And she stared and stared.

"It — oh, surely not!" she whispered, protesting against her understanding. She gave a little sob that had no immediate relation to tears. "Surely — *surely* — not!" It was of no use; understanding came, and came clearly, pitilessly. Many things — trifles, all of them — to which she had given no thought at the time, or which she had forgotten immediately, came back to her of their own accord; things she tried *not* to remember.

The cow stared at her for a minute, and, when she made no hostile move, turned its attention back to its bereavement. Once again it thrust its moist muzzle between two rails, gave a preliminary, vibrant *mmm — mmmmm — m*, and then, with a spasmodic heaving of ribs and of flank, burst into a long-drawn *baww — aw — aw — aw*, which rose rapidly in a tremulous crescendo and died to a throaty rumbling.

Val started nervously, though her eyes were fixed upon

the cow and she knew the sound was coming. It served, however, to release her from the spell of horror which had gripped her. She was still white, and when she moved she felt intolerably heavy, so that her feet dragged; but she was no longer dazed. She went slowly around to the gate, reached up wearily and undid the chain fastening, opened the gate slightly, and went in.

Four of the calves were huddled together for mutual comfort in a corner. They were blatting indefatigably. Val went over to where the fifth one still stood beside the fence, as near the cow as it could get, and threw a small stone, that bounced off the calf's rump. The calf jumped and ran aimlessly before her until it reached the half-open gate, when it dodged out, as if it could scarcely believe its own good fortune. Before Val could follow it outside, it was nuzzling rapturously its mother, and the cow was contorting her body so that she could caress her offspring with her tongue, while she rumbled her satisfaction.

Val closed and fastened the gate carefully, and went back to where the cow still lingered. With her lips drawn to a thin, colorless line, she drove her across the coulee and up the hill, the calf gamboling close alongside. When they had gone out of sight, up on the level, Val turned back and went slowly to the house. She stood for a minute staring stupidly at it and at the coulee, went in and gazed around her with that blankness which follows a great mental shock. After a minute she shivered, threw up her hands before her face, and dropped, a pitiful, sorrowing heap of quivering rebellion, upon the couch.

CHAPTER XIX

POLYCARP JENKS came ambling into the coulee, rapped perfunctorily upon the door-casing, and entered the kitchen as one who feels perfectly at home, and sure of his welcome; as was not unfitting, considering the fact that he had "chored around" for Val during the last year, and longer.

"Anybody to home?" he called, seeing the front door shut tight.

There was a stir within, and Val, still pale, and with an almost furtive expression in her eyes, opened the door and looked out.

"Oh, it 's you, Polycarp," she said lifelessly. "Is there anything — "

"What 's the matter? Sick? You look kinda peaked and frazzled out. I met Man las' night, and he told me you needed wood; I thought I 'd ride over and see. By granny, you do look bad."

"Just a headache," Val evaded, shrinking back guiltily. "Just do whatever there is to do, Polycarp. I think —

I don't believe the chickens have had anything to eat to-day — "

"Them headaches are sure a fright; they 're might' nigh as bad as rheumatiz, when they hit you hard. You jest go back and lay down, and I 'll look around and see what they is to do. Any idee when Man 's comin' back?"

"No." Val brought the word out with an involuntary sharpness.

"No, I reckon not. I hear him and Fred De Garmo come might' near havin' a fight las' night. Blumenthal was tellin' me this mornin'. Fred 's quit the Double Diamond, I hear. He 's got himself appointed dep'ty stock inspector — and how he managed to git the job is more 'n I can figure out. They say he 's all swelled up over it — got his headquarters in town, you know, and seems he got to lordin' it over Man las' night, and I guess if somebody had n't stopped 'em they 'd of been a mix-up, all right. Man was n't in no shape to fight — he 'd been drinkin' pretty — "

"Yes — well, just do whatever there is to do, Polycarp. The horses are in the upper pasture, I think — if you want to haul wood." She closed the door — gently, but with exceeding firmness, and Polycarp took the hint.

"Women is queer," he muttered, as he left the house. "Now, she knows Man drinks like a fish — and she knows everybody else knows it — but if you so much as mention sech a thing, why — " He waggled his head disapprovingly and proceeded, in his habitually laborious manner, to take a chew of tobacco. "No matter how much they may know a thing is so, if it don't suit 'em you can't never git 'em to stand right up and face it out — seems like, by granny, it comes natural to 'em to make believe things is different. Now, she knows might' well she can't fool *me*. I've hearn Man swear at her like — "

He reached the corral, and his insatiable curiosity turned his thoughts into a different channel. He inspected the four calves gravely, wondered audibly where Man had found them, and how the round-up came to miss them, and criticized his application of the brand; in the opinion of Polycarp, Manley either burned too deep or not deep enough.

"Time that line-backed heifer scabs off, you can't tell what's on her," he asserted, expectorating solemnly before he turned away to his work.

From a window, Val watched him with cold terror. Would he suspect? Or was there anything to suspect? "It's silly — it's perfectly idiotic," she told herself impatiently; "but if he hangs around that corral another minute, I shall scream!" She watched until she saw him mount his horse and ride off toward the upper pasture. Then she went out and began apathetically picking seed pods off her sweet-peas, which the early frosts had spared.

"Head better?" called Polycarp, half an hour later, when he went rattling past the house with the wagon, bound for the river bottom where they got their supply of wood.

"A little," Val answered inattentively, without looking at him.

It was while Polycarp was after the wood, and while she was sitting upon the edge of the porch, listlessly arranging and rearranging a handful of long-stemmed blossoms, that Kent galloped down the hill and up to the gate. She saw him coming and set her teeth hard together. She did not want to see Kent just then; she did not want to see anybody.

Kent, however, wanted to see her. It seemed to him at least a month since he had had a glimpse of her, though it was no more than half that time. He watched her covertly while he came up the path. His mind, all the way over from the Wishbone, had been very clear and very decided. He had a certain thing to tell her, and a certain thing to do; he had thought it all out during the nights when he could not sleep and the days when men called him surly, and there was no going back, no reconsideration of the matter. He had been telling himself that, over and over, ever since the house came into view and he saw her sitting there on the porch. She would probably want to argue, and perhaps she would try to persuade him, but it would be absolutely useless; absolutely.

"Well, hello!" he cried, with more than his usual buoyancy of manner — because he knew he must hurt her later on. "Hello, Madam Author*ess*. Why this haughty air? This stuckupiness? Shall I get a ladder and climb up where you can hear me say howdy?" He took off his hat and slapped her gently upon the top of her head with it. "Come out of the fog!"

"Oh — I wish you would n't!" She glanced up at him so briefly that he caught only a flicker of her yellow-brown eyes, and went on fumbling her flowers. Kent stood and looked down at her for a moment.

"Mad?" he inquired cheerfully. "Say, you look awfully savage. On the dead, you do. What do *you* care if they sent it back? You had all the fun of writing it — and you know it 's a dandy. Please smile. *Pretty* please!" he wheedled. It was not the first time he had discovered her in a despondent mood, nor the first time he had bantered and badgered her out of her gloom. Presently it dawned upon him that this was more serious; he had never seen her quite so colorless or so completely without spirit.

"Sick, pal?" he asked gently, sitting down beside her.

"No-o — I suppose not." Val bit her lips, as soon as she had spoken, to check their quivering.

"Well, what is it? I wish you 'd tell me. I came over here full of something I had to tell you — but I can't, now; not while you 're like this." He watched her yearningly.

"Oh, I can't tell you. It 's nothing." Val jerked a sweet-pea viciously from its stem, pressed her hand against her mouth, and turned reluctantly toward him. "What was it you came to tell me?"

He watched her narrowly. "I 'll gamble you 're down in the mouth about something hubby has said or done. You need n't tell me — but I just want to ask you if you think it 's worth while? You need n't tell me that, either. You know blamed well it ain't. He can't deal you any more misery than you let him hand out; you want to keep that in mind."

Another blossom was demolished. "What was it you came to tell me?" she repeated steadily, though she did not look at him.

"Oh, nothing much. I 'm going to leave the country, is all."

"Kent!" After a minute she forced another word out. "Why?"

Kent regarded her somberly. "You better think twice before you ask me that," he warned; "because I ain't much good at beating all around the bush. If you ask me again, I 'll tell you — and I 'm liable to tell you without any frills." He drew a hard breath. "So I'd advise you not to ask," he finished, half challengingly.

Val placed a pale lavender blossom against a creamy white one, and held the two up for inspection.

"When are you going?" she asked evenly.

"I don't know exactly — in a day or so. Saturday, maybe."

She hesitated over the flowers in her lap, and selected a pink one, which she tried with the white and the lavender.

"And — *why* are you going?" she asked him deliberately.

Kent stared at her fixedly. A faint, pink flush was creeping into her cheeks. He watched it deepen, and knew that his silence was filling her with uneasiness. He wondered how much she guessed of what he was going to say, and how much it would mean to her.

"All right — I'll tell you why, fast enough." His tone was grim. "I'm going to leave the country because I can't stay any longer — not while you're in it."

"Why — Kent!" She seemed inexpressibly shocked.

"I don't know," he went on relentlessly, "what you think a man's made of, anyhow. And I don't know what *you* think of this pal business; I know what I think: It's a mighty good way to drive a man crazy. I've had about all of it I can stand, if you want to know."

"I'm sorry, if you don't — if you can't be friends

any longer," she said, and he winced to see how her eyes filled with tears. "But, of course, if you can't — if it bores you —"

Kent seized her arm, a bit roughly. "Have I got to come right out and tell you, in plain English, that I — that it's because I'm so deep in love with you I can't. If you only knew what it's cost me this last year — to play the game and not play it too hard! What do you think a man's made of? Do you think a man can care for a woman, like I care for you, and — Do you think he wants to be just pals? And stand back and watch some drunken brute abuse her — and never — Here!" His voice grew tender. "Don't do that — don't! I didn't want to hurt you — God knows I didn't want to hurt you!" He threw his arm around her shoulders and pulled her toward him.

"Don't — pal. I'm a brute, I guess, like all the rest of the male humans. I don't mean to be — it's the way I'm made. When a woman means so much to me that I can't think of anything else, day or night, and get to counting days and scheming to see her — why — being friends — like we've been — is like giving a man a teaspoon of milk and water when he's starving to death, and thinking that oughta do. But I shouldn't have let it hurt you. I tried to stand for it, little woman. There were times when I just had to fight myself not

to take you up in my arms and carry you off and keep
you. You must admit," he argued, smiling rather wanly,
"that, considering how I 've felt about it, I 've done
pretty tolerable well up till now. You don't — you
never will know how much it 's cost. Why, my nerves
are getting so raw I can't stand anything any more.
That 's why I 'm going. I don't want to hang around
till I do something — foolish."

He took his arm away from her shoulders and moved
farther off; he was not sure how far he might trust
himself.

"If I thought you cared — or if there was anything
I could do for you," he ventured, after a moment, "why,
it would be different. But —"

Val lifted her head and turned to him.

"There is something — or there was — or — oh, I
can't think any more! I suppose" — doubtfully — "if
you feel as you say you do, why — it would be — wicked
to stay. But you don't; you must just imagine it."

"Oh, all right," Kent interpolated ironically.

"But if you go away —" She got up and stood before
him, breathing unevenly, in little gasps. "Oh, you must n't
go away! Please don't go! I — there 's something
terrible happened — oh, Kent, I need you! I can't tell
you what it is — it 's the most horrible thing I ever heard
of! You can't imagine anything more horrible, Kent!"

She twisted her fingers together nervously, and the blossoms dropped, one by one, on the ground. "If you go," she pleaded, "I won't have a friend in the country, not a real friend. And — and I never needed a friend as much as I do now, and you must n't go. I — I can't let you go!" It was like her hysterical fear of being left alone after the fire.

Kent eyed her keenly. He knew there must have been something to put her into this state — something more than his own rebellion. He felt suddenly ashamed of his weakness in giving way — in telling her how it was with him. The faint, far-off chuckle of a wagon came to his ears. He turned impatiently toward the sound. Polycarp was driving up the coulee with a load of wood; already he was nearing the gate which opened into the lower field. Kent stood up, reached out, and caught Val by the hand.

"Come on into the house," he said peremptorily. "Polly 's coming, and you don't want him goggling and listening. And I want you," he added, when he had led her inside and closed the door, "to tell me what all this is about. There 's something, and I want to know what. If it concerns you, then it concerns me a whole lot, too. And what concerns me I 'm going to find out about — what is it?"

Val sat down, got up immediately, and crossed the

room aimlessly to sit in another chair. She pressed her palms tightly against both cheeks, drew in her breath as if she were going to speak, and, after all, said nothing. She looked out of the window, pushing back the errant strand of hair.

"I can't — I don't know how to tell you," she began desperately. "It's too horrible."

"Maybe it is — I don't know what you'd call too horrible; I kinda think it would n't be what I'd tack those words to. Anyway — what is it?" He went close, and he spoke insistently.

She took a long breath.

"Manley's a thief!" She jerked the words out like an automaton. They were not, evidently, the words she had meant to speak, for she seemed frightened afterward.

"Oh, that's it!" Kent made a sound which was not far from a snort. "Well, what about it? What's he done? How did you find it out?"

Val straightened in the chair and gazed up at him. Once more her tawny eyes gave him a certain shock, as if he had never before noticed them.

"After all our neighbors have done for him," she cried bitterly; "after giving him hay, when his was burned and he could n't buy any; after building stables, and corral, and — everything they did — the kindest, best neighbors a man ever had — oh, it 's too shameful for utterance! I might forgive it — I might, only for that. The — the ingratitude! It 's too despicable — too —"

Kent laid a steadying hand upon her arm.

"Yes — but what is it?" he interrupted.

Val shook off his hand unconsciously, impatient of any touch.

"Oh, the bare deed itself — well, it 's rather petty, too — and cheap." Her voice became full of contempt. "It was the calves. He brought home five last night — five that had n't been branded last spring. Where he found them *I* don't know — I did n't care enough about it to ask. He had been drinking, I think; I can usually tell — and he often carries a bottle in his pocket, as I happen to know.

"Well, he had me make a fire and heat the iron for him, and he branded them — last night; he was very touchy about it when I asked him what was his hurry. I think now it was a stupid thing for him to do. And — well, in the night, some time, I heard a cow bawling around close, and this morning I went out to drive her away; the fence is always down somewhere — I suppose she found a place to get through. So I went out to drive her away." Her eyes dropped, as if she were making a confession of her own misdeed. She clenched her hands tightly in her lap.

"Well — it was a Wishbone cow." After all, she said it very quietly.

"The devil it was!" Kent had been prepared for something of the sort; but, nevertheless, he started when he heard his own outfit mentioned.

"Yes. It was a Wishbone cow." Her voice was flat and monotonous. "He had stolen her calf. He had it in the corral, and he had branded it with his own brand — with a VP. *With my initials!* " she wailed suddenly, as if the thought had just struck her, and was intolerably bitter. "She had followed — had been hunting her calf; it was rather a little calf, smaller than the others. And it was crowded up against the fence, trying to get to her. There was no mistaking their relationship. I tried to think he had made a mistake; but it's of no use — I know he did n't. I know he *stole* that calf. And for all I know, the others, too. Oh, it's perfectly horrible to think of!"

Kent could easily guess her horror of it, and he was sorry for her. But his mind turned instantly to the practical side of it.

"Well — maybe it can be fixed up, if you feel so bad about it. Does Polycarp — did he see the cow hanging around?"

Val shook her head apathetically. "No — he did n't come till just a little while ago. That was this morning.

And I drove her out of the coulee — her and her calf.
They went off up over the hill."

Kent stood looking down at her rather stupidly.

"You — *what?* What was it you did?" It seemed
to him that something — some vital point of the story —
had eluded him.

"I drove them away. I did n't think they ought to
be permitted to hang around here." Her lips quivered
again. "I — I did n't want to see him — get — into
any trouble."

"You drove them away? Both of them?" Kent was
frowning at her now.

Val sprang up and faced him, all a-tremble with indig-
nation. "Certainly, both! *I 'm* not a thief, Kent Burnett! When I knew — when there was no possible doubt
— why, what, in Heaven's name, *could* I do? It was n't
Manley's calf. I turned it loose to go back where it
belonged."

"With a VP on its ribs!" Kent was staring at her
curiously.

"Well, I don't care! Fifty VP's could n't make the
calf Manley's. If anybody came and saw that cow,
why —" Val looked at him rather pityingly, as if she
could not quite understand how he could even question
her upon that point. "And, after all," she added for-
lornly, "he 's my husband. I could n't — I had to do

what I could to shield him — just for sake of the past,
I suppose. Much as I despise him, I can't forget that
— that I cared once. It's because I wanted your
advice that I —"

"It's a pity you did n't get it sooner, then! Can't
you see what you 've done? Why, think a minute! A
VP calf running with a Wishbone cow — why, it's —
you could n't advertise Man as a rustler any better if
you tried. The first fellow that runs onto that cow and
calf — well, he won't need to do any guessing — he 'll
know. It's a ticket to Deer Lodge — that VP calf. Now
do you see?" He turned away to the window and stood
looking absently at the brown hillside, his hands thrust
deep into his pockets.

"And there 's Fred De Garmo, with his new job, ranging around the country just aching to cinch somebody
and show his authority. It's a matter of days almost.
He 'd like nothing better than to get a whack at Man,
even if the Wishbone —"

Outside, they could hear Polycarp throwing the wood
off the wagon; knowing him as they did, they knew it
would not be long before he found an excuse for coming
into the house. He had more than once evinced a good
deal of interest in Kent's visits there, and shown an unmistakable desire to know what they were talking about.
They had never paid much attention to him; but now

even Val felt a vague uneasiness lest he overhear. She had been sitting, her face buried in her arms, crushed beneath the knowledge of what she had done.

"Don't worry, little woman." Kent went over and passed his hand lightly over her hair. "You did what looked to you to be the right thing — the honest thing. And the chances are he 'd get caught before long, anyhow. I don't reckon this is the first time he 's done it."

"Oh-h — but to think — to think that *I* should do it — when I wanted to save him! He — Kent, I despise him — he has killed all the love I ever felt for him — killed it over and over — but if anybody finds that calf, and — and if they — Kent, I shall go crazy if I have to feel that *I* sent him — to — prison. To think of him — shut up there — and to know that I did it — I can't bear it!" She caught his arm. She pressed her forehead against it. "Kent, is n't there some way to get it back? If I should find it — and — and shoot it — and pay the Wishbone what it 's worth — oh, *any* amount — or shoot the cow — or —" she raised her face imploringly to his — "tell me, pal — or I shall go stark, raving mad!"

Polycarp came into the kitchen, and, from the sound, he was trying to enter as unobtrusively as possible, even to the extent of walking on his toes.

"Go see what that darned old sneak wants," Kent

commanded in an undertone. "Act as if nothing happened — if you can." He watched anxiously, while she drew a long breath, pressed her hands hard against her cheeks, closed her lips tightly, and then, with something like composure, went quietly to the door and threw it open. Polycarp was standing very close to it, on the other side. He drew back a step.

"I wondered if I better git another load, now I 've got the team hooked up," he began in his rasping, nasal voice, his slitlike eyes peering inquisitively into the room. "Hello, Kenneth — I *thought* that was your horse standin' outside. Or would you ruther I cut up a pile? I dunno but what I 'll have to go t' town t'-morrer or next day — mebby I better cut you some wood, hey? If Man ain't likely to be home, mebby —"

"I think, Polycarp, we 'll have a storm soon. So it would be good policy to haul another load, don't you think? I can manage very well with what there is cut until Manley returns; and there are always small branches that I can break easily with the axe. I really think it would be safer to have another load hauled now while we can. Don't you think so?" Val even managed to smile at him. "If my head was n't so bad," she added deceitfully, "I should be tempted to go along, just for a close sight of the river. Mr. Burnett is going directly — perhaps I may walk down later on. But you had better not wait — I should n't want to keep you working till dark."

Polycarp, eying her and Kent, and the room in all its details, forced his hand into his trousers pocket, brought up his battered plug of tobacco and pried off a piece, which he rolled into his left cheek with his tongue.

"Jest as you say," he surrendered, though it was perfectly plain that he would much prefer to cut wood and so be able to see all that went on, even though he was denied the gratification of hearing what they said. He waited a moment, but Val turned away, and even had the audacity to close the door upon his unfinished reply. He listened for a moment, his head craned forward.

"Purty kinda goings-on!" he mumbled. "Time Man had a flea put in 'is ear, by granny, if he don't want to lose that yeller-eyed wife of hisn." To Polycarp, a closed door — when a man and woman were alone upon the other side — could mean nothing but surreptitious kisses and the like. He went stumbling out and drove away down the coulee, his head turning automatically so that his eyes were constantly upon the house; from his attitude, as Kent saw him through the window, Polycarp expected an explosion, at the very least. His outraged virtue vented itself in one more sentence: "Purty blamed nervy, by granny — to go 'n' shut the door right in m' face!"

Inside the room, Val stood for a minute with her back against the door, as if she half feared Polycarp would break in and drag her secret from her. When she heard him leave the kitchen she drew a long breath, eloquent in itself: when the rattle of the wagon came to them there, she left the door and went slowly across the room until she stood close to Kent. The interruption had steadied them both. Her voice was a constrained calm when she spoke.

"Well — is there anything I can do? Because I suppose every minute is dangerous."

Kent kept his eyes upon the departing Polycarp.

"There's nothing you can do, no. Maybe I can do something; soon as that granny gossip is outa sight, I'll go and round up that cow and calf — if somebody has n't beaten me to it."

Val looked at him with a certain timid helplessness.

"Oh! Will you — won't it be against the law if you — if you kill it?" She grew slightly excited again. "Kent, you shall not get into any trouble for — for his sake! If it comes to a choice, why — let him suffer for his crime. You shall not!"

Kent turned his head slowly and gazed down at her. "Don't run away with the idea I'm doing it for him," he told her distinctly. "I love Man Fleetwood like I love a wolf. But if that VP calf catches him up, you'd fight your head over it, God only knows how long. I know you! You 'd think so much about the part you played that you 'd wind up by forgetting everything else. You 'd get to thinking of him as a martyr, maybe! No — it 's for you. I kinda got you into this, you recollect? If I 'd let you see Man drunk, that day, you 'd never have married him; I know that now. So I 'm going to get you out of it. My side of the question can wait."

She stared up at him with a grave understanding.

"But you know what I said — you won't do anything that can make you trouble — won't you tell me, Kent, what you 're going to do?"

He had already started to the door, but he stopped and smiled reassuringly.

"Nothing so fierce. If I can find 'em, I aim to bar out that VP. Sabe?"

CHAPTER XX

A T the brow of the hill, which was the western rim of the coulee, Kent turned and waved a farewell to Val, watching him wistfully from the kitchen door. She had wanted to go along; she had almost cried to go and help, but Kent would not permit her — and beneath the unpleasantness of denying her anything, there had been a certain primitive joy in feeling himself master of the situation and of her actions; for that one time it was as if she belonged to him. At the last he had accepted the field glasses, which she insisted upon lending him, and now he was tempted to take them from their worn, leathern case and focus them upon her face, just for the meager satisfaction of one more look at her. But he rode on, out of sight, for the necessity which drove him forth did not permit much loitering if he would succeed in what he had set out to do.

Personally he would have felt no compunctions whatever about letting the calf go, a walking advertisement of Manley's guilt. It seemed to him a sort of grim retribution, and no more than he deserved. He had not exaggerated his sentiments when he intimated plainly to her his hatred of Manley, and he agreed with her that the fellow was making a despicable return for the kindness his neighbors had always shown him. No doubt he had stolen from the Double Diamond as well as the Wishbone.

Once Kent pulled up, half minded to go back and let events shape themselves without any interference from him. But there was Val — women were so queer about such things. It seemed to Kent that, if any man had caused him as much misery as Manley had caused Val, he would not waste much time worrying over him, if he tangled himself up with his own misdeeds. However, Val wanted that bit of evidence covered up; so, while Kent did not approve, he went at the business with his customary thoroughness.

The field glasses were a great convenience. More than once they saved him the trouble of riding a mile or so to inspect a small bunch of stock. Nevertheless, he rode for several hours before, just at sundown, he discovered the cow feeding alone with her calf in a shallow depression near the rough country next the river. They were wild, and he ran them out of the hollow and up on high ground before he managed to drop his loop over the calf's head.

"You sure are a dandy-fine sign-post, all right," he observed, and grinned down at the staring VP brand.

"It's a pity you can't be left that way." He glanced cautiously around him at the great, empty prairie. A mile or two away, a lone horseman was loping leisurely along, evidently bound for the Double Diamond.

"Say — this is kinda public," Kent complained to the calf. "Let's you and me go down outa sight for a minute." He started off toward the hollow, dragging the calf, a protesting bundle of stiffened muscles pulling against the rope. The cow, shaking her head in a half-hearted defiance, followed. Kent kept an uneasy eye upon the horseman, and hoped fervently the fellow was absorbed in meditation and would not glance in his direction. Once he was almost at the point of turning the calf loose; for barring out brands, even illegal brands, is justly looked upon with disfavor, to say the least.

Down in the hollow, which Kent reached with a sigh of relief, he dismounted and hastily started a little fire on a barren patch of ground beneath a jutting sandstone ledge. The calf, tied helpless, lay near by, and the cow hovered close, uneasy, but lacking courage for a rush.

Kent laid hand upon his saddle, hesitated, and shook his head; he might need it in a hurry, and a cinch ring takes time both in the removal and the replacement — and is vitally important withal. His knife he had lost on the last round-up. He scowled at the necessity, lifted his heel, and took off a spur. "And if that darned ginny don't get too blamed curious and come fogging over this way —" He spoke the phrase aloud, out of the middle of a mental arrangement of the chance he was taking.

To heat the spur red-hot, draw it across the fresh VP again and again, and finally drag it crisscross once or twice to make assurance an absolute certainty, did not take long. Kent was particular about not wasting any seconds. The calf stopped its dismal blatting, and when Kent released it and coiled his rope, it jumped up and ran for its life, the cow ambling solicitously at its heels. Kent kicked the dirt over the fire, eyed it sharply a moment to make sure it was perfectly harmless, mounted in haste, and rode up the sloping side down which he had come. Just under the top of the slope, he peered anxiously out over the prairie, ducked precipitately, and went clattering away down the hollow to the farther side; dodged around a spur of rocks, forced his horse down over a wicked jumble of bowlders to level land below, and rode as if a hangman's noose were the penalty for delay.

When he reached the river — which he did after many windings and turnings — he got off and washed his spur, scrubbing it diligently with sand in an effort to remove the traces of fire. When the evidence was at least less conspicuous, he put it on his heel and jogged down the

To draw the red hot spur across the fresh VP did not take long

Page 274.

river bank quite innocently, inwardly thankful over his escape. He had certainly done nothing wrong; but one sometimes finds it rather awkward to be forced into an explanation of a perfectly righteous deed.

"If I 'd been stealing that calf, I 'd never have been crazy enough to take such a long chance," he mused, and laughed a little. "I 'll bet Fred thought he was due to grab a rustler right in the act — only he was a little bit slow about making up his mind; deputy stock inspectors had oughta think quicker than that — he was just about five minutes too deliberate. I 'll gamble he 's scratching his head, right now, over that blotched brand, trying to *sabe* the play — which he won't, not in a thousand years!"

He gave the reins a twitch and began to climb through the dusk to the lighter hilltop, at a point just east of Cold Spring Coulee. At the top he put the spurs to his horse and headed straight as might be for the Wishbone ranch. He would like to have told Val of his success, but he was afraid Manley might be there, or Polycarp; it was wise always to avoid Polycarp Jenks, if one had anything to conceal from his fellows.

CHAPTER XXI

IT was the middle of the next forenoon when Manley came riding home, sullen from drink and a losing game of poker, which had kept him all night at the table, and at sunrise sent him forth in the mood which meets a grievance more than half-way. He did not stop at the house, though he saw Val through the open door; he did not trouble to speak to her, even, but rode on to the stable, stopping at the corral to look over the fence at the calves, still bawling sporadically between half-hearted nibblings at the hay which Polycarp had thrown in to them.

Just at first he did not notice anything wrong, but soon a vague disquiet seized him, and he frowned thoughtfully at the little group. Something puzzled him; but his brain, fogged with whisky and loss of sleep, and the reaction from hours of concentration upon the game, could not quite grasp the thing that troubled him. In a moment, however, he gave an inarticulate bellow, wheeled about, and rode back to the house. He threw himself from the horse almost before it stopped, and rushed into the kitchen. Val, ironing one of her ruffled white aprons, looked up quickly, turned rather pale, and then stiffened perceptibly for the conflict that was coming.

"There's only four calves in the corral — and I brought in five. Where's the other one?" He came up and stood quite close to her — so close that Val took a step backward. He did not speak loud, but there was something in his tone, in his look, that drove the little remaining color from her face.

"Manley," she said, with a catch of the breath, "why did you do that horrible thing? What devil possessed you? I—"

"I asked you 'where is that other calf'? Where is it? There's only four. I brought in five." His very calmness was terrifying.

Val threw back her head, and her eyes were — as they frequently became in moments of stress — yellow, inscrutable, like the eyes of a lion in a cage.

"Yes, you brought in five. One of the five, at least, you — stole. You put your brand, Manley Fleetwood, on a calf that did not belong to you; it belonged to the Wishbone, and you know it. I have learned many disagreeable things about you, Manley, in the past two years; yesterday morning I learned that you were a *thief*. Ah-h — I despise you! Stealing from the very men who helped you — the men to whom you owe nothing but gratitude and — and friendship! Have you no manhood whatever? Besides being weak and shiftless, are you a criminal as well? *How* can you be so utterly lacking in — in common decency, even?" She eyed him as she would look at some strange monster in a museum about which she was rather curious.

"I asked you where that other calf is — and you'd better tell me!" It was the tone which goes well with a knife thrust or a blow. But the contempt in Val's face did not change.

"Well, you'll have to hunt for it if you want it. The cow — a Wishbone cow, mind you! — came and claimed it; I let her have it. No stolen goods can remain on this ranch with my knowledge, Manley Fleetwood. Please remember —"

"Oh, you turned it out, did you? You turned it out?" He had her by the throat, shaking her as a puppy shakes a purloined shoe. "I could — *kill* you for that!"

"Manley! Ah-h-h —" It was not pleasant — that gurgling cry, as she struggled to get free.

He had the look of a maniac as he pressed his fingers into her throat and glared down into her purpling face.

With a sudden impulse he cast her limp form violently from him. She struck against a chair, fell from that to the floor, and lay a huddled heap, her crisp, ruffled skirt just giving a glimpse of tiny, half-worn slippers, her yellow hair fallen loose and hiding her face.

He stared down at her, but he felt no remorse — she had jeopardized his liberty, his standing among men. A cold horror caught him when he thought of the calf turned loose on the range, his brand on its ribs. He rushed in a panic from the kitchen, flung himself into the saddle, and went off across the coulee, whipping both sides of his horse. She had not told him — indeed, he had not asked her — which way the cow had gone, but instinctively he rode to the west, the direction from which he had driven the calves. One thought possessed him utterly; he must find that calf.

So he rode here and there, doubling and turning to search every feeding herd he glimpsed, fearing to face the possibility of failure and its inevitable consequence.

The cat with the white spots on its sides — Val called her Mary Arabella, for some whimsical reason — came into the kitchen, looked inquiringly at the huddled figure upon the floor, gave a faint mew, and went slowly up, purring and arching her back; she snuffed a moment at Val's hair, then settled herself in the hollow of Val's arm, and curled down for a nap. The sun, sliding up to midday, shone straight in upon them through the open door.

Polycarp Jenks, riding that way in obedience to some obscure impulse, lifted his hand to give his customary tap-tap before he walked in; saw Val lying there, and almost fell headlong into the room in his haste and perturbation. It looked very much as if he had at last stumbled upon the horrible tragedy which was his one daydream. To be an eyewitness of a murder, and to be able to tell the tale afterward with minute, horrifying detail — that, to Polycarp, would make life really worth living. He shuffled over to Val, pushed aside the mass of yellow hair, turned her head so that he could look into her face, saw at once the bruised marks upon her throat, and stood up very straight.

"Foul play has been done here!" he exclaimed melodramatically, eying the cat sternly. "Murder — that's what it is, by granny — a foul murder!"

The victim of the foul murder stirred slightly. Polycarp started and bent over her again, somewhat disconcerted, perhaps, but more humanly anxious.

"Mis' Fleetwood — Mis' Fleetwood! You hurt? It's Polycarp Jenks talkin' to you!" He hesitated, pushed the cat away, lifted Val with some difficulty, and carried her into the front room and deposited her on the couch. Then he hurried after some water.

"Come might' nigh bein' a murder, by granny — from the marks on 'er neck — come might' nigh, all right!"

He sprinkled water lavishly upon her face, bethought him of a possible whisky flask in the haystack, and ran every step of the way there and back. He found a discarded bottle with a very little left in it, and forced the liquor down her throat.

"That 'll fetch ye if anything will — *he-he!*" he mumbled, tittering from sheer excitement. Beyond a very natural desire to do what he could for her, he was extremely anxious to bring her to her senses, so that he could hear what had happened, and how it had happened.

"Betche Man got jealous of her'n Kenneth — by granny, I betche that's how it come about — hey? Feelin' better, Mis' Fleetwood?"

Val had opened her eyes and was looking at him rather stupidly. There was a bruise upon her head, as well as upon her throat. She had been stunned, and her wits came back slowly. When she recognized Polycarp, she tried ineffectually to sit up.

"I — he — is — he — gone?" Her voice was husky, her speech labored.

"Man, you mean? He's gone, yes. Don't you be afeared — not whilst I'm here, by granny! How came it he done this to ye?"

Val was still staring at him bewilderedly. Polycarp repeated his question three times before the blank look left her eyes.

"I — turned the calf — out — the cow — came and — claimed it — Manley —" She lifted her hand as if it were very, very heavy, and fumbled at her throat. "Manley — when I told him — he was a — thief —" She dropped her hand wearily to her side and closed her eyes, as if the sight of Polycarp's face, so close to hers and so insatiably curious and eager and cunning, was more than she could bear.

"Go away," she commanded, after a minute or two. "I'm — all right. It's nothing. I fell. It was — the heat. Thank you — so much —" She opened her eyes and saw him there still. She looked at him gravely, speculatively. She waved her hand toward the bedroom. "Get me my hand glass — in there on the dresser," she said.

When he had tiptoed in and got it for her, she lifted it up slowly, with both hands, until she could see her throat. There were distinct, telltale marks upon the tender flesh — unmistakable finger prints. She shivered and dropped the glass to the floor. But she stared steadily up at Polycarp, and after a moment she spoke with a certain fierceness.

"Polycarp Jenks, don't ever tell — about those marks. I — I don't want any one to know. When — after a while — I want to think first — perhaps you can help me. Go away now — not away from the ranch, but —

let me think. I'm all right — or I will be. Please go."

Polycarp recognized that tone, however it might be hoarsened by bruised muscles and the shock of what she had suffered. He recognized also that look in her eyes; he had always obeyed that look and that tone — he obeyed them now, though with visible reluctance. He sat down in the kitchen to wait, and while he waited he chewed tobacco incessantly, and ruminated upon the mystery which lay behind the few words Val had first spoken, before she realized just what it was she was saying.

After a long, long while — so long that even Polycarp's patience was feeling the strain — Val opened the door and stood leaning weakly against the casing. Her throat was swathed in a piece of white silk.

"I wish, Polycarp, you'd get the team and hitch it to the light rig," she said. "I want to go to town, and I don't feel able to drive. Can you take me in? Can you spare the time?"

"Why, certainly, I c'n take you in, Mis' Fleetwood. I was jest thinkin' it wa'n't safe for you out here —"

"It is perfectly safe," Val interrupted chillingly. "I am going because I want to see Arline Hawley." She raised her hand to the bandage. "I have a sore throat," she stated, staring hard at him. Then, with one of her impulsive changes, she smiled wistfully.

"You'll be my friend, Polycarp, won't you?" she pleaded. "I can trust you, I know, with my — secret. It is a secret — it *must* be a secret! I'll tell you the truth, Polycarp. It was Manley — he had been drinking again. He — we had a quarrel — about something. He did n't know what he was doing — he did n't mean to hurt me. But I fell — I struck my head; see, there is a great lump there." She pushed back her hair to show him the place. "So it's a secret — just between you and me, Polycarp Jenks!"

"Why, certainly, Mis' Fleetwood; don't you be the least mite oneasy; I'm your friend — I always have been. A feller ain't to be held responsible when he's drinkin' — by granny, that's a fact, he ain't."

"No," Val agreed laconically, "I suppose not. Let us go, then, as soon as we can, please. I'll stay overnight with Mrs. Hawley, and you can bring me back to-morrow, can't you? And you'll remember not to mention — anything, won't you, Polycarp?"

Polycarp stood very straight and dignified.

"I hope, Mis' Fleetwood, you can always depend on Polycarp Jenks," he replied virtuously. "Your secret is safe with me."

Val smiled — somewhat doubtfully, it is true — and let him go. "Maybe it is — I hope so," she sighed, as she turned away to dress for the trip.

All through that long ride to town, Polycarp talked and talked and talked. He made surmises and waited openly to hear them confirmed or denied; he gave her advice; he told her everything he had ever heard about Manley, or had seen or knew from some other source; everything, that is, save what was good. The sums he had lost at poker, or had borrowed; the debts he owed to the merchants; the reputation he had for "talking big and doing little;" the trouble he had had with this man and that man; and what he did not know for a certainty he guessed at, and so kept the subject alive.

True, Val did not speak at all, except when he asked her how she felt. Then she would reply dully, "Pretty well, thank you, Polycarp." Invariably those were the words she used. Whenever he stole a furtive, sidelong glance at her, she was staring straight ahead at the great, undulating prairie with the brown ribbon, which was the trail, thrown carelessly across to the sky line.

Polycarp suspected that she did not see anything — she just stared with her eyes, while her thoughts were somewhere else. He was not even sure that she heard what he was saying. He thought she must be pretty sick, she was so pale, and she had such wide, purple rings under her eyes. Also, he rather resented her desire to keep her trouble a secret; he favored telling everybody, and organizing a party to go out and run Man Fleetwood out of the country, as the very mildest rebuke which the outraged community could give and remain self-respecting. He even fell silent during the last three or four miles, while he dwelt longingly upon the keen pleasure there would be in leading such an expedition.

"You 'll remember, Polycarp, not to speak of this?" Val urged abruptly when he drew up before the Hawley Hotel. "Not a hint, you know until — until I give you permission. You promised."

"Oh, certainly, Mis' Fleetwood. Certainly. Don't you be a mite oneasy." But the tone of Polycarp was dejected in the extreme.

"And please be ready to drive me back in the morning. I should like to be at the ranch by noon, at the latest." With that she left him and went into the hotel.

CHAPTER XXII

"AND so," Val finished, rather apathetically, pushing back the fallen lock of hair, "it has come to that. I can't remain here and keep any shred of self-respect. All my life I've been taught to believe divorce a terrible thing — a crime, almost; now I think it is sometimes a crime *not* to be divorced. For months I have been coming slowly to a decision, so this is really not as sudden as it may seem to you. It is humiliating to be compelled to borrow money — but I would much rather ask you than any of my own people. My pride is going to suffer enough when I meet them, as it is; I can't let them know just how miserable and sordid a failure —"

Arline gave an inarticulate snort, bent her scrawny body nearly double, and reached frankly into her stocking. She fumbled there a moment and straightened triumphantly, grasping a flat, buckskin bag.

"I'd feel like shakin' you if you went to anybody else but me," she declared, untying the bag. "I know what men is — Lord knows I see enough of 'em and their meanness — and if I can help a woman outa the clutches

of one, I 'm tickled to death to git the chancet. I ain't
sayin' they 're all of 'em bad — I c'n afford to give the
devil his due and still say that men is the limit. The
good ones is so durn scarce it ain't one woman in fifty
lucky enough to git one. All I blame you for is stayin'
with him as long as you have. I 'd of quit long ago; I
was beginnin' to think you never would come to your
senses. But you had to fight that thing out for yourself;
every woman has to.

"I 'm glad you 've woke up to the fact that Man
Fleetwood did n't git a deed to you, body and soul, when
he married you; you 've been actin' as if you thought
he had. And I 'm glad you 've got sense enough to pull
outa the game when you know the best you can expect
is the worst of it. There ain't no hope for Man Fleetwood;
I seen that when he went back to drinkin' again after you
was burnt out. I did think that would steady him down,
but he ain't the kind that braces up when trouble hits
him — he 's the sort that stays down ruther than go to
the trouble of gittin' up. He 's hopeless now as a rotten
egg, and has been for the last year. Here; you take the
hull works, and if you need more, I can easy git it for you
by sendin' in to the bank."

"Oh, but this is too much!" Val protested when she
had counted the money. "You 're so good — but really
and truly, I won't need half — "

Arline pushed away the proffered money impatiently. "How'n time are you goin' to tell how much you'll need? Lemme tell you, Val Peyson — I ain't goin' to call you by his name no more, the dirty cur! — I've been packin' that money in my stockin' for six months, jest so'st to have it handy when you wanted it. Divorces cost more'n marriage licenses, as you'll find out when you git started. And —"

"You — why, the idea!" Val pursed her lips with something like her old spirit. "How could *you* know I'd need to borrow money? I did n't know it myself, even. I —"

"Well, I c'n see through a wall when there's a knothole in it," paraphrased Arline calmly. "You may not know it, but you've been gittin' your back-East notions knocked outa you pretty fast the last year or so. It was all a question of what kinda stuff you was made of underneath. You c'n put a polish on most anything, so I could n't tell, right at first, what there was to you. But you're all right — I've seen that a long time back; and so I knowed durn well you'd be wantin' money to pull loose with. It takes money, though I know it ain't polite to say much about real dollars 'n' cents. You'll likely use every cent of that before you're through with the deal — and remember, there's a lot more growin' on the same bush, if you need it. It's only waitin' to be picked."

Val stared, found her eyes blurring so that she could not see, and with a sudden, impulsive movement leaned over and put her arms around Arline, unkempt, scrawny, and wholly unlovely though she was.

"Arline, you're an angel of goodness!" she cried brokenly. "You're the best friend I ever had in my life — I've had many who petted me and flattered me — but you — you *do* things! I'm ashamed — because I haven't loved you every minute since I first saw you. I judged you — I mean — oh, you're pure, shining gold inside, instead of —"

"Oh, git out!" Arline was compelled to gulp twice before she could say even that much. "I don't shine nowhere — inside er out. I know that well enough. I never had no chancet to shine. It's always been wore off with hard knocks. But I like shiny folks all right — when they're fine clear through, and —"

"Arline — dear, I do love you. I always shall. I —"

Arline loosened her clasp and jumped up precipitately.

"Git out!" she repeated bashfully. "If you git me to cryin', Val Peyson, I'll wish you was in Halifax. You go to bed, 'n' go to sleep, er I'll —" She almost ran from the room. Outside, she stopped in a darkened corner of the hallway and stood for some minutes with her checked gingham apron pressed tightly over her face, and several times she sniffed audibly. When she finally returned to the kitchen her nose was pink, her eyelids were pink, and she was extremely petulant when she caught Minnie eying her curiously.

Val had refused to eat any supper, and, beyond telling Arline that she had decided to leave Manley and return to her mother in Fern Hill, she had not explained anything very clearly — her colorless face, for instance, nor her tightly swathed throat, nor the very noticeable bruise upon her temple.

Arline had not asked a single question. Now, however, she spent some time fixing a tray with the daintiest food she knew and could procure, and took it upstairs with a certain diffidence in her manner and a rare tenderness in her faded, worldly-wise eyes.

"You got to eat, you know," she reminded Val gently. "You 're bucking up ag'inst the hardest part of the trail, and grub 's a necessity. Take it like you would medicine — unless your throat 's too sore. I see you got it all tied up."

Val raised her hands in a swift alarm and clasped her throat as if she feared Arline would remove the bandages.

"Oh, it 's not sore — that is, it is sore — I mean not very much," she stammered betrayingly.

Arline set down the tray upon the dresser and faced Val grimly.

"I never asked you any questions, did I?" she demanded. "But you act for all the world as if — do you want me to give a guess about that tied-up neck, and that black 'n' blue lump on your forehead? I never asked any questions — I did n't need to. Man Fleetwood's been maulin' you around. I was kinda afraid he 'd git to that point some day when he got mad enough; he 's just the brand to beat up a woman. But if it took a beatin' to bring you to the quitting point, I 'm glad he done it. *Only*," she added darkly, "he better keep outa my reach; I 'm jest in the humor to claw him up some if I should git close enough. And if I happened to forget I 'm a lady, I 'd sure bawl him out, and the bigger crowd heard me the better. Now, you eat this — and don't get the idee you can cover up any meanness of Man Fleetwood's; not from me, anyhow. I know men better 'n you do; you could n't tell me nothing about 'em that would su'prise me the least bit. I 'm only thankful he did n't murder you in cold blood. Are you going to eat?"

"Not if you keep on reminding me of such h-horrid things," wailed Val, and sobbed into her pillow. "It 's bad enough to — to have him ch-choke me without having you t-talk about it all the time!"

"Now, honey, don't you waste no tears on a brute like him — he ain't w-worth it!" Arline was on her bony knees beside the bed, crying with sympathy and self-reproach.

So, in truly feminine fashion, the two wept their way back to the solid ground of everyday living. Before they reached that desirable state of composure, however, Val told her everything — within certain limits set not by caution, but rather by her woman's instinct. She did not, for instance, say much about Kent, though she regretted openly that Polycarp knew so much about it.

"Hope never needed no newspaper so long as Polycarp lives here," Arline grumbled when Val was sitting up again and trying to eat Arline's toast, and jelly made of buffalo berries, and sipping the tea which had gone cold. "But if I can round him up in time, I'll try and git him to keep his mouth shet. I'll scare the liver outa him some way. But if he caught onto that calf deal —" She shook her head doubtfully. "The worst of it is, Fred's in town, and he's always pumpin' Polycarp dry, jest to find out all that's goin' on. You go to bed, and I'll see if I can find out whether they're together. If they are — but you need n't to worry none. I reckon I'm a match for the both of 'em. Why, I'd dope their coffee and send 'em both to sleep till Man got outa the country, if I had to!"

She stood with her hands upon her angular hips and glared at Val.

"I sure would do that very thing — for *you*," she reiterated solemnly. "I don't purtend I'd do it for Man —

but I would for you. But it 's likely Kent has fixed things up so they can't git nothing on Man if they try. He would if he said he would; that there 's *one* feller that 's on the square. You go to bed now, whilst I go on a still hunt of my own. I 'll come and tell you if there 's anything to tell."

It was easy enough to make the promise, but keeping it was so difficult that she yielded to the temptation of going to bed and letting Val sleep in peace; which she could not have done if she had known that Polycarp Jenks and Fred De Garmo left town on horseback within an hour after Polycarp had entered it, and that they told no man their errand.

Over behind Brinberg's store, Polycarp had told Fred all he knew, all he suspected, and all he believed would come to pass. "Strictly on the quiet," of course — he reminded Fred of that, over and over, because he had promised Mrs. Fleetwood that he would not mention it.

"But, by granny," he apologized, "I did n't like the idee of keepin' a thing like that from *you;* it would kinda look as if I was standin' in on the deal, which I ain't. Nobody can't accuse me of rustlin', no matter what else I might do; you know that, Fred."

"Sure, I know you 're honest, anyway," Fred responded quite sincerely.

"Well, I considered it my duty to tell you. I 've kinda

had my suspicions all fall, that there was somethin' scaly goin' on at Cold Spring. Looked to me like Man had too blamed many calves missed by spring round-up — for the size of his herd. I dunno, of course, jest where he gits 'em — you 'll have to find that out. But he 's brung twelve er fourteen to the ranch, two er three at a time. And what she said when she first come to — told me right out, by granny, 'at Man choked her because she called 'im a thief, and somethin' about a cow comin' an' claimin' her calf, and her turnin' it out. That oughta be might' nigh all the evidence you need, Fred, if you find it. She don't know she said it, but she would n't of told it, by granny, if it was n't so — now would she?"

"And you say all this happened to-day?" Fred pondered for a minute. "That 's queer, because I almost caught a fellow last night doing some funny work on a calf. A Wishbone cow it was, and her calf fresh burned — a barred-out brand, by thunder! If it was to-day, I 'd say Man found it and blotched the brand. I wish now I 'd hazed them over to the Double Diamond and corralled 'em, like I had a mind to. But we can find them, easy enough. But that was last night, and you say this big setting came off to-day; you *sure*, Polly?"

"'Course I 'm sure." Polycarp waggled his head solemnly. He was enjoying himself to the limit. He was the man on the inside, giving out information of the greatest importance, and an officer of the law was hanging anxiously upon his words. He spoke slowly, giving weight to every word. "I rode up to the house — Man's house — somewhere close to noon, an' there she was, layin' on the kitchen floor. Did n't know nothin', an' had the marks of somebody's fingers on 'er throat; the rest of her neck 's so white they showed up, by granny, like — like —" Polycarp never could think of a simile. He always expectorated in such an emergency, and left his sentence unfinished. He did so now, and Fred cut in unfeelingly.

"Never mind that — you 've gone over it half a dozen times. You say it was to-day, at noon, or thereabouts. Man must have done it when he found out she 'd turned the calf loose — he would n't unless he was pretty mad, and scared. He is n't cold-blooded enough to wait till he 'd barred out the brand, and then go home and choke his wife. He did n't know about the calf till to-day, that 's a cinch." He studied the matter with an air of grave importance.

"Polycarp," he said abruptly, "I 'm going to need you. We 've got to find that bunch of cattle — it ought to be easy enough, and haze 'em down into Man's field where his bunch of calves are — see? Any calf that 's been weaned in the last three weeks will be pretty likely to claim its mother; and if he 's got any calves branded that claim cows with some other brand — well —" He threw out his hands in a comprehensive gesture. "That 's the quickest way I know to get him," he said. "I want a witness along, and some help. And you," he eyed Polycarp keenly, "ain't safe running around town loose. All your brains seem to leak out your mouth. So you come along with me."

"Well — any time after to-morrer," hedged Polycarp, offended by the implication that he talked too much. "I 've got to drive the team home for Mis' Fleetwood to-morrer. I tol' her I would — "

"Well, you won't. You 're going to hit the trail with me just as soon as I can find a horse for you to ride. We 'll sleep at the Double Diamond, and start from there in the morning. And if I catch you letting a word outa you about this deal, I 'll just about have to arrest you for — " He did not quite know what, but the very vagueness of the threat had its effect upon Polycarp.

He went without further argument, though first he went to the Hawley Hotel — with Fred close beside him as a precaution against imprudent gossip — and left word in the office that he would not be able to drive Mrs. Fleetwood home, the next morning, but would be back to take her out the day after that, if she did not mind staying in town. It was that message which Arline deliberately held back from Val until morning.

"You better stay here," she advised then. "Polycarp

an' Fred 's up to some devilment, that 's a cinch; but whatever it is, you 're better off right here with me. S'posen you should drive out there and run into Man — what then?"

Val shivered. "I — that 's the only thing I can't bear," she admitted, as if the time for proud dignity and reserve had gone by. "If I could be sure I would n't need to meet him, I 'd rather go alone; really and truly, I would. You know the horses are perfectly safe — I 've driven them to town fifty times if I have once. I had to, out there alone so much of the time. I 'd rather not have Polycarp spying around. I 've got to pack up — there are so many things of no value to — to *him*, things I brought out here with me. And there are all my manuscripts; I can't leave them lying around, even if they are n't worth anything; especially since they are n't worth anything." She pushed back her hair with a weary movement. "If I could only be sure — if I knew where *he* is," she sighed.

"I 'll lend you my gun," Arline offered in good faith. "If he comes around you and starts any funny business again, you can stand him off, even if you got some delicate feelin's about blowin' his brains out."

"Oh, I could n't. I 'm deadly afraid of guns." Val shuddered.

"Well, then you can't go alone. I 'd go with you, if

you could git packed up so as to come back to-day. I guess Min could make out to git two meals alone."

"Oh, no. Really and truly, Arline, I'd just as soon go alone. I would rather, dear."

Arline was not accustomed to being called "dear." She surrendered with some confusion and a blush.

"Well, you better wait," she admonished temporizingly. "Something may turn up."

Presently something did turn up. She rushed breathlessly into Val's room and caught her by the arm.

"Now's your chancet, Val," she hissed in a loud whisper. "Man jest now rode into town; he's over in Pop's place — I seen him go in. He's good for the day, sure. I'll have Hank hitch right up, an' you can go down to the stable and start from there, so 'st he won't see you. An' I'll keep an eye out, 'n' if he leaves town I won't be fur behind, lemme tell you. He won't, though; there ain't one chancet in a hundred he'll leave that saloon till he's full — an' if he tries t' go then, I'll have somebody lock 'im up in the ice house till you git back. You want to hurry up that packin', an' git in here quick's you can."

She went to the stable with Val, her apron thrown over her head for want of a hat. When Val was settling herself in the seat, Arline caught at the wheel.

"Say! How 'n time you goin' to git your trunks loaded into the wagon?" she cried. "You can't do it alone."

Val pursed her lips; she had not thought of that.

"But Polycarp will come, by the time I am ready," she decided. "You could n't keep him away, Arline; he would be afraid he might miss something, because I suppose ours is the only ranch in the country where the wheels are n't turning smoothly. Polycarp and I can manage."

Hank, grinning under his ragged, brown mustache, handed her the lines. "I 've got my orders," he told her briefly. "I 'll watch out the trail 's kept clear."

"Oh, thank you. I 've so many good friends," Val answered, giving him a smile to stir his sluggish blood. "Good-bye, Arline. Don't worry about me, there 's a dear. I shall not be back before to-morrow night, probably."

Both Arline and Hank stood where they were and watched her out of sight before they turned back to the sordid tasks which made up their lives.

"She 'll make it — she 's the proper stuff," Hank remarked, and lighted his pipe. Arline, for a wonder, sighed and said nothing.

CHAPTER XXIII

AFTER two nights and a day of torment unbearable, Kent bolted from his work, which would have taken him that day, as it had done the day before, in a direction opposite to that which his mind and his heart followed, and without apology or explanation to his foreman rode straight to Cold Spring Coulee. He had no very definite plan, except to see Val. He did not even know what he would say when he faced her.

Michael was steaming from nose to tail when he stopped at the yard gate, which shows how impatience had driven his master. Kent glanced quickly around the place as he walked up the narrow path to the house. Nothing was changed in the slightest particular, as far as he could see, and he realized then that he had been uneasy as well as anxious. Both doors were closed, so that he was obliged to knock before Val became visible. He had a fleeting impression of extreme caution in the way she opened the door and looked out, but he forgot it immediately in his joy at seeing her.

"Oh, it 's you. Come in, and — you won't mind if I close the door? I 'm afraid I 'm the victim of nerves, to-day."

"Why?" Kent was instantly solicitous. "Has anything happened since I was here?"

Val shook her head, smiling faintly. "Nothing that need to worry *you*, pal. I don't want to talk about worries. I want to be cheered up; I have n't laughed, Kent, for so long I 'm afraid my facial muscles are getting stiff. Say something funny, can't you?"

Kent pushed his hat far back on his head and sat down upon a corner of the table. "Such is life in the far West — and the farther West you go, the livelier —" he began to declaim dutifully.

"The livelier it gets. Yes, I 've heard that a million times, I believe. I can't laugh at that; I never did think it funny." She sighed, and twitched her shoulders impatiently because of it. "I see you brought back the glasses," she remarked inanely. "You certainly were n't in any great hurry, were you?"

"Oh, they had us riding over east of the home ranch, hazing in some outa the hills. I 'm supposed to be over there right now — but I ain't. I expect I 'll get the can, all right —"

"If you 're going away, what do you care?" she taunted.

"H'm — sure, what do I care?" He eyed her from

under his brows while he bent to light a match upon the sole of his boot. Val had long ago settled his compunctions about smoking in her presence. "You seem to be all tore up, here," he observed irrelevantly. "Cleaning house?"

"Yes — cleaning house." Val smiled ambiguously.

"Hubby in town?"

"Yes — he went in yesterday, and has n't come back yet."

Kent smoked for a moment meditatively. "I found that calf, all right," he informed her at last. "It was too late to ride around this way and tell you that night. So you need n't worry any more about that."

"I 'm not worrying about that." Val stooped and picked up a hairpin from the floor, and twirled it absently in her fingers. "I don't think it matters, any more. Yesterday afternoon Fred De Garmo and Polycarp Jenks came into the coulee with a bunch of cattle, and turned all the calves out of the river field with them; and, after a little, they drove the whole lot of them away somewhere — over that way." She waved a slim hand to the west. "They let out the calves in the corral, too. I saw them from the window, but I did n't ask them any questions. I really did n't need to, did I?" She grazed him with a glance. "I thought perhaps you had failed to find that calf; I 'm glad you did, though — so it was n't that started them hunting around here — Polycarp and Fred, I mean."

Kent looked at her queerly. Her voice was without any emotion whatever, as if the subject held no personal interest for her. He finished his cigarette and threw the stub out into the yard before either of them spoke another word. He closed the door again, stood there for a minute making up his mind, and went slowly over to where she was sitting listlessly in a chair, her hands folded loosely in her lap. He gripped with one hand the chairback and stared down at her high-piled, yellow hair.

"How long do you think I'm going to stand around and let you be dragged into trouble like this?" he began abruptly. "You know what I told you the other day — I could say the same thing over again, and a lot more; and I'd mean more than I could find words for. Maybe you can stand this sort of thing — I can't. I'm not going to try. If you're bound to stick to that — that gentleman, I'm going to get outa the country where I can't see you killed by inches. Every time I come, you're a little bit whiter, and a little bigger-eyed — I can't stand it, I tell you!

"You weren't made for a hell like you're living. You were meant to be happy — and I was meant to make you happy. Every morning when I open my eyes — do you know what I think? I think it's another day we oughta be happy in, you and me." He took her suddenly by the shoulder and brought her up, facing him, where he could look into her eyes.

"We 've only got just one life to live, Val!" he pleaded. "And we could be happy together — I 'd stake my life on that. I can't go on forever just being friends, and eating my heart out for you, and seeing you abused — and what for? Just because a preacher mumbled some words over you two! Only for that, you would n't stay with him over-night, and you know it! Is *that* what ought to tie two human beings together — without love, or even friendship? You hate him; you can't look me in the eyes and say you don't. And he 's tired of you. Some other woman would please him better. And I could make you happy!"

Val broke away from his grasp, and retreated until the table was between them. Her listlessness was a thing forgotten. She was panting with the quick beating of her heart.

"Kent — don't, pal! You must n't say those things — it 's wicked."

"It 's true," he cried hotly. "Can you look at me and say it ain't the truth?"

"You 've spoiled our friendship, Kent!" she accused, while she evaded his question. "It meant so much to me — just your dear, good friendship."

"My love could mean a whole lot more," he declared sturdily.

"But you must n't say those things — you must n't feel that way, Kent!"

"Oh!" He laughed grimly. "Must n't I? How are you going to stop me?" He stared hard at her, his face growing slowly rigid. "There 's just one way to stop me from saying such wicked things," he told her. "You can tell me you don't care anything about me, and never could, not even if that down-east conscience of yours did n't butt into the game. You can tell me that, and swear it 's the truth, and I 'll leave the country. I 'll go so far you 'll never see me again, so I 'll never bother you any more. I can't promise I 'll stop loving you — but for my own sake I 'll sure try hard enough." He set his teeth hard together and stood quiet, watching her.

Val tried to answer him. Evidently she could not manage her voice, for he saw her begin softly beating her lips with her fist, fighting to get back her self-control. Once or twice he had seen her do that, when, womanlike, the tears would come in spite of her.

"I don't want you to go a-away," she articulated at last, with a hint of stubbornness.

"Well, what *do* you want? I can't stay, unless —" He did not attempt to finish the sentence. He knew there was no need; she understood well enough the alternative.

For long minutes she did not speak, because she could not. Like many women, she fought desperately against the tears which seemed a badge of her femininity. She sat down in a chair, dropped her face upon her folded arms, and bit her lips until they were sore. Kent took a step toward her, reconsidered, and went over to the window, where he stood staring moodily out until she began speaking. Even then, he did not turn immediately toward her.

"You need n't go, Kent," she said with some semblance of calm. "Because I 'm going. I did n't tell you — but I 'm going home. I 'm going to get free, by the same law that tied me to him. You are right—I have a 'down-east' conscience. I think I was born with it. It demands that I get my freedom honestly; I can't steal it — pal. I could n't be happy if I did that, no matter how hard I might try — or you."

He turned eagerly toward her then, but she stopped him with a gesture.

"No — stay where you are. I want to solve my problem and — and leave you out of it; you 're a complication, pal — when you talk like — like you 've just been talking. It makes my conscience wonder whether I 'm honest with myself. I 've got to leave you out, don't you see? And so, leaving you out, I don't feel that any woman should be expected to go on like I 'm doing. You don't know — I could n't tell you just how — impossible — this marriage of mine has become. The day after — well, yesterday — no, the day before yesterday — he came home and found out — what I 'd done. He — I could n't stay here, after that, so —"

"What did he do?" Kent demanded sharply. "He did n't dare to lay his hands on you — did he? By —"

"Don't swear, Kent — I hear so much of that from him!" Val smiled curiously. "He — he swore at me. I could n't stay with him, after that — could I, dear?" Whether she really meant to speak that last word or not, it set Kent's blood dancing so that he forgot to urge his question farther. He took two eager steps toward her, and she retreated again behind the table.

"Kent, don't! How can I tell you anything, if you won't be good?" She waited until he was standing rather sulkily by the window again. "Anyway, it does n't matter now what he has done. I am going to leave him. I 'm going to get a divorce. Not even the strictest 'down-east' conscience could demand that I stay. I 'm perfectly at ease upon that point. About this last trouble — with the calves — if I could help him, I would, of course. But all I could say would only make matters worse — and I 'm a wretched failure at lying. I can help him more,

I think, by going away. I feel certain there's going to be trouble over those calves. Fred De Garmo never would have come down here and driven them all away, would he, unless there was going to be trouble?"

"If he came in here and got the calves, it looks as if he meant business, all right." Kent frowned absently at the white window curtain. "I've seen the time," he added reflectively, "when I'd be all broke up to have Man get into trouble. We used to be pretty good friends!"

"A year ago it would have broken my heart," Val sighed. "We do change so! I can't quite understand why I should feel so indifferent about it now; even the other day it was terrible. But when I felt his fingers — " she stopped guiltily. "He seems a stranger to me now. I don't even hate him so very much. I don't want to meet him, though."

"Neither do I." But there was a different meaning in Kent's tone. "So you're going to quit?" He looked at her thoughtfully. "You'll leave your address, I hope!"

"Oh, yes." Val's voice betrayed some inward trepidation. "I'm not running away; I'm just going."

"I see." He sighed, impatient at the restraint she had put upon him. "That don't mean you won't ever come back, does it? Or that the trains are going to quit carrying passengers to your town? Because you can't *always* keep me outa your 'problem,' let me tell you. Is it against the rules to ask when you 're going — and how?"

"Just as soon as I can get my trunks packed, and Polycarp — or somebody — comes to help me load them into the spring wagon. I promised Arline Hawley I would be in town to-night. I don't know, though — I don't seem to be making much progress with my packing." She smiled at him more brightly. "Let 's wade ashore, pal, and get to work instead of talking about things better left alone. I know just exactly what you 're thinking — and I 'm going to let you help me, instead of Polycarp. I 'm frightfully angry with him, anyway. He promised me, on his word of honor, that he would n't mention a thing — and he must have actually hunted for a chance to tell! He did n't have the nerve to come to the house yesterday, when he was here with Fred — perhaps he won't come to-day, after all. So you 'll have to help me make my getaway, pal."

Kent wavered. "You 're the limit, all right," he told her after a period of hesitation. "You just wait, old girl, till you get that conscience of yours squared! What shall I do? I can pack a warbag in one minute and three-quarters, and a horse in five minutes — provided he don't get gay and pitch the pack off a time or two, and somebody 's around to help throw the hitch. Just tell me where to start in, and you won't be able to see me for dust!"

"You seem in a frightful hurry to have me go," Val complained, laughing nevertheless with the nervous reaction. "Packing a trunk takes time, and care, and intelligence."

"Now is n't that awful?" Kent's eyes flared with mirth, all the more pronounced because it was entirely superficial. "Well, you take the time and care, Mrs. Goodpacker, and I 'll cheerfully furnish the intelligence, This goes, I reckon?" He squeezed a pink cushion into as small a space as possible, and held it out at arm's length.

"That goes — to Arline. *Don't* put it in there!" Val's laughter was not far from hysteria. Kent was pretending to stuff the pink cushion into her hand bag.

"Better take it; you 'll —"

The front door was pushed violently open and Manley almost fell into the room. Val gave a little, inarticulate cry and shrank back against the wall before she could recover herself. They had for the moment forgotten Manley, and all he stood for in the way of heartbreak.

A strange-looking Manley he was, with his white face and staring, bloodshot eyes, and the cruel, animal lines around his mouth. Hardly recognizable to one who had not seen him since three or four years before, he would have been. He stopped short just over the threshold, and glanced suspiciously from one to the other before he came farther into the room.

"Dig up some grub, Val — in a bag, so I can carry it on horseback," he commanded. "And a blanket — where did you put those rifle cartridges?" He hurried across the room to where his rifle and belt hung upon the wall, just over the little, homemade bookcase. "I had a couple of boxes — where are they?" He snatched down the rifle, took the belt, and began buckling it around him with fumbling fingers.

Mechanically Val reached upon a higher shelf and got him the two boxes of shells. Her eyes were fixed curiously upon his face.

"What has happened?" she asked him as he tore open a box and began pushing the shells, one by one, into his belt.

"Fred De Garmo — he tried to arrest me — in town — I shot him dead." He glanced furtively at Kent. "Can I take your horse, Kent? I want to get across the river before —"

"You shot — Fred —" Val was staring at him stupidly. He whirled savagely toward her.

"Yes, and I'd shoot any man that walked up and tried to take me. He was a fool if he thought all he had to do was crook his finger and say 'Come along.' It

was over those calves — and I 'd say you had a hand
in it, if I had n't found that calf, and saw how you burned
out the brand before you turned it loose. You might
have told me — I would n't have —" He shifted his
gaze toward Kent. "The hell of it is, the sheriff happened
to be in town for something; he 's back a couple of miles
— for God's sake, move! And get that flour and bacon,
and some matches. I 've got to get across the river. I
can shake 'em off, on the other side. Hurry, Val!"

She went out into the kitchen, and they heard her moving
about, collecting the things he needed.

"I 'll have to take your horse, Kent." Manley turned
to him with a certain wheedling tone, infinitely disgusting
to the other. "Mine 's all in — I rode him down, getting
this far. I 've got to get across the river, and into the
hills the other side — I can dodge 'em over there. You
can have my horse — he 's good as yours, anyway."
He seemed to feel a slight discomfort at Kent's silence.
"You 've always stood by me — anyway, it was n't so
much my fault — he came at me unawares, and says
'Man Fleetwood, you 're my prisoner!' Why, the very
tone of him was an insult — and I won't stand for being
arrested — I pulled my gun and got him through the
lungs — heard 'em yelling he was dead — Hurry up
with that grub! I can't wait here till —"

"I ought to tell you Michael 's no good for water,"

Kent forced himself to say. "He's liable to turn back on you; he's scared of it."

"He won't turn back with *me* — not with old Jake Bondy at my heels!" Manley snatched the bag of provisions from Val when she appeared, and started for the door.

"You better leave off some of that hardware, then," Kent advised perfunctorily. "You're liable to have to swim."

"I don't care how I get across, just so —" A panic seemed to seize him then. Without a word of thanks or farewell he rushed out, threw himself into Kent's saddle without taking time to tie on his bundle of bacon and flour, or remembering the blanket he had asked for. Holding his provisions under his arm, his rifle in one hand, and his reins clutched in the other, he struck the spurs home and raced down the coulee toward the river. Fred and Polycarp had not troubled to put up the wire gate after emptying the river field, so he had a straight run of it to the very river bank. The two stood together at the window and watched him go.

CHAPTER XXIV

"HE thought it was I burned out that brand; did you notice what he said?" Val, as frequently happens in times of stress, spoke first of a trivial matter, before her mind would grasp the greater issues.

"He'll never make it," said Kent, speaking involuntarily his thought. "There comes old Jake Bondy, now, down the hill. Still, I dunno — if Michael takes to the water all right —"

"If the sheriff comes here, what shall we tell him? Shall we —"

"He won't. He's turning off, don't you see? He must have got a sight of Man from the top of the hill. Michael's tolerably fresh, and Jake's horse isn't; that makes a big difference."

Val weakened unexpectedly, as the full meaning of it all swept through her mind.

"Oh, it's horrible!" she whispered. "Kent, what can we do?"

"Not a thing, only keep our heads, and don't give

way to nerves," he hinted. "It's something out of our reach; let's not go all to pieces over it, pal."

She steadied under his calm voice.

"I'm always acting foolish just at the wrong time — but to think he could —"

"Don't think! You'll have enough of that to do, managing your own affairs. All this doesn't change a thing for you. It makes you feel bad — and for that I could kill him, almost!" So much flashed out, and then he brought himself in hand again. "You've still got to pack your trunks, and take the train home, just the same as if this hadn't happened. I didn't like the idea at first, but now I see it's the best thing you can do, for the present. After awhile — we'll see about it. Don't look out, if it upsets you, Val. You can't do any good, and you've got to save your nerves. Let me pull down the shade —"

"Oh, I've got to see!" Perversely, she caught up the field glasses from the table, drew them from their case, and, letting down the upper window sash with a slam, focused the glasses upon the river. "He usually crosses right at the mouth of the coulee —" She swung the glasses slowly about. "Oh, there he is — just on the bank. The river looks rather high — oh, your horse doesn't want to go in, Kent. He whirls on his hind feet, and tried to bolt when Manley started in —"

Kent had been watching her face jealously. "Here, let me take a look, will you? I can tell —" She yielded reluctantly, and in a moment he had caught the focus.

"Tell me what you see, Kent — everything," she begged, looking anxiously from his face to the river.

"Well, old Jake is fogging along down the coulee — but he ain't to the river yet, not by a long shot! Ah-h! Man 's riding back to take a run in. That 's the stuff — got Michael's feet wet that time, the old freak! They came near going clean outa sight."

"The sheriff — is he close enough —" Val began fearfully. "Oh, we 're too far away to do a thing!"

Kent kept his eyes to the glasses. "We could n't do a thing if we were right there. Man 's in swimming water already. Jake ain't riding in — from the motions he 's ordering Man back."

"Oh, please let me look a minute! I won't get excited, Kent, and I 'll tell you everything I see — *please!*" Val's teeth were fairly chattering with excitement, so that Kent hesitated before he gave up the glasses. But it seemed boorish to refuse. She snatched at them as he took them from his eyes, and placed them nervously to her own.

"Oh, I see them both!" she cried, after a second or two. "The sheriff 's got his rifle in his hands — Kent, do you suppose he 'd —"

"Just a bluff, pal. They all do it. What —"

Val gave a start. "Oh, he shot, Kent! I saw him take aim — it looked as if he pointed it straight at Manley, and the smoke —" She moved the glasses slowly, searching the river.

"Well, he 'd have to be a dandy, to hit anything on the water, and with the sun in his eyes, too," Kent assured her, hardly taking his eyes from her face with its varying expression. Almost he could see what was taking place at the river, just by watching her.

"Oh, there 's Manley, away out! Why, your Michael is swimming beautifully, Kent! His head is high out of the water, and the water is churning like — Oh, Manley 's holding his rifle up over his head — he 's looking back toward shore. I wonder," she added softly, "what he 's thinking about! Manley! you 're my husband — and once I —"

"Draw a bead on that gazabo on shore," Kent interrupted her faint flaring up of sentiment toward the man she had once loved and loved no more.

Val drew a long breath and turned the glasses reluctantly from the fugitive. "I don't see him — oh, yes! He 's down beside a rock, on one knee, and he 's taking a rest across the rock, and is squinting along — oh, he can't hit him at that distance, can he, Kent? Would he dare — why, it would be murder, would n't it? Oh-h — *he shot again!*"

Kent reached up a hand and took the glasses from her eyes with a masterful gesture. "You let me look," he said laconically. "I 'm steadier than you."

Val crept closer to him, and looked up into his face. She could read nothing there; his mouth was shut tight so that it was a stern, straight line, but that told her nothing. He always looked so when he was intent upon something, or thinking deeply. She turned her eyes toward the river, flowing smoothly across the mouth of the coulee. Between, the land lay sleeping lazily in the hazy sunlight of mid-autumn. The grass was brown, the rocky outcroppings of the coulee wall yellow and gray and red — and the river was so blue, and so quiet! Surely that sleepy coulee and that placid river could not be witnessing a tragedy. She turned her head, irritated by its very calmness. Her eyes dwelt wistfully upon Kent 's half-concealed face.

"What are they doing now, Kent?" Her tone was hushed.

"I can't — exactly —" He mumbled absently, his mind a mile away. She waited a moment.

"Can you see — Manley?"

This time he did not answer at all; he seemed terribly far off, as if only his shell of a body remained with her in the room.

"Why don't you talk?" she wailed. She waited until

she could endure no more, then reached up and snatched the glasses from his eyes.

"I can't help it — I shall go crazy standing here. I 've just got to see!" she panted.

For a moment he clung to the glasses and stared down at her. "You better not, sweetheart," he urged gently, but when she still held fast he let them go. She raised them hurriedly to her eyes, and turned to the river with a shrinking impatience to know the worst and have it over with.

"E-everything j-joggles so," she whimpered complainingly, trying vainly to steady the glasses. He slipped his arms around her, and let her lean against him; she did not even seem to realize it. Just then she had caught sight of something, and her intense interest steadied her so that she stood perfectly still.

"Why, your horse —" she gasped. "Michael — he 's got his feet straight up in the air — oh, Kent, he 's rolling over and over! I can't see —" She held her breath. The glasses sagged as if they had grown all at once too heavy to hold. "I — I thought I saw —" She shivered and hid her face upon one upflung arm.

Kent caught up the glasses and looked long at the river, unmindful of the girl sobbing wildly beside him. Finally he turned to her, hesitated, and then gathered her close in his arms. The glasses slid unheeded to the floor.

"Don't cry — it's better this way, though it's hard enough, God knows." His voice was very gentle. "Think how awful it would have been, Val, if the law had got him. Don't cry like that! Such things are happening every day, somewhere —" He realized suddenly that this was no way to comfort her, and stopped. He patted her shoulder with a sense of blank helplessness. He could make love — but this was not the time for love-making; and since he was denied that outlet for his feelings, he did not know what to do, except that he led her to the couch, and settled her among the cushions so that she would be physically comfortable, at least. He turned restlessly to the window, looked out, and then went to the couch and bent over her.

"I'm going out to the gate — I want to see Jake Bondy. He's coming up the coulee," he said. "I won't be far. Poor little girl — poor little pal, I wish I could help you." He touched his lips to her hair, so lightly she could not feel it, and left her.

At the gate he met, not the sheriff, who was riding slowly, and had just passed through the field gate, but Arline and Hank, rattling up in the Hawley buckboard.

"Thank the good Lord!" he exclaimed when he helped her from the rig. "I never was so glad to see anybody in my life. Go on in — she's in there crying her heart out. Man 's dead — the sheriff shot him in the river — oh, there 's been hell to pay out here!"

"My heavens above!" Arline stared up at him while she grasped the significance of his words. "I knowed he 'd hit for here — I followed right out as quick as Hank could hitch up the team. Did you hear about Fred —"

"Yes, yes, yes, I know all about it!" Kent was guilty of pulling her through the gate, and then pushing her toward the house. "You go and do something for that poor girl. Pack her up and take her to town as quick as God 'll let you. There 's been misery enough for her out here to kill a dozen women."

He watched until she had reached the porch, and then swung back to Hank, sitting calmly in the buckboard, with the lines gripped between his knees while he filled his pipe.

"I can take care of the man's side of this business, fast enough," Kent confessed whimsically, "but there 's some things it takes a woman to handle." He glanced again over his shoulder, gave a huge sigh of relief when he glimpsed Arline's thin face as she passed the window and knelt beside the couch, and turned with a lighter heart to meet the sheriff.

THE END

Other titles by B. M. Bower
available in Bison Books editions

CHIP OF THE FLYING U

FLYING U RANCH

THE HAPPY FAMILY OF THE FLYING U